ASSASSIN'S CREED

FRAGMENTS

THE HIGHLANDS CHILDREN

Also in the *Assassin's Creed – Fragments* series
available from Titan Books:

The Blade of Aizu

The Witches of the Moors
(upcoming)

ASSASSIN'S CREED

FRAGMENTS

THE HIGHLANDS CHILDREN

ALAIN T. PUYSSÉGUR

TITAN BOOKS

Assassin's Creed – Fragments: The Highlands Children
Print edition ISBN: 9781803363554
E-book edition ISBN: 9781803365794

Published by Titan Books
A division of Titan Publishing Group Ltd
144 Southwark Street, London SE1 0UP
www.titanbooks.com

First edition: November 2023
1 3 5 7 9 10 8 6 4 2

Ⓞ UBISOFT   ORIGINALS

Map design by Darth Zazou.
Translation by Jessica Burton.

A CIP catalogue record for this title is available from
the British Library.

Printed and bound in the United Kingdom by
CPI Group (UK) Ltd, Croydon CR0 4YY.

1296

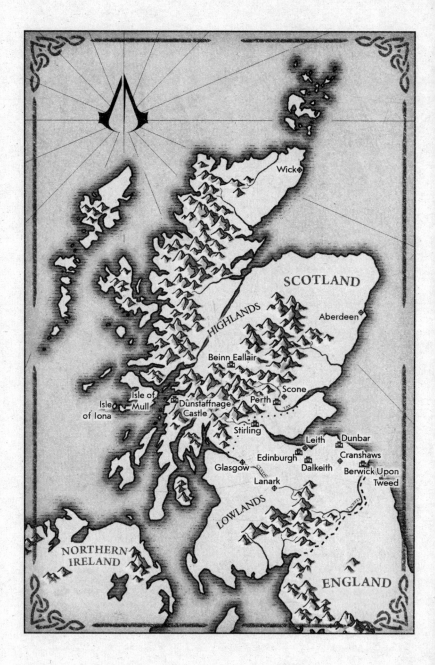

1

SHADOWS

The door opened with a bang, rattling the frame and breaking the lock, which gave way. The bell jingled, breaking the silence of the night. The shop was swathed in darkness. A single candle flickered, trying to chase away the darkness while making shadows dance up the walls.

An imposing man wearing a black cape with a rolled-down hood slipped inside. He barely had time to catch his breath before he shivered, as he felt a blade press against his jugular and one of his arms pushed into his back at a painful angle.

"What—"

The pressure on his arm increased and the man let out a gasp.

"It's me, Glenn, the goldsmith!"

His headgear was pushed back, unveiling a face lined with pain. His eyes were bulging in terror.

He was forced closer to the candle and, straining his neck, he could just make out the face of a young woman with emerald eyes.

"Ailéas? My god, what's the matter with you?"

The young woman let go of his arm and withdrew the scissors' blade from his neck. She readjusted her long ginger mane and continued to glare questioningly at the goldsmith; the scar which ran across her forehead made her seem even scarier.

"Precautionary measure," she replied. "You did just break down the door."

She gestured at the door which had just swung shut with a concerning creak. Glenn dumbly observed the metal lock hanging off with his mouth open.

"I… I thought it was stuck."

Ailéas rolled her eyes in exasperation.

An amused voice from behind the timbers spoke up.

"You're a brute, Glenn. It's no wonder you work on jewels instead of armor!"

A man slid out of the shadow produced by the shop counter. He was middle-aged, sported a gray beard and wore a dark embroidered doublet which accentuated his square shoulders.

"Alastair!" gasped the goldsmith in shock. "My god! Why this welcome? I almost wet myself!"

The bearded man let out a laugh and nodded.

"Your apprentice is better at cutting up a man with scissors than a garment! A real wild cat."

"Watch yourself, Glenn, cats scratch," snarled the girl.

She sprung forwards to light the other candles. The goldsmith moved aside with a fearful look. From the halo of the candlelight, he took in the chaos of the shop. Fabrics were piled here and there. Sections of the large and luxurious furnace had been strewn in a ball on the floor. A broken wooden table lay not far from that destruction.

"Did they try to rob you, too?"

Alastair Aitken nodded in affirmation. He was the most respected tailor in the south of Scotland, and certainly the richest. His dresses were known right up to the Highlands[*], and some of his overcoats were worth their weight in gold in the markets of Glasgow and Edinburgh. That someone tried to rob him wasn't exactly surprising, especially right now.

"Luckily Ailéas was here."

"The bastard ran away like a little coward," she said with a smirk.

"I see," replied the goldsmith, wiping his brow.

"What brings you here?"

"What brings me here? Good lord, Alastair! Three days!

---

[*] The Highlands are the mountainous region in the north and west of Scotland. The natural border of the Highlands runs from Arran to Stonehaven.

The town has been under siege for three days. And you ask what brings me here? What the hell are you still doing here?"

The master tailor leaned against one of the bolts of vermillion fabric.

"The Guild…" he started.

"Beck got killed in his damned bunker," Glenn cut him off. "Oh, you didn't know, huh? Well, he did! He was a bloody idiot and bad at business, but he didn't deserve that."

The goldsmith paced around the shop. He wrung his hands, with his many rings all clinking together.

"I almost got eviscerated myself on my way here! People have gone mad! But at the same time, I get it. Have you heard the screams from beyond the walls?"

Ailéas felt a shiver run down her spine.

Four days earlier, the English army had been spotted coming from the south. The young woman had climbed up to the watchtower above the ramparts and had seen the organized battalions advancing through the hills. The weapons and armor of the soldiers glistened in the spring sunshine, and the wind fluttered their banners.

The terrified screams of those who had managed to find refuge behind the city walls had come just before those who didn't make it to safety. Ailéas half-wondered what they were doing to people to make them scream like that, not really wanting to know the answer.

Since then, tents had sprouted up everywhere, like red and

gold petals on the jade moors. It had been three days since Berwick-upon-Tweed, the economic heart of the southern Scottish Lowlands*, was under siege and a maritime blockade.

Ailéas understood why the city, *her* city, had found itself in this catastrophic situation. Alastair had made it a point of pride to explain it to her. It was all about a military campaign, organized by Edward I, King of England, in retaliation for treason by the King of Scotland, John Balliol. The latter, in agreement with Parliament, had rejected a call to arms from the English crown to go up against the French. Even worse, he had then forged a military alliance with the King of France.

She was pulled out of her thoughts as a young man appeared in the doorframe of the shop. Just like her, he had emerald eyes, a wild and tangled mane of red hair, and a thin nose and mouth.

"Ah, Fillan! At least you won't welcome me by trying to slaughter me?" Glenn quipped.

"A public danger is more than enough for that!" retorted the new man with a mischievous look at his twin sister, who made an obscene gesture in return. "What are you doing here?" he continued, shaking hands with the goldsmith.

"Did you hit all your heads? I've come to do what the

---

* The Scottish Lowlands stretch from the south of Scotland to the east of the natural border of the Highlands between Stonehaven and Helensburgh.

Merchants Guild should have done long ago and make us leave Berwick!"

He almost shouted it, frowning deeply at Alastair.

"Calm down, Glenn."

"Calm down?" he shouted for real this time. "Damn it! Alastair, I just learned that that son of a bitch Douglas is going to hand over the keys to the city to Clifford!"

"Right, we—"

"Do you know what awaits us? Douglas will abdicate with no conditions. They'll gut us like pigs!"

"Will you let me speak?!" interrupted the tailor. "We leave tonight. I was about to send the kids to tell you."

The 'kids' gave each other an annoyed look. At sixteen years old, they detested being treated like children.

"Ah, ok. OK. But we must leave right away. Immediately! You haven't rushed them enough; you've handled all this badly!"

Fillan frowned.

"And no thanks to you, things have been arranged," he started icily. "You should show more respect, Glenn!"

"And you," interrupted his master, "should learn to shut your mouth and mind your own business. Go put this in my luggage."

He was holding an old piece of fabric in his arms. Ailéas knew it was just an excuse to make her brother leave the room. She watched him exit with his head bowed.

"This is how we'll proceed," started Alastair to Glenn.

While he outlined how they would leave the city, using the quays, the young woman was lost in thought about the shop.

She'd miss this place. A lot.

Her eyes turned towards each wooden beam, each dusty corner, and every bit of furniture that held so many memories. She and her brother had lived here for eight years. They had grown up here and rebuilt themselves between the overflowing wardrobes. They came from the north of Scotland, and Alastair had taken them in after their parents were massacred. The master tailor had taken care of them with all his signature kindness and offered them a new life of luxury in Berwick. Ailéas was grateful to him, as he had helped to give them a future by making them his apprentices.

Yes, the smell of the dyes, the rays of sunshine on the edges of the quays, her escapades on the city walls – she would miss all of it.

She had no idea what the future held for her now and it was terrifying. She hoped their journey might bring them to the sweeping, savage, and mountainous countries of her childhood, her memories of which were slowly fading. At the same time, she hated that the hope was a possibility. Thanks to the Guild, and money, they survived while thousands of others had met their ends during this atrocity.

Her throat and her stomach were dry.

Glenn left with a wave, and she went to find Fillan in the back of the shop with Alastair, before buckling up their packs. A heavy silence hung in the air. It was so heavy that Ailéas felt her sense of guilt growing.

"It's not fair," she said with a frown.

"What's that?" asked Alastair.

"That we get to leave the city while so many others can't."

The tailor looked at her with his kind eyes, full of sympathy.

"Don't be so stupid," retorted her brother, annoyed. "What do you want? To stay here and be massacred? Take more with us who would get us caught? Think about it!"

He was right, and she knew it. There was no other choice.

"Do you know what soldiers do to women during a siege?" he continued.

"Calm yourself, Fillan," soothed Alastair, who was used to their bickering. "Being cruel is no help to you. Ailéas, listen to me. When war comes, the only thing that matters is survival. And you cannot lose your will to survive."

The teenager bit her lip. Her master's words eased the knot in her stomach. A little. But not enough.

"Now you've finished, go warn Nollan."

"The cobbler?" asked Fillan.

"He's the last one to know."

Mounting cries resounded from just a few streets away. They all exchanged worried looks.

"Be careful," he carried on. "Douglas has called back the garrison. The streets aren't safe."

"We know what's coming," retorted Ailéas, arming herself with a walking stick.

Fillan shrugged his shoulders and snarled.

"You're like a dog! No, that's unfair to dogs. You're even worse!"

Her brother gave her a mean look as they kept going. They turned at a fork in the road, where it was darker because of the timber buildings.

"You're so annoying with your stupid thoughts," he said. "Plus, you woke me up last night again."

"Sooo sorry for having a nightmare, oh great sir."

"Hmm."

"Don't you ever relive it?"

"Relive what?"

She held back a sigh. He knew perfectly well what she was talking about. It wasn't the first time she'd had this sort of dream.

"The night our parents died."

"Damn, Ailéas! We're sixteen. It was years ago! Get over it!"

This time she wanted to break his nose.

As they came out of the shadows of the street, Fillan saw the rage-filled eyes of his sister.

"No one said we had to talk," he said.

He went silent once more and pressed on.

They were the mirror image of one another, but their characters were complete opposites.

Ailéas was poised and reflective, and preferred solitude to futile friendships. Fillan was impetuous and arrogant, loved to mingle, and knew everyone in town.

They kept going as though they were shadows. After two steps, they ducked into a porch to avoid the groups of local thugs who were trying to find a poor soul on whom to take out their nerves. From time to time, a scream rang out. The rest of the city was petrified in anticipation and terror, frozen by indecision.

It was suffocating.

They came into view of the workshop and spread out. The moon had finally managed to pierce through the clouds and they could make out the shopfront. On the cobblestones, near the dark threshold, a scarlet pool gleamed.

They each took a direction, listening intently.

Nothing.

They crept along to the entry. The trail of blood was flowing from outside to inside. Ailéas gripped her stick, which did nothing for the erratic beating of her heart.

They entered the shop in one step, but found nothing.

Nothing alive.

"Is that… Master Nollan?"

Fillan thought he was going to be sick, the bile burning his throat, and his sister reached out for his hand.

There was blood everywhere, to the point that even the walls were streaked with red. The awful smell of iron enveloped the whole room. The cobbler, a man the same age as Alastair, was laid out on the counter. Several of his tools surrounded his body. Along with several of his organs.

"They jumped him in front of his door," observed the young man. "Then they pushed him inside…"

"They've stolen everything," said Ailéas taking in the devastation on the counter.

"Such animals! What difference will money make when the English have their heads on spikes?"

The eerie silence fell once more, but it was broken almost immediately by dozens of shouts exploding from the west of the city. Roused by the same instincts, brother and sister looked at each other. Their fear was visceral and instinctive, and shone in their eyes.

As they exited the shop, a man slipped onto the blood-covered floor in mid-run. He cast a furtive look in the direction of two growing shadows and gave a start upon discovering the twins.

"The English are in the city!" he screamed from the ground.

Residents fearfully looked out of their windows and some even dared open their doors.

"Douglas has surrendered! The soldiers are killing everyone!"

The man shouted the words with a haunted look. It was only as Ailéas tried to help him up that she noticed the spear in his back.

"Get out of here! Go!" he shouted as he tried to flee.

The teenagers took off without a word.

2

MASSACRE

Berwick awoke to the sound of screaming, only to be plunged into horror. With every passing minute new voices were added to the loud and unbearable racket, as more and more of the screams of those about to die rang out. The north of the city was a hellscape of atrocities. The flickering red light of the first fires began along with the furling black smoke to confirm their existence. The smell of burning wood started to spread, harsh and choking.

Fillan dodged a puddle of blood and wiped the corner of his mouth with the back of his hand. He fell to the ground from a blow he couldn't have seen coming.

As he and his sister fled through the streets to try and get back to Alastair's shop, three young novices of the guard had come upon them. They had business to settle with the young man who had humiliated them a week earlier in one of the city's taverns. They were using the general panic to do what the law normally forbade.

Ailéas begged her brother not to rise to their provocation. Each new scream was a stark reminder that their time was running out. They were close—too close—to one of the city gates where English soldiers could burst through at any moment. As always, Fillan ignored her and shook his head. If she'd known for sure that she could carry him afterwards, she'd have knocked him out.

"Oh, not so smart, are you?" taunted the biggest of the three novices as he massaged his reddened fist.

The young woman watched her brother, who still hadn't gotten up. He looked miserable. The worst thing was that he'd forbidden her from interfering, even though out of the two of them, she was the only one who knew how to fight.

"I stand by what I said," said Fillan with a laugh. "You're stupider than goats."

The novice's eyes glinted. He pulled out a sharp blade from under his coat.

"I've been waiting days for this—"

His jaw cracked with a horrific sound, preventing him from finishing that thought. Losing patience, Ailéas had leapt forward with her stick. With the weapon thrust from her shoulders, she used the distance to hit him again in the temple. The novice stumbled and fell, and his dagger made a metallic clink as it hit the ground.

Four seconds, five maximum, passed slowly.

The trainees stayed where they were, hesitant to move. The redheaded girl advanced on them with determination. They stumbled and fled, disappearing onto Main Street, where a cohort of residents were shouting and trying to save themselves.

She held out her hand to help her brother up, but he shoved it away violently.

"Leave me alone! I told you to stay out of it!"

"He was going to split you in half."

"So what! I'm sick of you always jumping to my rescue. I know how to defend myself."

It was completely untrue, laughable even, but Ailéas didn't respond. Her brother went out of his way to annoy her. You'd think he hated her.

"Oh, get up," was all she replied.

They set off once more but had to cut through a crossing of the main roads. The chaos was unimaginable. People were running in all directions. Some forgot to jump over the bodies of the unfortunate souls who'd already been killed. All around, men, women, and children clustered together to form a magma of impenetrable movement that wasn't getting them anywhere. A child stuck under the axle of a wagon frantically beckoned with his tiny hands, his face streaked with tears. No one paid any attention to him. When she noticed him, Ailéas almost ran to his aid but Fillan put out his arm to stop her. Barging with his large shoulders, he forged a path through the kerfuffle and helped them reach the opposite side.

The soles of their leather boots clattered along the ground and their lungs were on fire, but they didn't slow down at all and soon reached the southeast of the city. The terror hadn't completely taken over there yet. The only trace was the waves of smoke carried by a light breeze.

They had almost reached the merchants' column where the shop was located when they distinctly heard the cry of their master, followed by a thud that could only mean he'd been hit.

"I don't know what you're talking about!"

It was the weak and breathless voice of Alastair.

The twins risked a look over the wall, angled from the alley they'd just passed.

The old man was on his knees in the middle of the street. A warrior in shining armor stood in front of him. The warrior was wearing a long red cape that draped down his back and to the floor. In the moonlight it looked like the color of blood. His head was covered by a resplendent helmet mounted with metallic antlers. Ailéas found them both magnificent and terrifying.

Three soldiers came out of the shop. Each was wearing an identical red cape, but their armor was less impressive and their heads were uncovered. Ailéas observed their behavior and realized that the one with the helmet was in command.

They weren't part of the English army, she was sure. They were too well equipped, and the advance guard hadn't yet reached this part of town.

"He's lying," said one of them. "I found luggage in the back room."

"Plus beds upstairs," added another.

The man with the antlers grabbed Alastair by the throat and lifted him up. The old man had been beaten nearly to death. His arm was broken at a strange angle. He could barely stand and his stricken face was covered in blood.

"For the last time, we know you worked with the Brotherhood. Where are the Children of Fal?"

Ailéas had never heard such a cold voice. If a dead man could talk, he would have done so in the same tone. She sought her brother's hand but couldn't find it. He was pressed against the wall, trembling.

The tailor replied with something they couldn't hear. His lips could barely get out a murmur. The grip on his throat tightened and he let out a horrific gargle.

"As you wish."

The warrior in the helmet let him go, pulled out a sword that glinted in the moonlight, and without an ounce of hesitation, plunged it into Alastair's chest.

Time stood still. The faraway screams disappeared. The air itself seemed to dissipate.

Ailéas remembered meeting the master tailor the day a

man in a helmet brought them to him. He had joked with her and 'stolen' her nose. The memories flooded in as her throat went dry. She relived him teaching her to pin an old chiffon, him taking her to the herbalist the first time she bled, him consoling her as her nightmares plagued her. A final image remained in her mind: a hug, which he wouldn't ever be able to give again.

Time started again with a cry.

Fillan's cry.

Ailéas met her master's eyes and heard him gasp a 'no' of deep sadness as Fillan was discovered. But maybe it was just her imagination, as the lifeless body of the old man dropped limply to the ground. The soldiers turned to face their direction. The one with the helmet didn't even need to speak; he just pointed the sword, the tip of which still dripped with Alastair's blood.

Fillan stayed in the middle of the street, paralyzed. Ailéas had to shove him to get him to react.

"We head for the quays!" she yelled, thinking of the Guild's plan.

In the middle of her panicked shouts, her brother agreed with a nod.

After a few steps they came face to face with a horde of men and women, crashing like a wave towards them. Their screams barely covered the clinking of the weapons of the detachment of English soldiers pursuing them.

The compacted crowd was blocking their only escape. Seeing their crazed eyes, Ailéas didn't hesitate in pushing them aside to get past.

The clinking of armor was right at their backs.

"Split up!" she shouted.

She took the lead, jumped onto a wooden crate, and grabbed a signpost of a building. With cat-like agility, she scaled the facade of the building with the help of imperfections in the wood and windows. Her brother followed suit and they were on the roof within a few seconds.

They had a terrible shock when they saw the full city, though each reacted in their own way. Fillan let out a curse which involved the mothers of the English, while Ailéas tried to wipe away the tears pooling in the corners of her eyes.

Most of the city was ablaze. The consuming ghost-like flames had spread from the ramparts through the city as though the buildings were nothing but kindling. Berwick was no more than a monster of fire, embers, and death. The sky had disappeared under the thick, black, suffocating smoke.

Regaining their wits, they set off over the straw-covered roofs, moving from side to side to avoid the immovable chimney obstacles. Ailéas was more agile, even running along the central beams without needing to hold out her arms for balance. They sometimes zigzagged between flames that were engulfing the wooden beams below their feet. The breeze and the heat spurred them on.

"After them!" ordered the warrior with the helmet. "Don't let them get away!"

The soldiers in red capes pressed forwards below without taking their eyes off them. The residents did everything they could to get out of their way. Some were too slow, others paralyzed in fear, and were pushed aside or impaled on swords.

The twins ran quickly. They had learned to explore the city from this angle the first year they arrived here, hungry for the thrills of adventure and freedom. They knew the best places to step, how hard to tread on the tiles without them giving way. They had learned to judge the distance to jump between buildings, in a leap of faith against the emptiness below them.

With a quick look back, Ailéas saw that they had lost their pursuers.

"Go left," she ordered, aiming towards the quays.

She crossed a roof enveloped in flames that gave way just after she ran across.

"I'm cut off!" shouted Fillan, who could no longer follow her.

"Go along Fishmongers row, then!"

"What do you think I am, an idiot? I know where to go, damn it."

"We'll meet at the warehouses!" replied Ailéas with a cold glare.

The young man wiped away the soot and sweat that was tickling his nose and started to run again. His sister got further away and disappeared into the thickening smoke. He felt a tremendous terror rise up in him, a wave of fear that almost made him step on a false tile. He regained his balance, adrenaline running through his whole body.

And then, a scream that resounded above all the others.

A cry he'd heard a thousand times. The one that woke him at night and that he knew by heart.

"Ailéas?!" he called as he stopped.

But only the horror of the city and the cries of the dying answered him.

3

RUPTURE

Fillan held himself on the edge of darkness, on the edge of a roof ravaged by flames. A powerful terror devoured him from within.

There was just one scream. Long, pained, and fearful. And then nothing.

His heart stopped beating, even though only a second ago it had been racing from the intensity of his run. His body reacted first because his mind was laden with fear and doubt. He leapt down quickly from the roof without looking where he was landing. He pushed on through the street, shoving aside the crowds and being shoved in turn, almost oblivious of his surroundings.

Fillan set off down the street where the scream had come from, driven by an instinct that could not be explained. He pressed forwards, occasionally putting his hands up to protect his face from the floating embers. He squinted at the shadows pooled at the end of the alley, and through the smoke he saw a figure trying to get up.

"Ailéas!" he gasped.

He had no strength left in his voice, which was filled with despair.

He pressed on and almost tripped over the body of an English soldier with a burnt face, but slipped on the blood that covered the ground. He arrived in time to help the shadow up. Both relief and anguish washed over him; the shadow was just a man, a city resident whose slit throat was oozing blood in weak droplets.

The man gave a last gargle. A bubbly and foul-smelling gasp. Fillan pushed the body away in horror, barely registering his own shaking hands. He looked around him for the body of his sister, praying to the gods he wouldn't find her there. He couldn't see her and let out a sigh of relief.

Which ended with a sharp intake of breath.

His eyes landed on a specific spot in the street a yard away. The ground was falling away under his feet. The pavestones, the mud, the blood, the bodies, everything was disappearing.

"No," was all he could try to say, but his lips barely moved and no sound came out.

His knees hit the floor with a wet sound.

His emotions were all over the place, contradictory and

violent. They made no sense to him but flowed all the same. He could no longer contain them, as though he was a prisoner to them.

He could only crawl. With a trembling hand he reached over the fluids on the ground and touched a ripped piece of fabric.

"Ailéas…" he rasped.

It was a fragment of the shirt his sister had been wearing. It was torn. In the only places not covered by blood, he recognized the blue-gray color. On the fabric there were strands of red hair clumped together in the sticky mess, confirming the unthinkable truth.

His stomach churned and his throat contracted but he had no time to vomit. A clack resounded from down the street. He raised his tear-filled eyes, that were red from the heat, and found his sister's face. It was rigid and still. Instead of calming him down, this sight destroyed him. He wanted to scream, scream enough to drive himself mad.

A man exited the alley. He was fleeing the devouring fire at pace. Judging by his armor he was an English soldier. Over his shoulder was slung Ailéas's limp body. His twin's arm swung lifelessly. Her head, upside down and covered in blood with her mouth hanging open, did the same. Fillan searched his sister's face for even the slightest trace of life but saw only still and cold death.

His legs began to move by themselves. He took a first step and almost fell.

He was still screaming to himself. Ailéas couldn't be dead. It wasn't possible! Not today. Not now. Not after all the horrors that he'd seen on her face.

He took another step. His legs were trembling and spasming. The man was about to disappear around the corner.

The teenager pushed through the terror invading him.

"Aileeeeeeeeeaaa—"

A hand violently grabbed his neck.

"Now I've got you!" enthused one of the warriors in the red capes. "Come with me, and no funny business, or…"

He simply raised his sword, which glowed in the light of the flames.

Ailéas disappeared along with every ounce of willpower from Fillan. He let himself be led away, unable to hear what the man was saying to him as he pushed him along. A building collapsed in front of him with a rumbling and cracking, covering the soldier. Fillan was deafened and flung his arms up to his face as the city continued to scream out its agony. The flames were licking up against his skin and he could barely even feel it.

Get to the quays!

Right. Get to the quays. He started to stumble like a drunk, then found the strength to run, and fled without a backward glance at the soldier struggling under the burning wood. He felt like his whole body was suffering, but denial invaded his soul and made him forget everything. He ran through terrible scenes without even really seeing them.

The survivors continued to flee, crazed and trampling over the dead. They hoped not to die as prisoners of the flames, or worse, to be massacred out in the open. Nothing represented better the massacre that took place that first night of April. The English had progressed and spread terror. They burned, pillaged, and raped. They let out screams of rage and bloodlust. They laughed like animals amid a frenetic killing spree, high on the hunt, blood and death.

Fillan pushed through it all with agility. He dodged a horse that almost knocked him over as it reared up with neighs of pain. An old man lying on the ground with only one leg tried to reach out for him, but Fillan ignored him. Carried on ignoring everything. He thought about getting back up onto the roofs, but there was no point; everything was on fire and full of smoke.

He reached the main city square, the trading heart of the city where different markets took place during the week. Here, unlike the rest of the city, a group of townspeople had stopped fleeing to regroup and challenge the English, with the senseless hope of surviving for just a little longer.

The resistance had already confronted the English and formed a compact wall in the center of the square.

It was useless, in vain. They should have fled, thought

Fillan, with no idea as to where. He ran along the line of melee to the right but came face to face with Charles, the blacksmith of the square. Wielding a giant sword, he taught an English soldier respect, dodging his attacks like a fawn. His crossed red and black tartan* made him look even fiercer in the flames. In a large sweeping movement, he disarmed the soldier, whose sword flew through the air. The blacksmith pivoted, and in the same movement, decapitated his opponent.

Fillan did everything he could to dodge the body that fell on him, but it hit him so hard it knocked the wind out of him. He found himself lying in the middle of a pile of bodies. He felt time slow down and wondered if it would be better to stay here and play dead. Maybe he'd figure out a way to get out of it later.

It was a stupid idea.

Using the last of his strength, he pushed away the body whose blood was pooling in its mouth.

He didn't know who he was anymore. Maybe he was just a shadow, trying to escape the horror. He got up and started running again.

"It's the kid!" shouted an English soldier as he spotted him. "He murdered the captain!"

---

* Tartan is a checkered and colored wool fabric typical to Scotland. The word also denotes the garment made from the fabric.

"What? Don't let him get away! Bring me the murdering bastard!"

Fillan ignored them. He dived, ducked, and even dropped to the ground to avoid everyone fighting, those who were screaming, and the dying. On his way, he spotted Glenn, swimming in a sea of blood and surrounded by other bodies. The goldsmith had no rings left on his fingers.

A new sprint, another street.

The chaos of the fight grew quieter. The interior quays, at last, came into view. The sea air and its freshness were so soothing in comparison to the heat of the city. Fillan even felt drops of water on his face. He had started to cry.

He approached the east wall of the city, not far from where all the ships were docked in the port. They would soon catch fire and become giant torches. He saw no one on the way to the ramparts. The residents, like the English soldiers, surely knew there was no reason to come here, because there was nothing here.

Think. He had to think. Remember.

The denial in his head blurred everything, but a few fragments came back to him.

The quays. The east wall. The drains.

He boarded a long wooden pontoon that hadn't yet been devoured by flames and paddled towards an opening that led to the waters of the Tweed.

"Hey ho!" he tried, without shouting.

No one.

His throat and his lungs were burning.

"Is anybody there? I know Alastair!"

His denial broke at these words, because he'd spoken of the master in the present tense, though his master was dead. He gritted his teeth and inhaled the port air and waited. Still no one.

As he watched the shadows on the wall, the clinking of armor made him jump. One of the English soldiers from the square had followed him and was approaching him with a dagger in hand.

"Time to die, Scottish bastard!"

Fillan once again found himself paralyzed, unable to make the slightest movement. Everything spun in his head. The severe glare from Alastair as he reprimanded him: The sound the weapon had made as it had entered Alastair's chest. Berwick, the hub of fire and death. And Ailéas, or worse still, her lifeless face. A blow struck the back of his head and the world started spinning.

As he was dying, he hoped to rejoin his sister.

4

MERCENARIES

Fillan awoke to a crow's squawk.

It was dark and humid. Upon hearing the rustling of leaves, the cracking of twigs, and the occasional tweeting of birds, he realized he was in a forest. Dawn had not yet risen. Underneath his cheek he felt the freshness of grass with hints of flowers. This feeling soothed his sore skin a little, but another more unpleasant sensation took over: a tight cord around his wrists. His hands were tied behind his back.

He tried to wriggle out of the knots in the rope with a discreet movement but soon gave up. Voices murmured nearby.

He closed his eyes and fell still. Listening closely.

There were two of them, a man and a woman.

"Are you sure we didn't make a mistake?" said the

female voice. "What does the Brotherhood want with this kid?"

"No idea," replied the other, in a gravelly and authoritative masculine voice.

Fillan opened his eyes but couldn't recognize anyone. All around him, between the dark trees, were more trees. The people speaking were behind him.

"And the sister?"

"Given the state of the city, she got left behind."

Fillan felt his whole body tense. He couldn't follow the rest of this conversation. His brain was screaming.

Ailéas.

Just one thought invaded his mind. He'd abandoned her. He hadn't even tried to fight, to find her after the battle. All he had done was flee like a coward.

A tear rolled down his cheek.

"The kid's awake," said a third voice with a northern accent.

A firm hand dragged Fillan a few yards across the ground. They helped him sit up and he found himself leaning against a tree. A sharp pain flared in his lower back. Amidst the darkness of the woods, he could make out three silhouettes.

"I think he woke up because of you, Edan!" said the woman, a touch of amusement in her voice. "Look how alert he is!"

"Yeah well, who cares!"

Fillan found himself nose to nose with the one who'd shot him at the quays and had just spoken—a man of around thirty who, it seemed, was named Edan. He had a bald head and his long brown beard had traces of red. A strong smell of alcohol wafted from his whole body. The old tartan with a simple motif that covered his simple leather armor was dotted with dried blood. On his belt, a dagger hung to one side and a sword on the other.

He was a mercenary—or, even worse, a bandit.

"Come on, tell us your name," Edan started, trying to be jovial, but it made him look even more terrifying.

Fillan felt the fear rising in him. Who were these people who'd captured him? What did they want? Did they work for the English? Not knowing if they were expecting a full name, and unable to respond, he simply turned his head and stayed quiet.

"Cat got your tongue?" continued the man, giving him a soft slap on the back of his head.

Fillan shifted his weight, but it hurt him even more. He tried to keep a neutral expression, but inside he was shaking in terror.

"I had to hit him pretty hard," said the mercenary as he returned to the others. "He's gone deaf."

Now it was the other man's turn to approach. Fillan felt the very ground rumbling beneath him. He was enormous, as big as a mountain. He wasn't scary like Edan. No, he was absolutely terrifying. Fillan thought he must have Norwegian heritage, from those who were once conquering Vikings. He was no doubt a direct descendant. You could see his chest was bigger than an ox's and the outline showed nothing but muscle, even in the darkness. His hair was blond with white streaks and hung down his back in a long ponytail. An old scar, which Fillan first mistook for a strand of hair, ran down the right side of his face. He had a long beard, the tip of which was bunched up in an iron ring.

The teenager had never met anyone who gave off such an aura. Confidence. Violence. Serenity. Death.

"I don't care what your name is," said the Norwegian in a growl. "But I want you to tell me what happened before we got you out of the city."

"Are you the Guild?" asked Fillan hopefully.

"No. And I'm the one asking questions. Answer me. What happened?"

His tone was calm and collected, and his demeanor made it clear that this request could not be refused. *Plus, it wasn't a request*, thought Fillan, *it was an order*. He didn't dare imagine what would happen if he didn't comply, so he did.

He gathered his strength and tried to explain all he had gone through since they'd seen Glenn in the shop as best he could. He stuttered over his words, interrupted himself and couldn't finish his sentences. Everything was confusion, fleeting visions, and scattered memories. The most difficult thing was trying to retrace the events in order. Alastair's escape plan. His murder by the English soldiers. The run along the roofs with Ailéas, whose name he couldn't speak.

When he got to that point in his story, he had to stop. He didn't want to cry. Especially not in front of these strangers who'd surely judge him. He couldn't show the slightest weakness. His teeth chattered.

The Norwegian, who'd listened to his tale without the slightest reaction or comment, met his gaze. For just a moment Fillan thought he saw a trace of emotion in those blue-gray eyes, but the man just gave a grunt as he got up.

"The old tailor was betrayed," he said once he got back to the others.

"By whom?" asked the woman. "The Guild?"

"Maybe…"

"Deorsa won't be happy. We were supposed to deliver the twins. Both of them."

"I know the job; I take care of my business."

Fillan listened with an attentive ear, and the more he listened the more he felt like a piece of merchandise. That wasn't good. He tried to assess his strength. He was battered and exhausted, but he thought he might be able to get up and run. But probably not much more than that.

Ailéas.

The denial in him bubbled up once more. He must do everything to find her. She wasn't dead. She couldn't be.

He took a deep breath and pushed his crossed legs to get up. He got up quicker than he would have thought possible, and everything spun for a second.

He sprinted.

"And just where do you think you're going?"

His body screamed in pain as he hit the floor. He hadn't even made it a yard.

A woman had tripped him as he ran. She must have been behind him the whole time. He hadn't noticed her, hadn't even felt her presence. She wielded a long walking stick upon which dried flowers, amulets and bones hung. That was probably what had tripped him. She wore a fitted tunic and a red sash with sewn ornaments that covered her shoulders: clothing typical of a druid.

"Deafened, huh?" said the younger woman in the direction of the bald man. "So you say! He's faster than a hare!"

He shrugged with a grumble in return.

The Norwegian came close to Fillan.

"That's exactly the type of idiocy you should avoid, kid."

"I'm not a kid!" retorted Fillan, getting a little mud in his mouth.

"If you want us to call you something different, you just need to tell us your name."

"Fillan."

"Fillan. Good. A bit of advice: trying to escape with your hands tied is a kid's reaction. Want to tell me where you thought you were heading?"

In a clear memory, the young man saw two lifeless green eyes.

"Berwick… My sister…" he gasped, trying unsuccessfully to get off the floor.

"It's no use. She's dead."

The words were cold, emotionless.

"NO. No, I—"

"I'm telling you, it's no use!"

Fillan tried to crawl across the ground, the earth staining his tunic.

"Would you look at that," chuckled Edan. "A real nature boy!"

"Shut it!"

Everyone watched him try to carry on, at the very end of his strength. The crow let out another squawk.

"You're coming with me," said the Norwegian as he grabbed the teenager.

"We'd better get going," sulked the bald man. "A part of the army will keep advancing, and we've already lost enough time. Plus—"

With a stern look, the leader of the mercenaries shut him up.

"Be ready to leave when I get back."

Edan gave a disapproving glare, then went to pee against a tree. Fillan was shocked that he wasn't concerned about doing it in front of the two women who could see him and judge him.

The Norwegian led him into the forest, sometimes almost carrying him as his strength failed him.

"You have to see sense, kid. There's nothing left—do you hear? There's nothing left for you in Berwick."

Despite the harshness of his words, his tone had softened.

"There is! I have to—"

"No, believe me."

Fillan saw the hint of warmth in the man's eyes. The kind you show to those to whom you're about to give bad news.

"Now be quiet and come here."

They had reached the edge of the woods. The man pushed aside a branch covered in leaves.

The dawn was rising, bathing the horizon in a wave of orange shades. The same shades of orange were all over Berwick, where the flames still ravaged the largest buildings beyond the ramparts. Fillan realized where they were: in the deep forest a mile from the northwest of the city. Berwick was breathing its last breath. As he took in the huge columns of smoke and the city gate, he understood the scale of the massacre.

"Fillan, listen to me."

But he wasn't listening to him. His mind was overtaken by the chaos on the city walls.

The Norwegian snapped his fingers in front of Fillan's nose.

"Why didn't you leave me there?" Fillan said. "Who are you?"

"My name is Sören. We were the ones who were supposed to help you get out of the city. But there was only you left…"

Fillan didn't believe a word. He was lying.

"You took me."

"We were in a rush. We hadn't expected Douglas to cede the city in the night."

"What do you want from me?"

"Us? Nothing, but the people who hired us worked with the Guild to plan the escape from the city."

"Which people?"

"They call them the Brotherhood. They only agreed to help the merchants on the condition that we would take you and your sister to Dalkeith."

The word Brotherhood rang a bell for Fillan, but he couldn't remember where he'd heard it before.

"What do they want with me?"

"They didn't tell me."

Sören wasn't telling him everything. Fillan had learned to sense these types of things in the shop. But the little he had learned already told him a lot. An exchange. Him and Ailéas were just a form of currency, a way to get the merchants out. How could Alastair do this to them?

"If you want answers," interrupted Sören as he sensed his contemplative air, "you'll only be able to find them in Dalkeith. You'll be safe with us."

He helped him get up.

"Unless you keep trying to escape," he added with a twinge of humor.

Not having the strength to do otherwise, Fillan was inclined to believe him.

They returned to the camp in the woods together and found Sören's companions ready to leave.

5

HUNTED

Fillan prided himself on certain qualities.

For starters, he was an excellent speaker and knew how to use his words to convince hesitant clients in the shop. He was also a skilled climber who had scaled most of the buildings in Berwick. Heights didn't scare him. He was a charmer, and both of the aforementioned skills had come in handy in this regard: the first to win someone over and the second to turn heel and run from them.

However, he couldn't say that he was a good horseman. He was the opposite, in fact. As far back as he could remember, he had never liked horses, and horses had never liked him. A scar in the shape of a horseshoe on his left butt cheek was a testament to that fact. He even felt the pain of that scar reawaken as he learned that they would be leaving the woods on horseback.

But he couldn't argue: they had to put distance between them and Berwick.

He snorted almost as loudly as the black stallion whose reins they'd given him, and stood frozen while the others mounted their own horses.

"Try not to panic," advised Moira the druid as she came over. "If you panic, he'll sense it and he'll panic too."

"And what if I panic because he's panicking?"

Moira forced a smile, thinking he was joking, though in fact he was deadly serious.

A few mean comments and an insult from Edan left him feeling terribly alone. He finally decided to put his foot in the stirrup and pull himself up. There was a neigh and then a yelp. Whether it was the stallion or Fillan who panicked first, no one could say, but the horse took off at a triple gallop and barely missed decapitating his rider on a low-hanging branch.

"We drew the short straw with this idiot. I told you so!" The bald man roared with laughter so loud that a few birds fell out of their nests.

They followed Fillan at pace and his mount slowed in the presence of the other horses. He felt even more miserable and out of place as he watched Sören and his companions—he was barely clinging on to his imposing beast while they sat proud and impressive atop theirs. Once they left the woods, he turned one last time to see the silhouette of Berwick in the sunrise. The thick cloud of smoke, and everything it represented, seemed to follow him like a bad omen.

"Farewell…" he whispered to himself.

The word was lost on the wind.

He had no idea what he was feeling. He thought he couldn't feel anymore. All the same, tears streamed down his cheeks.

From dawn to dusk, they rode at a fierce pace, spurred on by the wind and rain. Sören was at the head leading them, avoiding the main routes. Whenever he could, he cut through woods, zigzagging between thickets and ditches. After the fields and pastures came valleys and vast plains that were green despite the overcast weather.

Fillan soon realized that he'd been wrong to hate horses his whole life. These beasts weren't so bad after all. Sure, they smelled terrible, but he'd been in enough taverns. No, the worst thing was how much pain he was in from riding. He discovered buttock muscles he never knew existed. Muscles which begged for mercy.

When night fell, they stopped in a forest clearing far from any dwellings. Sören forbade Edan from lighting a fire, which provoked several insults.

When she saw Fillan shivering, Moira lent him an old tartan blanket that smelled stronger than all the horses put together. But he didn't care, since all he wanted was to sleep.

He was exhausted. But just as he was lying down on the grass, Sören called him over.

"Come over here and eat something before you go to sleep."

He placed a portion of dried meat into his hands.

Everyone except the druid was also chewing a piece, all sat together on the ground. A leather flask was being passed around.

"You should get to know those you ride with," said the Norwegian.

Fillan nodded in agreement as he chewed the meat. It had a nice salty taste. He tried to stretch out his legs and almost groaned.

"This brute here," said Sören, indicating the bald one, "is Edan. He won't be nice to you. He isn't nice to anyone. A panther is more friendly."

"Oh, yeah. Yeah!" replied the concerned party with a finger up his nose as though he was searching for treasure. "This guy isn't exactly cheery either!"

"I bet you haven't ever even seen silk," said the young woman with the plait as she threw a branch at him.

"You nearly took my eye out!"

"Don't exaggerate, you wimp."

"And that's Kyle," continued Sören. "I would advise that you don't annoy her, or you'll regret it."

"Huh?" gasped Kyle. "I'm not a monster, either!"

Fillan took a swig of the flask he was handed. A harsh liquid burned his throat. He spluttered, his nose on fire.

"Oh, you're worse than that!" Edan cackled. "Yeah, way worse than a panther yourself!"

"Ah, but that doesn't mean anything!" retorted Kyle, completely ignoring the teenager choking next to her.

"I say what I want! Give back the booze, little maggot!"

Kyle and Edan carried on bickering as Sören and Moira watched them in amusement.

Fillan took the time to watch Kyle.

She mustn't have been much older than him. She must be eighteen, maximum, but she acted with a confidence that made her seem like she was at least twenty. She had thin eyebrows above a blue stare that could be sweet but tried hard to be stern. A few strands of her auburn hair had fallen out of her braid across her face. She kept blowing them out of her face through the corner of her mouth.

"And the druid is Moira," concluded the Norwegian.

The young man was burning to ask them a thousand questions, but he could barely keep his eyes open.

He laid his head on the ground.

"We'd all do well to get some sleep," said Sören.

"The kid's already asleep," finished Moira.

"So shut up. Edan. First guard duty."

"Ah, crap!"

Fillan did not sleep peacefully. He woke up three times,

convinced he'd find himself in his own bed under the beams of the roof of the shop in Berwick. The biting cold of the night and the nocturnal noises always brought him back to harsh reality and brought a tear to his eye every time. He fell back into his fears, always pulled by strong arms. Everything was smoke and screams.

The second day was exactly like the first, split between riding and brief rests, but the only difference was that two other mercenaries joined them on the way. One was a stocky warrior by the name of Craig who wore a strange axe on his back. The other, Fergus, didn't seem to be a great fighter and traveled with a spruce-wood lute.

As dusk fell, Sören let them know they'd be stopping in the approaching woods for the night. He briefly conversed with Kyle mid-gallop. A little while later, Fillan was surprised to see the warrior departing the group to take a different direction. He dared not ask questions in the middle of a ride.

He noted nonetheless that an incredible tension had fallen over the group. Edan, who this time had the go-ahead to light a fire, was more restless than ever. Everyone kept their hands near their weapons, as though a threat was nearby. Only Fergus, leaning against a tree and occasionally playing a few notes on his instrument, seemed at ease.

They ate sparingly and night fell.

Exhausted and rocked to sleep by the warmth and crackling of the fire, Fillan soon passed out. With no idea of how much time had passed, he jumped up at the sound of clashing metal. The stillness of the night was broken.

A string of curses rang out from somewhere in the forest.

Sören quickly unsheathed his sword. Edan and Craig, too. Fillan expected Moira to brandish her walking stick and Fergus his lute, but both remained peacefully by the fire as though nothing was wrong.

Another sound rung out. One sword hit another.

Fillan wished he had a weapon. He grabbed the first branch he could get his hands on.

Between two trees and in the light of the fire, an English soldier appeared. Fillan almost threw his stick at his face, but then he saw a dagger glinting against the man's throat.

Kyle was standing just behind him.

"You took your time!" grumbled Edan to the young woman. "I've been needing to pee for an hour."

"There were three of them following us. I came as quickly as I could. Move, you!"

She pushed the English man into the light.

"Add another log to the fire," ordered Sören, "so we can see him better."

Fergus complied, sending up a few sparks.

Sören saw the branch in Fillan's hand and smiled.

"You wouldn't have needed it," he chuckled. "We've known we were being followed since yesterday afternoon. We don't leave anything to chance."

Fillan understood. He realized that the fire had attracted the English like moths to a flame. The tension from the group was because of the risk of an attack. During that time, Kyle had taken them by surprise.

They tied up the soldier and made him sit on a tree stump.

"You and your friends are following us. Why?" demanded Sören in an icy tone.

Fillan didn't even see the hit. The noise, however, reverberated clearly in the forest.

"I'll repeat my question, but I warn you, every time I have to ask, I'll hit harder. And not just with my fist."

The soldier stayed firm. For the first minute.

He decided to cooperate when Sören pushed a dagger into his thigh as he gagged.

Fillan almost ran for the hills as he watched such a show, but Moira sat by him in support.

The soldier looked at him with hatred.

"The kid."

"What do you mean, 'the kid'?"

"He's the one we're following. We recognized him when you passed through Deans Burn. His description has been passed on from the commanders. They're after him."

Sören glanced at Fillan.

"Do you know why?"

"No. Orders from the very top."

"Do you know who he is?"

"No."

The Norwegian pulled out his dagger and got up to discuss with the others.

"What is this crap?" growled Edan. "They recognized this idiot?"

"From a simple description," added Kyle with a furrowed brow.

"You're right," said Sören, scratching his beard.

What followed happened very quickly.

Sören unsheathed the soldier's sword and ran him through. The man didn't even have time to cry out. There was just a small gargle that made Fillan want to be sick. Then the Norwegian jumped on him just as the Englishman's body fell.

Fillan was frozen in terror, seeing the weapon come down on him in the firelight. He felt the pain, the blood in his mouth, and passed out.

9

A dream. No. A nightmare.

It's always been a nightmare.

Fire crackles to the unsteady rhythm of the wind.

You recognize a small village, brighter than a beacon. Everywhere, the flames gnaw through the wood with a crackling sound. The fire spews up waves of smoke and sparks that vanish into the air with a shimmer.

Something is moving: a dark, gigantic shape. It looks like a predator and blocks the clouds, which fly above houses with the same slowness as the stars.

Everything is a mixture of threatening light and darkness, each seemingly fleeing the other.

The sound of a cracking beam reverberates. More embers fly away in whirlwinds.

A cry rings out.

6

CAPTIVITY

The shout resounded around the camp, breaking the quiet of the night. It hovered above the tent for a few long seconds.

A loud bellow followed.

"Will you just die and shut your damn mouth, for everyone's sake!"

The words were atrocious, cruel and unthinkable.

Not in a military camp. There, the injured person on the point of death cried out in distress and every time, the better-off soldiers screamed at them to shut up so they could get some sleep. They needed a good night's sleep to wage war and win fights. This had been the rule for all time.

In their bed on the floor, the injured person moved weakly, trying to regain their strength. They had moved so quickly as they woke up that the wound on their abdomen had reopened. Blood was already soaking through the bandages. The pain of it made them wince.

The images from the nightmare, ephemeral and terribly frightening, continued to plague them as though projected onto the fabric of the tent. The person closed their eyes and bit their tongue. They could only wait. Wait for the pain, all the pain, to get better or take them from this world. They could not cry out, for they didn't know what the soldiers were capable of.

Someone cleared their throat at the entrance of the tent like the sound of a bear scratching. It was the man with the gray beard. He did that every time he came into the tent to announce himself. He pulled aside the tent opening and entered, carrying a beaker of steaming liquid. The day before he'd been wearing armor, but today he was just in a simple tunic tied with a belt. This made him seem much less terrifying, but he was still impressive given his imposing height.

Bradley.

He said his name was Bradley.

"Don't pay any attention to them," he said with a hint of annoyance. "They're drunk, but they're not bad guys. They're just exhausted."

The war. The massacre. The murders. Sure, they had every reason to be exhausted, thought the injured person bitterly.

They were beasts, savage animals of blood and violence. Even the fiercest of beasts needed rest.

"How do you feel?" asked Bradley.

The injured person sat in obstinate silence in their bed. How did they feel? Rage and terror were boiling within.

He hadn't hurt them at all. In fact, he'd done everything he could to save their life. These last three days, he had cleaned their wounds and stitched them back together. He had even helped them to eat when they couldn't do it for themselves. All the same, this camp was filled with warriors and English banners by the dozen, with their threatening lion heads, so the mistrust would not disappear so easily.

Bradley put the beaker on the floor and pointed to the bandage.

"You opened up your stitches again," he said in a soft tone.

Red droplets were soaking through the gray fabric.

He moved his enormous, thin, calloused hands forwards. Warrior's hands. Hands made for killing, not for healing. The injured person wondered how many men, women, and children's lives those hands had taken. The person flinched. Like always.

"It's okay," whispered Bradley, "I have to make sure you didn't completely pull the stitches out and then clean them, or it will get infected."

He had the strength of a bear, but his movements were

soft and cautious without being imprecise. He gently pulled the bandage apart and dabbed a little hot water where the dried blood had stuck to the fabric.

"The stitches have held, that's something."

He cleaned the flesh. The injured person tried not to cry or jump up.

"I know it's been difficult," said Bradley. "I mean, everything that's happened."

"No, you don't."

The words were barely a voice, just a whisper.

He had no idea how difficult it was. No. He couldn't know. The injured person was sure of that. They chose to stare at Bradley for a few seconds. In the weak light of the lantern placed on a wooden stump, his face was impassive, but his eyes shone with rage.

"You're wrong, but I won't tell you my life story," said the man.

In any case, the injured person didn't want to hear it.

"You have to be careful," he continued, "extremely careful."

He glanced around the tent. Three other injured souls were also there, but they were so badly hurt that they were unconscious. They would surely die in a day or two. Three at the most.

Bradley hadn't chosen this tent by accident.

He paused to find the right words.

"It's a question of life or death. No one must notice you for the moment."

The English soldier had never been so talkative. During his last visits, he had barely spoken a few words. Not today. Because of what had happened.

He began his lecture, not in the tone of a sermon but with a hint of worry.

"What you did last night was careless. Very dangerous, even."

The injured person averted their eyes to the darkness of the tent.

"Both of us could have been killed."

That would have been better, thought the injured person. Preferable to all of this.

In the middle of the previous night, they had regained enough strength after waking up from their comatose state after two days. They waited for Bradley to fall asleep and for the patrol to compete their rounds before they sprung from the tent to escape. The cold was biting on their skin. They were only wearing a simple shirt and pants as thin as a sheet, and worse, they had bare feet.

Despite the shivers that made their teeth chatter, they'd used the cover of darkness to dodge between the tents. Twice, they'd almost been seen and had barely made it to the hastily constructed palisade, completely out of breath.

Once they were out of the camp, their heartbeat racing as

though they were already galloping across the surrounding fields dimly lit by the moonlight, they had run in the grass with no concern for the stones they stepped on or the bristles that caught their legs. They held their side with their hand as the wound made them suffer. Thinking they'd gotten far enough away from the camp and at the end of their strength, they stopped by a small body of water for a break, breathing in the air of freedom. Their surroundings were in complete darkness. No villages or lights. Only the oppressive shadow of the city that finally stopped smoking on the other side of the Tweed.

"Who goes there?" shouted someone as a sword crossed their path.

It was an English patrolman.

When the injured person was spotted, they thought about running, but soon realized they wouldn't get very far. The last of their strength would be gone in a few steps.

They were too far away for their face to be seen and recognized.

Another, more authoritative voice came across the splashing of the water.

"It's nothing, I can vouch for him."

It was Bradley. He had come to stand next to the injured person who had turned their face slightly into the shadows on purpose. As he saw the soldier coming closer, he whispered that he wasn't one of his own men.

"Who goes there?"

"It's me, Bradley. Second in command."

As he closed the distance, the soldier squinted before giving a salute.

"Commander. My apologies, I didn't know he was with you. My mission is to—"

"What's your name?"

"Pete, commander."

"I know your mission, Pete, and you're doing it very well."

"No one normally leaves the camp."

The soldier couldn't hide a note of suspicion in his voice.

"He's an injured soldier. He hallucinated and ran."

"Injured?"

Bradley's lie hung by a thread. No commander would have run after a simple wounded soldier.

"What, don't you understand the word? I'm taking him back to camp. You'd do best to continue your patrol."

Pete gave a quick salute and, fearing rebuttal, let them go. Bradley led the injured one by the shoulder to support them and they began to walk back. They had barely made it three yards when the soldier seemed to come to his senses.

"Wait a minute! My report!"

He jogged to catch up with them.

"They'll ask me for the soldier's name for my reports!"

As he reached them, he pulled the injured soldier by

the arm to face him and then saw them very clearly in the moonlight.

"Huh? But that's no soldier, that's…"

A sword slit his throat.

The injured person would remember Pete's expression of surprise and terror forever.

The commander hadn't hesitated for a second. He got rid of the body—the injured person wasn't sure how, since they were frozen in fear from what they'd just witnessed—and they returned to the camp. Neither one of them opened their mouths on the way back.

"Are you listening to me?" continued Bradley, dragging the injured person out of their memories. "Next time—and there better not be a next time—I won't be able to save you."

The injured person suddenly wanted to scream. To scream so loud that every single soldier in the camp would order them to shut up.

They felt trapped.

Berwick.

They hadn't even been able to say goodbye to Berwick and everything it held.

Everything they had lost.

After he'd finished with the bandages, Bradley readjusted the dressing that covered the injured person's right wrist, which wasn't covering an injury.

"Never take it off," he reminded them. "No one can see what's underneath."

Defeated, the wounded person withdrew into themselves in an icy silence.

Bradley only patted their shoulder. He tried to find the words, but nothing came to mind. After pulling the covers back over their thin body, he left the tent and returned to join the soldiers who were still awake.

The injured person tried to return to sleep. There was nothing else to do anyway. They prayed they wouldn't be plunged once more into nightmares of the past.

7

CRANSHAWS

Fillan fought off the darkness, only half-conscious.

Rain drops hit his cheek. The wind dried them rapidly. He was draped over the back of a horse at gallop. Two arms pinned him to stop him from falling. Green countryside unfolded below a cloudy sky. He thought he saw a crow and wanted to raise his eyes to get a better look, but he felt a terrible pain in his face and was plunged once more into the abyss.

Dreams and reality intermingled; moments of consciousness were followed by darkness in a nauseating rhythm. The sunset seemed to show an unfathomable shimmering mirage of an army on the march. Darkness. Edan and Sören arguing over this famous Brotherhood. Darkness. Thunder rumbling without lightning, shaking the whole of Scotland. Darkness. An immense stag chasing a child. Darkness.

Every time, he did everything he could to stay in the moment, but tumultuous waves always dragged him in deeper.

Until finally, he broke out of the chaotic cycle and opened his eyes, disoriented to see the face of Moira inches from his own. He could see wrinkles that were normally hidden behind her black hair. The druid must have been at least thirty, maybe older.

She raised her eyebrows and smiled.

"I thought you'd never wake up!"

"How long was I…"

"Two days. I volunteered to carry you on my horse. I had to keep an eye on you."

Fillan couldn't work out what she was talking about at first, but as he tried to sit more comfortably, he thought his head was going to explode with the pain. He grimaced and put a hand to his face.

Moira gently knocked away his fingers.

"Don't touch," she said. "Unless you want it to get infected…"

"What did…?"

"You got sliced, remember?"

A shiver of horror ran down his spine as he remembered the icy eyes of the Norwegian.

"But why…?"

"It's harder to recognize you now."

Fillan hated to be interrupted. In normal times, Moira would have gotten on his nerves. He would have made a snide comment and carried on his sentence. But there was nothing normal about this situation, and every word he spoke exacerbated his injury. So, he chose to stay quiet, with a level of willpower Alastair would have been proud of.

"I'll admit," carried on the druid, "there was perhaps a less... barbaric... way. But, well. Sören..."

She left his name hanging with a shrug, as though Sören and barbarism went hand in hand.

Once again, they'd made camp in the woods. Edan and Craig were taking care of the horses, debating the quality of the services offered at a brothel in Glasgow. Kyle and Sören were talking in low voices, leaning against a tree. Fergus was running his fingers over his lute and singing softly.

When Fillan got up, wobbling, only the Norwegian looked over in his direction.

"Come on," said Moira. "Let's go to the river so you can wash up. Your face looks awful."

The young man believed her.

"Are we far from Dalkeith?" he asked as they walked.

"About halfway."

As he asked the question, he realized that Dalkeith was his only goal. He had to know what this Brotherhood Sören talked about wanted with him. The mystery kept him going; he had nothing else to hold on to.

The stream appeared under an embankment. Moira left him alone but kept an eye on him.

He bent down, curious to see the extent of the damage, and his eyes widened in shock. What had they done to him? A stranger stared back at him from the reflective water. A paste dressing covered the wound up to his right eyebrow, went across his nose and ended at the corner of his mouth. His hair, which the day before had reached down to his shoulders, was now only up to his ears. By some strange spell it was no longer red, but brown.

"It's only superficial," called Moira. "You'll heal quick enough."

"And will my hair heal too?"

She gave him a sad look.

"Hair grows back!" shouted Sören as he joined them. "That's Kyle's handiwork! Don't worry, she still finds you attractive like that."

Fillan was embarrassed. He hadn't thought for one moment that Kyle might like him. The warrior had paid him no more mind than the flies behind her horse.

"Good to see you're doing better," added the Norwegian as he reached him.

Doing better? He'd never felt so bad! Sören had disfigured him. Fillan wanted to whack him in the face to return the favor, even if it broke all his fingers against the mercenary's stone jaw.

"You're one to talk," grumbled the teenager.

"You were putting us in danger."

He didn't even try to say sorry. Fillan shot him a furious glare and tried to get away from him, but Sören grabbed him by the arm.

"What do the English want with you?"

"I don't know!" he replied.

His own voice annoyed him. It sounded weak and wobbly, with no confidence. It was the voice of a kid, which squeaked in comparison to the echoing rumble of the Norwegian.

"Think!"

Fillan pulled himself away and stared along the water. He didn't want to think too deeply into his memories. The image of the main square in Berwick came to mind, burning hotter than a furnace.

"They think I killed a captain. I think."

Sören raised an eyebrow.

"You think?"

"Yes, but they got it wrong. It was the blacksmith."

"I don't doubt that."

The young man realized that Sören thought him incapable of bearing a weapon. That wasn't untrue, but it annoyed him all the same.

"Whether they were mistaken or not, the English won't let such an insult go unpunished."

He looked the boy up and down.

"Alright, we'll get going, but make sure you get a good wash. Or Kyle and Moira will make me abandon you in a field... because of the smell."

He left and Fillan washed quickly. The icy water made him shiver, but it also did him good. While he washed away the blood, sweat, and mud from his body, Moira pretended to cook mushrooms. He wasn't stupid: she was watching him.

When they returned to the others, Sören addressed the group.

"We make a stop at Cranshaws," he said. "We'll be there by nightfall."

"Isn't that risky?" grumbled Craig, with an accusatory glance at Fillan.

"I doubt the English have ventured so far into the country."

"Worst we could do is make some heads roll," chortled Edan.

Fillan wanted to mount his horse by himself, but Moira forbade it. She wanted to keep an eye on his health and made him ride with her.

"Ah, the magic of the Lowlands," cackled Edan as he spurred on his horse. "A maggot turned into an ugly damsel."

He laughed heartily. From atop her horse, Kyle was watching Fillan. He didn't see her doing it, because his blood was boiling, unable to bear being insulted or treated like an invalid. The young woman threw something at Edan's face that made him fall off his horse.

"God damn it!" he shouted as he set off in pursuit, shouting insults that grew progressively more inventive.

"Fillan, would you please stop squeezing so hard."

In his anger he'd dug his fingernails into the druid's leg. Ashamed, he babbled an incoherent apology.

⚔

They rode at speed all day. The hilly country calmed him. Along the route they saw lines of peasants fleeing the war in an exodus. Fillan figured they must have been hoping for safety in the north.

When Sören made them stop to regroup at the mouth of another valley, night had already fallen half an hour earlier. The only sounds disturbing the night's calm were the sounds of animals and the pattering of rain on the branches.

"Cranshaws is just over there," he said, pointing a finger at the shadows down below.

"It's darker than inside a horse's ass!" said Edan.

Fillan was beginning to think the bald man had been staring too long at the animals' rears. But he wasn't wrong. In the darkness, you could barely make out the buildings in the village. The moon was hidden by the clouds.

Sören pensively stroked his beard.

"We'd better not take any risks. Craig, go ahead as scout."

The warrior spurred on his horse, axe in hand, and disappeared into the night.

They waited in silence and darkness. An owl hooted from somewhere. As the seconds passed, the air seemed to grow more oppressive. Fillan couldn't say how long the mercenary had been gone, but it felt like an eternity. Another longer hoot reverberated around them.

"Something's not right," Moira whispered to Sören.

"What?"

Another hoot.

"That's not a bird…"

The trumpeting of a horn from the village interrupted them.

"Damn it!" shouted Edan.

They urged their mounts in the direction of the village. When they arrived in the town square, it was Kyle's turn to curse.

"Damn it!" she repeated.

Craig was fighting the English soldier who'd just raised the alarm. He split his head in two with a vertical swipe and sent a spurt of black liquid into the night. Another soldier lay at his feet with his face caved in.

"By the Sidh*…" gasped Moira.

---

* The Sidh is the Other World in Celtic mythology.

The village was a monstrous devastation, doors and windows of houses all battered in. Plagues of flies circled the bodies of the residents that bathed in their own blood.

The sound of footsteps approached.

"It's a trap!" shouted Kyle.

But it was too late. Other soldiers were arriving, torches in hand.

"Fergus, you stay behind with the kid!" ordered Sören, "The rest of you, with me!"

He jumped off his horse; everyone but the bard and Fillan followed suit.

"You don't move from there!" ordered Moira, poking him with her stick.

The teenager complied, turned the reins, and retreated with the bard, who was taking care of all the rest of the horses under an enormous elm tree.

The English threw their torches to the ground and the fight began. Painful memories assaulted Fillan. He nervously tried to chase them away by shaking his head.

Sören and his companions were battling seven English soldiers around the wells in the center of the village. The clashing of weapons echoed against the buildings and violently broke the night's silence.

The Norwegian was up against two enemies. Fillan had never seen a battle like it. It was hypnotizing. Sören dodged their blows with an incomparable agility, folding his body and diving. When it was his turn to strike, he did not hesitate to run through one of his opponents by turning. The teenager had no idea how he'd managed it, but he'd even been able to impale the second soldier on the sword that stuck through his comrade.

Kyle, Moira, Craig, and Edan weren't doing too badly either. They each gave the impression of fighting completely independently from each other, but when you looked closer, they were doing a *danse macabre* completely in sync with one another, twisting and turning to keep swapping positions and throw off their enemies. Soon there was only one English soldier still alive.

"Ah, the dogs!" spat Kyle, snorting like a bull.

An old cottage caught fire from one of the torches. At the same moment, another horn rang out from the shadows surrounding the village. Another battalion was filing through the south gate on foot.

That's when Fillan saw him. The antler-helmeted warrior. His long blood-colored cape flew in the wind. Just like in the alley in Berwick, he pointed with his sword at Sören's group as a signal for his men to attack, and the fight began again. Without knowing how, Fillan found himself off his horse, sword in hand. He was face to face with the man who had killed Alastair. The man who'd caused Ailéas's death. He paid no attention to Fergus, who called after him while he tried to hold on to the horses. He didn't listen to Sören, screaming at him, anguish piercing his icy voice. He ran straight at the warrior.

The young man was only a few yards away when the man in the helmet stared at him with his black eyes.

Hatred was replaced with an unbearable terror and Fillan was frozen on the spot.

8

LANN FALA

The fire spread through the whole village due to the humidity. It devoured all the thatched roofs from within, lighting up the night sky with a circle of flames around the town square. It even spread to the human remains, leaving behind the terrible smell of burning flesh.

The warrior with the antlers pressed forwards. His helmet and the plates of his armor glimmered, reflecting the flames. He raised his gigantic sword. Fillan was frozen in fear and tried with all his might to move, but couldn't budge an inch. The memory of Ailéas's scream echoed in his head and vibrated in his eardrums.

"Craig!" screamed Sören, up against two more English soldiers.

The mercenary intervened just in time, blocking the blade with the handle of his axe. The contact made a deafening noise. The warrior in the helmet slipped out of the hold on his weapon, aiming for Craig's neck and barely missing his carotid.

"Get out of here!" the mercenary cried to the teenager.

He pushed his opponent back and soon followed up with a furious spinning of his axe, held with his arms outstretched. Despite the impressive distance, the warrior leapt backwards and was able to raise his guard with the steel of his blade on his shoulder. At the end of his movement, Craig also sank into a defensive stance. The two warriors were measuring each other up.

The rain poured, calming the fires and tapping on armor.

Fillan was pulled violently from behind, forcing him to turn around.

"Idiot!" shouted Moira, covered in blood that wasn't her own. "What did I say?!"

He was still deafened and still terrified, but he also felt ashamed to be lectured this way.

A soldier jumped on them. The druid dealt him a devastating blow with her stick and sliced his throat with a curved knife. Fillan would never have guessed she was carrying such a weapon. She stowed it quickly back in her clothes.

More English were flooding into the village, and they'd soon be overrun.

"Oh, crap!" exclaimed Kyle.

"Let's get out of here!" shouted Craig, twirling his axe in the air.

His opponent laughed at another masterfully choreographed attack. Fillan and Moira made it back to Fergus and jumped on their mounts. They spurred on their horses and headed towards the darkness in haste. The rain soaked their faces. Kyle, Sören and Edan were right at their heels. Just before they reached the edge of the village, Fillan turned. In the light of the last flames, he saw the knight decapitate Craig with one brutal movement of his sword. The mercenary had sacrificed himself to buy them time.

"Craig! They murdered Craig!" moaned Kyle.

"Sören!" Edan screamed as he fled into the night. "Sören, you hear? What the hell are we doing? We should go back and make them pay!"

"No! Shut it and follow me!"

For the first time, Fillan felt the Norwegian was losing control of himself. The one who was normally icier than a loch* in winter now had a trembling voice.

They carried on all night in closed formation, holding tightly onto their horses and trusting Sören's horse, who knew the region and led the way. More often than not, they

---

* A loch is a type of long lake typical in Scotland, formed at the crossing of valleys.

could only go at a trot because it was the only way to prevent their horses from breaking a leg in the darkness. They crossed many rivers and often changed direction. Sometimes they even separated into two groups only to meet up again later. Fillan realized Sören was doing everything he could to make it impossible to follow their trail.

They didn't stop until dawn at the top of a leaden hill in the region. There stood the ruins of a broch*, of which only an old wall and an arch remained. All their faces were marked by the terrible events at Cranshaws.

"Do you think they'll pick up our trail?" asked Moira worriedly.

Sören, deep in thought, did not respond.

"No way," said Edan on his behalf. "We've come twelve miles, I'd say. Plus, they were all on foot as far as I could see. We can relax. Sören, I..."

The Norwegian pushed past him without even a glance. He headed right for Fillan and pulled him off the horse, making him violently hit the floor.

"Idiot! What the hell were you thinking!"

"I'm sorry," babbled Fillan in a terrified voice.

"Did you know who that was?!"

"Who?"

---

* A broch is a round and hollow tower made of drystone dating from the British Iron Age to the early Middle Ages – i.e. between 100 BC and 300 AD.

"The antler knight!" growled the mercenary.

"He was the one who killed my master."

Surprise flooded the Norwegian's face.

"Do you mean to tell me you saw him in Berwick?!"

"Yeah, he was the one in front of the shop."

"Were there any more of them?"

"Three, with red capes."

Sören had him by the neck and pulled him right to his face to scream at him.

"WHY DIDN'T YOU SAY SO BEFORE?"

"I did… The English soldiers and…"

"HE AND HIS MEN HAVE NOTHING TO DO WITH THE ENGLISH SOLDIERS!"

His eyes were like a madman's. A madman dying of fear.

"What do they want with you?!"

Fillan glanced around the group. They were all watching with a worried look, the type you'd give a condemned man.

"The captain… They think I killed the cap–"

"But the *Lann Fala* wouldn't care about that!"

"Lann Fala?"

"Merciless trackers! The warrior you charged at is their leader! Cornavii!"

Fillan had never heard the name, nor that of the Lann Fala. He felt completely lost and tried with all his might to calm the anguish of his memories.

"What did they want with your master?"

He had no idea. All he could remember was the sight of the giant sword plunging into Alastair's body and his own cry of despair.

"I don't know," he burst out, spitting at Sören's face.

The fear somehow made him want to lash out.

The mercenary shook him one last time before letting go of him. He paced away in agitation.

"Sören," called Edan, "how many times have I told you? We never know what kind of shit the Brotherhood gets us into. This story stinks of something fishy."

"I know."

"We'd be better off leaving him. The Templars will…"

"Out of the question!" interrupted the Norwegian. "I won't look like a quitter in front of the Brotherhood."

"But Craig…"

"Out of the question, I said."

He let out a guttural scream that echoed around the waters. All the birds went still. Silence hung for a few moments over the group. They all watched the scene without moving. Fillan sat on the floor and saw that Sören was staring at him again with those signature wolf eyes. The mercenary withdrew a bloody sword from the bag on one of the horse's backs.

"So you think you can fight, huh? So, fight!" he screamed, throwing the sword at Fillan's feet.

He pulled out his own sword and flexed his arm muscles.

Fillan had only just managed to calm his breathing and acted with a reflex he never would have thought possible. He looked around for Ailéas. She was normally the one to come and fight in his place. "*You always get yourself in trouble, then it's up me to save your skin,*" she'd always joke. Deep down, she was always more than happy to come to his aid. He hated that; he hated the idea of her saving him for years. But in this moment, he wanted nothing more. All the emotions he'd been pushing down threatened to boil up to the surface: Ailéas, his twin, his mirror image. He missed her so much. His heart almost burst out of his chest.

"I don't…"

"Stand up!" bellowed Sören.

He shakily raised the weapon and stood up. His fingers were trembling.

"What are you waiting for? Attack!"

The steel was heavy at the end of his arm, and he shifted his other hand up to try and steady it. Fillan wanted to take a step forward but remained frozen in place.

"Well?" spat the Norwegian.

Fillan couldn't explain why he couldn't move. It was the same paralysis that had come over him in the street in Berwick and against the knight in Cranshaws. A deep-rooted terror.

The mercenary launched a high attack, and Fillan barely had the good sense to dodge. In shock, he threw the sword into the air.

"If you can't fight, you're an idiot to charge in!"

Ailéas's words were still ringing in his ears.

"Are you listening to me?" raged Sören. He whacked him in the face with the hand holding the sword hilt and Fillan felt his nose crack before stumbling back.

"Devil take you! I only just patched him up!" begged Moira, raising her arms to the sky.

The giant paid no attention to her. He came so close to his face that Fillan felt the hairs of his beard bristling against his chin.

"I lost one of my men because of you."

An ounce of sadness tinged his anger. He raised his fist once more, but Fillan was instinctively able to protect himself by throwing his arms out in front of him. He opened his eyes to Sören's furrowed brow, frowning deeper than ever before. His expression was indecipherable. Fillan saw he was staring at his wrist, where he had a birthmark.

"You…"

He fixed him with a more surprised look than Fillan had ever seen, as if the giant had seen a ghost. He walked away without another word.

"Sören!" yelled Edan. "Damn it! Sören!"

"Set up camp and leave me the hell alone," ordered the Norwegian before disappearing into the trees.

Someone held out their hand to help Fillan up. He expected to see Moira, but it was Kyle. Once he was up, he wiped away the blood dripping from his nose.

"What happened?" asked the young woman.

Fillan gave her a sulky look.

"He floored me, that's what happened. You were there, you saw it perfectly well."

She rolled her eyes.

"I mean, what did you say to make him leave like that?"

"Not a word."

"Nothing?"

His terror gave way to shame, and anger that the others had watched and made no move to intervene. He left, shrugging his shoulders, ignoring the glare from the warrior.

9

TRUST

A full morning passed with no sign of Sören.

The camp was set up at the base of the ruins in a somber atmosphere. Everyone slept a couple of hours, taking turns for guard duty, but despite the comfort of rest and sleep, everyone's faces were pained and set. With no river nearby, nobody could even wipe away the stains of Cranshaws, which made them look even worse.

Moira took care of Fillan's nose. It was a small comfort to find that neither the bone or the cartilage were broken. He still had to bite down on his fist as the druid reset it with her thumbs. The forest had spun for a moment and white slits appeared in his vision.

Craig's loss weighed heavily on them, but no one brought up the subject. Fergus just played a sad tune on his lute. Only Edan acted like normal, as though nothing had happened.

He kept complaining that they should have left ages ago. The lack of imagination in his insults, however, made it seem like he too was in a blaming mood.

Fillan felt uneasy in the group upon seeing all the accusatory looks shot his way. He sat apart from the others on an old tree trunk. His sleep was filled with nightmares, as they had been since the massacre in Berwick. When he woke up, the anger he felt towards Sören had been replaced with a deep sense of guilt. He regretted acting without thinking, not even knowing what came over him. It was his fault Craig was dead, killed by the antler knight.

Cornavii.

The name echoed in his ears. The Norwegian's words and his fury had only deepened the mystery surrounding the unknown knight. Fillan had trouble believing that this 'tracker' was after him. After all, he wasn't anything to anyone, though he couldn't help but wonder if there was a link between the Lann Fala and whatever was waiting for him in Dalkeith. He didn't believe in coincidences. What could this Brotherhood who seemed to have hired them be?

Fillan mulled over the little information he had to go on, trying to understand. A voice made him jump:

"Do you want me to tell you?"

It was Kyle.

Cranshaws hadn't left her unscathed either. The young mercenary had tried to rearrange her braid, but strands of bloodied hair fell down around her face. Traces of red and mud stained her forehead and cheeks.

"You won't turn that crap into mushrooms just by staring at it."

She smiled at her own joke.

Fillan blushed. Lost in his thoughts, he hadn't realized that he'd been staring at a steaming pile of horse poo.

The young woman plonked herself down next to him. Just like Sören, she intimidated him—there was just something about her.

"Sulking won't get you anywhere."

That sounded like Ailéas.

"I'm not sulking," he retorted.

"Oh? You play it well, then. You'd be a good actor."

The way she blatantly teased him was disconcerting.

"It wasn't your fault," she carried on. "Craig, I mean."

"Not true. It was totally my fault."

"Fine, I lied. You're right, it was largely your fault."

"I was trying to be nice."

"Why?"

She watched him for a moment.

"There's no sense in stewing all alone in your little corner."

"Hm."

"Oh, you're a quiet guy, huh?" She sighed, pretending to get up. "Well, if you want to stay here all alone…"

"I don't feel like I belong over there with you all."

Kyle hesitated and sat down again.

"I'm sorry," he murmured. "About Craig."

"He was a good fighter. We'll miss him. Especially Fergus."

"Why Fergus?"

"Craig was his cousin. They're part of the MacDougall clan."

Fillan felt even worse. Northern clan members were well-known for their close brotherhood. He glanced over at the bard who continued to play his chords aimlessly. He couldn't see his face but imagined it must be sad.

"He must hate me."

"I wouldn't go that far. For what it's worth, for Highlanders, death in combat is a glorious death."

"If it wasn't for me, he would have met that 'glory' much later."

"Maybe, maybe not. No one can know."

The young woman turned to face him.

"What were you thinking, running into the fight like that?"

"I don't know."

"This time I know you're lying."

He took a deep breath.

"That knight, Cornavii, he's the one who killed my master in Berwick."

"Yeah, I heard you tell Sören that. Was it also him who killed your sister?"

"Ailéas. My twin's name was Ailéas."

It was the first time he'd said her name out loud since Berwick. He tried to think about her as little as possible and ran from his emotions. In the middle of all the blood and mud, Kyle's eyes shone with sympathy. She kept quiet and maintained his stare, waiting for him to finish.

"Not directly," he carried on, "but he was responsible."

"You wanted revenge?"

"I don't know what I wanted…"

This time he wasn't lying.

A silence fell over them, but it wasn't an uncomfortable one.

Sören still hadn't returned, and instead of continuing to complain, Edan decided to eat. He pushed away the mushroom Moira offered him in disgust, preferring to chew on a stale piece of bread and a chunk of old cheese. Kyle traced Celtic rings in the ground with a stick. She decided to ask another question.

"How did you end up in Berwick?"

Fillan looked at her in surprise.

"Don't look at me like that! You don't think I believe that—with your face, build and hair—you come from the Lowlands?"

"No, you're right," he replied with a smile. "We were

born somewhere in the Highlands—I don't know where exactly—and we lived there until we were eight."

"What happened?"

"Our clan was attacked. We were the only survivors."

"That must have been awful!"

"I bet…"

"What do you mean 'you bet'? Don't you remember anything?"

"No."

"Oh…"

Another pause, then: "What's it like?"

"What?"

"Having a twin."

He watched the young woman and wondered why she was asking so many questions. Maybe it was her way of beating boredom?

"You have a lot of things in common. A lot of differences, too."

"Could you be any vaguer!" she exclaimed, and they both chuckled.

"Ah! It's hard to explain!" he started, taking a moment to think. "You know, it's like there's another you, a person who looks like you even down to your movements and expressions. Someone you have a strong bond with, that you don't have with anyone else, that can't be put into words. A person who's like a part of you, an extension of yourself. But at the same time, they're not you. You make up a whole together, but each has their own personality and character."

As he spoke, the weight he'd been carrying in his chest seemed to dissipate. Happy memories of him and Ailéas, inseparable and enjoying themselves in the streets of Berwick, came to mind.

"That must be incredible!" laughed Kyle. "I don't have any brothers or sisters."

"Oh, really?"

Only children were rare, and especially so for girls.

"My mother only had me, much to the disappointment of my father. There's a reason I have a boy's name."

She gave him a wink.

She brought the conversation back to him, as if they'd talked too much about her with just those few words.

"I bet you got on really well?"

A dark expression passed over Fillan's face. Everything he'd just said about his relationship with Ailéas was true. Most of it was. He thought about how he'd acted out against his sister, for no reason. The happy memories disappeared. He relived pushing her in the shop, out of pure cruelty, instead.

A mix of guilt and anger swirled around to reform the weight on his chest. The moment of peace was over.

"Why do you care so much?" he said in agitation.

Up against this change in attitude, Kyle's eyes darted around.

"I'm just intrigued," she admitted with sincerity.

Fillan let another silence hang for a moment.

"We didn't get on," he started, defeated. "We argued a lot, these last few years."

"What about?"

This girl was the epitome of prying questions.

"As we grew up, we became very different. Ailéas always dreamed of leaving Berwick to find our roots in the northern wilderness."

"And you?"

"I was the opposite. I like the pace of the city. When I finished my apprenticeship, I thought I'd open a shop in Edinburgh or Glasgow to build my reputation."

"So you grew apart?"

It was true, but there was something else. A past truth he knew deep down. Ailéas didn't care about their differences. They even made her laugh. It was him and only him who'd built an icy wall between them. The worst thing was that he didn't even understand why he'd done it.

"Do you miss her?"

"Yes."

Kyle didn't say anything, not even that she was sorry. Her expressive eyes said it all. The tweeting of birds echoed in the air. He watched the wind rustling the leaves.

"It seems so stupid now," he continued.

"What?"

"Talking about how we grew apart because of how we saw the future, when our destinies were destroyed in one night. I have no future; I have nothing now."

For a second, he looked pitiful, and Kyle stopped drawing on the ground to face him.

"I don't really know what's waiting for you in Dalkeith," she began.

He watched her out of the corner of his eye, wondering why she said that.

"But you want my advice? Be the master of your own destiny."

"That's a bit vague," he chuckled.

She smiled.

"What I mean is that the Fillan who sewed fabrics in Berwick has no more purpose, and he needs to go."

"What do you mean?"

"Because, due to that Fillan, a man died yesterday."

The young man frowned, hurt.

"Easy for you to say!" He grew annoyed. "You just said you didn't know what was waiting for me in Dalkeith."

"Does that make you think you have no future and react without thinking? The first time we met, you asked Sören not to treat you like a kid. This is the moment to show you aren't one. You're going to have to change and stop sulking."

She gave him a final look and got up and left. Was that what she'd wanted to say from the start?

Fillan stayed where he was. He was angry and wanted to believe that Kyle had only come to talk to him to chastise him and lecture him like a child. But that wasn't true. She only wanted to advise him and help him.

10

TRAINING

Fillan was awoken with a kick. He grumbled and rolled over. For once, he hadn't had any nightmares. Another, harder kick made him open his eyes. In the semi-darkness he saw Kyle above him with her hands on her hips.

"Up, slacker!" she said.

"Wh—what?"

Something heavy hit his throat, cutting his breath short. It was a sword stowed in its sheath.

"Pick it up and follow me," ordered the young woman.

He turned his head and watched the forest. The others were all fast asleep, wrapped in their tartans. Dawn had not yet risen.

"But why?" he said, rubbing his eyes.

"Shhhh," she whispered, beckoning him to follow her.

He got up with a wobble and almost fell on top of Sören,

who was snoring loudly. The day earlier, they'd left the banks of the broch when he returned around midday. They had ridden the whole day, and the Norwegian didn't say a word about what he'd been up to during his absence.

"Where are you taking me?" asked Fillan as he jogged to keep up.

"Training."

"What kind of training?"

"To cook mushrooms."

Surprised, he watched the mercenary, not realizing that she was teasing him.

"No, dummy. Training you to fight."

"But I know how to fight!"

"Oh, yeah? News to me."

"That's because you didn't see me…"

"Exactly. I didn't see you," she retorted, turning to poke him in the chest. "Even a stableboy would have ducked Cornavii. Worse! Even a wash maid could have dodged Sören if he tried to cut her throat."

"But I…"

"Shut up," she said with finality. "You don't know how to fight, and that's the end of it."

She watched him with her big blue eyes, eyebrows raised and daring him to argue. Fillan's mouth hung open, unable to find anything to say. He, so used to winning any argument with his words, couldn't find any.

They slid between tree trunks and branches and emerged in a clearing. The sky was beginning to turn red beyond the horizon of the trees.

"Here will do nicely," stated Kyle.

She picked up an old chopping block and threw it into the woods. The masculine clothes she wore were belted around her thin waist and accentuated her straight shoulders. Fillan could see thick biceps under the fabric on her arms. She was about his height but twice as muscled as him.

"To begin with," she said, "stand facing me and hold your sword."

He pulled out the sword from its sheath. The metal pinged against one of the trees.

"You do realize a sword is not a fishing rod?"

"Huh?"

"You're holding it all wrong!"

"No, I…"

Kyle swung onto one leg, pulled out her own sword and hit from above. Fillan tried to block, but his sword went flying into the air.

"Yes, you are," she said dryly.

As he went to pick up his sword, she smacked him on the hand with hers.

"Ow! What's the matter with you?"

"You are here to learn, because you know absolutely

nothing, so stop pretending like you know it all and listen to what I'm telling you."

Fillan clenched his jaw. The young mercenary kept hitting the mark. He didn't know how to hold a weapon. Alastair had tried to teach him the basics of swordsmanship, but Fillan had proven to be a danger to the public. Ailéas was the fighter, not him.

Once he got back in position, Kyle explained how to hold the sword.

"You won't always be able to use both hands. This hand here, loosen up! Not so close to the hilt. Your fist, make it looser, palm up! Are you even listening to me?"

"That's all I'm doing!"

"Don't argue!"

Finally, he got it. When Kyle made their blades collide once more, he held onto his.

"That's already something," continued Kyle. "Which is your lead foot?"

"My what?"

She went around his back and shoved him with her shoulder.

"Whaaargh!"

"I said, stop arguing, or I'll kick your ass. OK, left foot," she said. "That's the one you put forwards."

During the half hour that followed, she taught him the most common defensive position, the sixth. It wasn't an easy task. Fillan almost lost an eye with his own sword and discovered that you could get cramps even while standing still. Although his body was muscled thanks to his climbs in Berwick, he wasn't used to moving in this way. You had to be quick, precise, and balanced—while he was slow, imprecise, and clumsy.

"Relax your legs!" repeated Kyle. "You're stiffer than a new bagpipe!"

Fillan had finally stopped arguing and listened to her. When he blocked one of her attacks for the first time, he nearly jumped for joy.

"Did you see that?!" he said, beaming.

"Yeah, but don't get too cocky. I hit three times lighter than I would normally," she explained.

Fillan thought back to the way the group had fought at Cranshaws. He remembered their speed, their movement and coordination. He would never reach such a level.

He kept working on his defensive stance under a shower of blows and comments from the warrior.

"That's all wrong! Be more supple! You're too bent over! Your left foot! No, that's the right! Are you stupid or are you doing this on purpose? Please, tell me you're doing it on purpose!"

She only let him breathe once he was bruised and sweaty.

"I get the feeling Sören hates me," he began, breaking the silence.

Strangely, Kyle's presence made him feel like talking. The young woman watched him curiously, as though she couldn't understand the meaning of his words.

"Do you have a habit of thinking everyone hates you?" she asked. "First Fergus and now Sören? When you wake up stiff tomorrow, will I be next on the list?"

Fillan avoided her eyes. He'd already wondered the same thing a dozen times while they were training.

"He did cut up my face and almost break my nose," he argued. "I've seen better tokens of affection."

The forest was waking up with the tweeting of birds. The sky turned blue under the sun's rays, and Kyle passed him a goatskin flask. Fillan took a small sip and was relieved to find it was only water. The young woman saw him do it and smiled.

"I can tell you were raised in the south," she said. "A coward who loves to paint himself the victim and cares about feelings!"

"You mean he doesn't hate me?"

"I mean, it's got nothing to do with feelings. For Sören, you're a job. Have you ever had feelings for a job?"

"Well, I…"

"Don't hurt yourself looking for an answer, dummy, it wasn't really a question."

She drove the conversation back to fighting techniques and showed him the different parts of a sword and their uses.

The young man was surprised to find that he could position the blade to wield it better. She reeled off all the names of the techniques, but he was struggling to listen anymore.

"What do you know about the Lann Fala?" he asked.

"My word, you really can't concentrate, can you? Do I have to kick you up the butt to keep you focused? That's it, I'm going!"

"No! Don't! I'm just exhausted. Put yourself in my position, it's understandable!"

"Yeah… sure," she murmured. "Lann Fala means 'Bloodied Blade.'"

"Well, that already sends a message!" he interrupted.

Kyle shot him a dark look.

"They're a group of elite warriors. Their members are specialists in tracking and murder. They are extremely dangerous and very well trained. Sören didn't retreat from just anyone."

"Do they follow King Edward's orders?"

"No. Some aren't even English. They're the foot soldiers of a more important group, for whom borders are just imaginary lines they cross to extend their influence."

"A 'group?'"

Kyle pinched her lips together. She'd said too much.

"Enough chat!" she said to close the subject. *"En garde!"*

He barely had time to get into position before she attacked and he was forced to block.

"You could have dodged that one by taking a step to the side. The swords don't always have to touch."

She made the same attack, and he moved out of the way in time. The blade whooshed past as she missed him.

"Why are they after me?" he asked.

Kyle frowned in annoyance.

"Not a clue, but it's definitely not a good sign."

"How so?"

"Did you not hear what I just said? They're the best trackers in England and Scotland. If you're their prey, you're in deep trouble."

"And we are, too," she said with a pointed look. "Luckily, I doubt Cornavii recognized you in Cranshaws."

Fillan wasn't sure what worried him more—that he was the target of a mysterious and well-trained group of warriors, or that he didn't know why. What had Alastair been able to keep from him?

A tapping on his back brought him out of his reverie, and he found himself face to face with Sören as he turned around.

"Time to break camp," he told them.

The two mercenaries waited until Fillan was further away to talk in peace.

"Do you think the English or Cornavii will catch up with us?" questioned Kyle.

"No idea. I don't know what information they've been

able to gather. So, you've got a soft spot for our package?" chuckled the Norwegian, taking the sword she held out to him.

"He should at least be able to hold a sword."

He agreed with a silent nod.

"Is he any good?"

"About as good as a turkey might be."

They chuckled quietly, before Kyle became serious once more and decided to ask the question that haunted her the most.

"Sören, who is he?"

The Norwegian looked at her without replying, but a wrinkle of worry appeared on his forehead.

"Don't do that. I saw your face, after Cranshaws…"

"I think he might be a Child of Fal," he said, taking his time and scratching his beard. "That's why the Brotherhood didn't give us any information. And surely why Cornavii is after him."

Kyle's eyes widened. The danger was even worse than she'd imagined.

11

MEETING

It took them more than a week to get close to Dalkeith. Fillan let himself be carried by the repetitive rhythm of each new day. That helped him not think too much. Kyle's training was perfect for that. She would teach him how to wield a sword until Sören decided it was time to move on. With practice, the young man mastered the sixth. Next, he asked Kyle to teach him the defensive stance the Norwegian always used. It was a stance where he placed the sword under his head, with the tip pointed towards the ground.

During his lessons, his body turned different shades of black and blue. Kyle gave him an extra hit every time she struck a blow that could have killed him in a real fight. Edan enjoyed pressing on his bruises and laughed at the 'poor, delicate virgin' every time he cried out in pain. But Fillan

.was proud of his bruises; they were a sign of his hard work.

On the sixth day, he managed to hit Kyle for the first time. She seemed surprised and congratulated him, but he was convinced she'd done it on purpose so he wouldn't get discouraged. They celebrated with a sip out of a flask containing some alcohol. It still burned, though it didn't hurt for as long.

The rest of the day, they advanced towards Dalkeith, either on foot or on horse. Sören made them pass over difficult trails and walk their mounts. They were moving too slowly for Edan's tastes and he thew out insults whenever he could. The Norwegian paid no attention to him and took many precautions, fearing that the Lann Fala or the English might have patrols in the region.

When, on the seventh day, the towers of the Dalkeith fort came into view through the green and misty hills, Fillan grew nervous. He feared putting the group in danger again if they went into another town. He was so tense that he became irritable. Sören noticed and slowed his horse to keep pace with him, while they moved along the outskirts through an oat field.

"What's the matter with you?" he asked. "Are you worried?"

"Shouldn't I be?"

"That just shows you're not stupid. But we have nothing to fear in Dalkeith."

"Are you sure?"

"The town and the surrounding land is held by the Graham clan. Patrick of the Grahams of Kincardine is their leader. He's a purebred Scotsman. He would never let the English into his territory without a fight."

The first scattered cottages started to appear. The suburb wrapped around the fort that stood on a promontory. Sören made a *tsk* sound and everyone pulled down their hoods. Fillan didn't have one and simply looked around him. If he hadn't seen the horrors in Berwick and the massacred bodies of the Cranshaws residents, he might have believed that the war had not started. The residents here went about their business, oblivious.

"You'd think the English hadn't invaded Scotland here…"

"In any case, they're not here," said Sören. "So, calm down."

Passersby made way for them cheerfully. A party atmosphere was all around. Houses were decorated with banners that blew in the wind and most of the trees were decorated with ribbons. Here and there, shrines of wood and flowers were scattered around.

"What are they celebrating?" asked Fillan.

"Bealltainn*!" replied Moira, beaming. "The feast will take place in less than a week!"

---

* Bealltainn is the Gaelic name for Beltaine, or Beltane, a protohistoric Celtic festival that takes place on May 1st and marks the coming of the summer season.

The young man was shocked. It had been three weeks since he'd left Berwick! It seemed like only a few days had passed, but in reality, April was almost over. He'd tried so hard to suppress his emotions that he hadn't even felt the passage of time. He looked around with haggard eyes as the residents set up an immense wooden shack in the center of the town. The group branched off and turned away from Dalkeith Castle.

"Aren't we going to the fort?" said Fillan in surprise.

"No. Graham would welcome us with open arms, but he's not the one I have to bring you to. Feet on the ground! Follow me, and you others wait here for me."

Fillan had been anticipating this moment for a long time, but now Sören was saying it, he felt it was moving too quickly.

"Don't I get to say goodbye to the others?" he asked in a panic.

"You'll see them again. No one's going anywhere until after Bealltainn."

Fillan breathed a sigh of relief. He watched each member of the group. They all made up an anchor, to which he clung. Edan with his uncouth manners, Fergus with his gentleness and songs, Moira with her quiet attitude, and Kyle with her spontaneity. She stared at him with an expression he couldn't quite make out. All of them, even Sören, despite his beastly and unreadable moods.

He followed the mercenary to an inn where Sören

addressed a server, and they went around the back of the building. Fillan's heart was almost beating out of his chest. Who was he about to meet? What truth awaited him? The questions spun in his mind in step with his impatience.

A man pushed open a door behind the inn and approached them. He was almost as tall as Sören and wore a black robe that came down to his feet, accentuating the length of his body. As he noticed the embroidery on the man's habit, Fillan realized that this man was someone important. He had a small face, and the white of his shaved cheeks made his small and piercing eyes pop.

"My dear Sören," he started in a sickly sweet voice and extended his hand. "With no news, I might have thought you were all dead!"

"Deorsa," replied Sören icily, ignoring his outstretched hand. "It's just you?"

"James was sent elsewhere. You'll have to make do with my humble self."

The man bowed.

"A whole week I've been festering in this hole, Sören!" he complained. "Why on earth did you take so long?"

Fillan felt the mercenary stiffen.

"There were some snags… mainly Cornavii," he retorted with a death glare at the one named Deorsa.

The aforementioned kept a neutral expression, which made him look like a snake.

"He'd been on the kid's trail since Berwick!" raged Sören.

Deorsa opened his eyes a little wider while maintaining his impassive expression.

"You knew, and you didn't bother to say anything?" pressed the warrior.

"I told you what the Brotherhood decided you should know, nothing more and nothing less."

"Damn it, Deorsa! You threw me into the lion's den!"

"The Brotherhood had no choice. Information came in from the south. It was urgent. You never would have accepted the mission if you knew Cornavii was involved. And who knows what you might have revealed if you'd been captured."

"Are you kidding me?"

"Oh, stop complaining. You're the one who chose to leave the Brotherhood. Don't act surprised when you're treated like an outsider."

The Norwegian grabbed him by the neck, threatening.

"I lost one of my men because of your games!" he shouted, raising his fist ready to strike.

"Such impulsiveness. Always so impulsive, even after all these years! You never change. Maybe that kind of attitude helped your clan in the past..."

The tension was so thick that Fillan was afraid to even breathe too loudly. He waited for the blow to come, but was shocked to see Sören let go, defeated. Deorsa's words had struck deep. Deorsa, acting as though what just happened wasn't the slightest concern, turned his glance towards Fillan as though he'd only just appeared.

"You must be Fillan!"

He held out his hand and Fillan wasn't brave enough to ignore it.

"Yes," he said, defensively.

The man looked him up and down as he kept shaking his hand. He shook it for a long time before tilting his hand up to see the birthmark on his wrist.

"Excellent! But what is this terrible scar?"

The teenager's wound had completely healed thanks to Moira's obsessive care. The red line still ran across his face, but he decided it gave him a rebellious look. Plus, it reminded him of Ailéas.

"I told you," interrupted the Norwegian. "All the English were looking for him."

"You do have curious methods, Sören. And what a shame you couldn't manage to get the girl, too. Thomas will be disappointed."

The more this man spoke, the more Fillan hated him.

"Word on the grapevine, young man, is that you killed an English captain."

Fillan didn't answer right away. He had met plenty of this type of man in the markets, at his master's side. He knew he had to be careful with every word, or they could be used against him.

"That's not true."

"I'm sure!" chuckled Deorsa. "I just wanted you to confirm it. The best information comes directly from the source! Very good! Sören, I have to admit something, and you're not going to like it. Oh no, you won't like it at all…"

"Go on," snarled the Norwegian.

"As James isn't here, Dalkeith is just one step. As you can imagine, I'm not going to be the one to take care of the kid. You have to take him to Scone."

"What the hell are you saying?!"

"Yes, yes, I know! You'll have your little tantrum and threaten me, but eventually you'll agree."

"What makes you think that?"

"Your price will be doubled."

Sören scowled thoughtfully.

"This kid is a real pain," he said after a few seconds. "You really don't have anyone else to do it?"

The man forcefully shook his head.

Fillan knew the Norwegian's only wish was to be rid of him. He should have laughed at him, but it caused him pain.

"We'll take him to Scone, but you and I will have words later."

Sören didn't look at Fillan but he knew that 'later' meant 'without him.'

"Excellent!" said Deorsa joyfully. "You should stay for Bealltainn," he continued. "You need to rest. And as for me, it will give me the chance to scatter false trails in the region."

He gave them a broad smile and returned to the inn.

Fillan was terribly disappointed. He knew even less than when he started. A thousand questions burned on his lips, but given the huffing and grumbling of the Norwegian, he decided that this wasn't the time to ask them.

He felt lost, as though his own life was slipping through his fingers.

9

The nightmare goes on forever.

People are running in all directions. They are only dark, fleeting, inhuman shapes that wail in the night. Sometimes the cries die out suddenly, as their owners are caught in the glistening smoke and flames. Sometimes they get louder and even more terrible.

They tear through the night.

On the ground lie the dark, abandoned, and trampled masses of those who have been silenced. All around them the embers of the burning houses whip around.

The shape that is moving through the smoky darkness comes into focus. It is getting closer and closer. By the glow of flames, and to the rhythm of its heavy and terrifying steps, you think you see deer antlers.

As they move towards you, the air is filled with more screams of terror.

Again, the beam cracks.

And that cry. Always the same cry.

Where is it coming from?

12

TRUST

"Ailéas. My name is Ailéas."

Her voice was barely more than a whisper.

Bradley bowed his head as he closed the tent flap behind him and looked at her with his silver-gray eyes.

Given all the effort the man had gone through to save her life, Ailéas had finally decided to trust him. At least enough to tell him her name. If the English commander had wanted to hurt her, he would have done it long ago on one of the many times he'd had the chance. After her escape attempt, and despite the best efforts of the man to heal it, her wound had become infected, and she had teetered between life and death. The teenager had barely made it through, and she never tried to escape again. She remained in stony silence, simply trying to survive.

Bradley had tried everything to get her to talk. Every

day, he tried to start a conversation, on every imaginable subject, each one of them futile. He'd explained to her that after everything she had been through, talking was the best thing to do. Ailéas didn't share this opinion. For days, she simply stayed quiet and was content in her sulking. The day before, however, they'd had their first real discussion as the defensive walls she'd built up had started to come down.

The Englishman had come to find her, holding a handful of dice, just as he'd done for the past week. He'd explained the rules of the game of chance. At first, she'd resisted, but up against his insistence and his patience, she sulkily agreed to play. The other injured soldiers in the tent had died long ago. They were alone, and as the bone dice rattled, she finally asked the question she'd been wondering about for a long while:

"Why did you save me in Berwick?"

Bradley took the time to count the score before meeting her gaze. He didn't seem surprised, as though he'd been expecting the question.

"I acted how my honor told me to act," he said as he threw the dice, with a determined and sincere look.

Ailéas's memories reawakened. The blood that followed in the light of the flames in the alley. The bodies of her attackers, the bandits of Berwick, that spluttered out of existence with a gargle. The unbearable pain in her abdomen and her hand reaching for the outstretched arm of the one who'd come to save her. Yes, he was sincere about it, but she felt like he was hiding something from her, because for a few seconds on that night, he'd almost killed her, brandishing his sword. But something made him stop.

"Something stopped you from…" she murmured. "I'm not stupid."

"You're right," he admitted, crossing his fingers together in his lap. "And if I want you to trust me, I have to be completely honest with you."

He stroked his gray beard and pointed to the teenager's wrist, where a leather bracelet had replaced the bandage from the first few days.

"My birthmark?" she said, the confusion making the scar on her forehead fold up.

"That's not just any birthmark. It's the mark of fate. I know, I made the same face when I first heard about it. I even rolled my eyes. It was a very long time ago, before you were even born, I'd imagine. At the time, I wasn't a soldier, and I traveled a lot. I had a thirst for adventure and danger. I visited the Highlands for a few days because it was on my wish list. At the edge of a river where I was fishing for salmon, a bear attacked me and left me for dead. I only survived because a group of Highlanders were passing and took me to their clan."

Ailéas was captivated, just like every time she heard anything about the northern wilds, the clans, and her origins.

"When I woke up, the druid who had healed me made me promise one thing: to protect and help anyone who bore the mark she drew in the ground—the same mark you have on your wrist. Five years might go by, ten, it didn't matter. It was a lifelong debt. It bordered on prophecy. I accepted, not really believing in the obligations of the elder. But when I saw you in the alley, her old face swam in my memory, and I knew what I had to do."

The teenager pulled back the leather to look at the mark, an almost-perfect hollow brown circle with a straight line that ran a little up her arm.

A soldier called for Bradley with some urgent matter, and their discussion was cut short. Ailéas went over the story in her mind all night. She had never really believed in destiny. It was a vague and distant concept. But now she found herself face to face with the commander's revelation, and she couldn't help but wonder if the clan he spoke of might have been her own, before they were massacred.

She watched the old man who sat down in front of her and placed the wooden board and dice between them. The wind blew outside in the night air.

"Ailéas," he repeated. "Thank you for finally sharing it with me."

"After our talk yesterday, I thought I had nothing to fear," she said with a glance at him, as though she was asking a question.

"That's correct. I'll start the game, after you beat me yesterday…"

He threw the dice.

"Double pair!" he said. "Off to a good start."

Ailéas felt like he was doing everything he could to prevent her from bringing up the subject she really wanted to talk about.

"What's going to happen now?" she said, seizing the dice.

"This section of the army will soon follow the advance guard and head north. It's good timing, you're better and you can walk."

"Why would I come with you?" she said with an air of annoyance and holding the dice prisoner in her hand.

Bradley crossed his arms and looked at her in silence for a few seconds.

"Because you're in danger," he said calmly. "I haven't told you to keep your head down all this time for no reason. I found out people were hunting you during the Battle of Berwick."

The massacre of Berwick, she thought.

"Hunted? By who?"

"They call themselves the Lann Fala."

"'The Bloodied Blade?'"

"Ah, you know Gaelic. They're a group of hunters and mercenaries. They've existed in England and Scotland for over twenty years."

"Are they on the English side?"

Given their name, she doubted that was the case, but she couldn't understand the link with the attack on Berwick.

"Have you ever heard of the Order of the Templars?"

The teenager shook her head before weakly throwing the dice.

"I'd be surprised if you had. They're a very influential organization with influence in many countries. It's not an English group, but they have been linked with King Edward since he's been in power. The Lann Fala is their armed wing in Scotland."

"But what's all that got to do with me?"

"I have no idea, but whatever it might be, it can't be good. The Lann Fala are murderers above anything else. Not kidnappers or ransomers."

"And they're still looking for me?"

A note of panic crept into her voice.

"Your description has been circulated around all the English commanders. I received it myself. They're also looking for a young man. They say he's your double."

"Fillan?!" she exclaimed, her heart about to explode. "He's alive?!"

"You know him?" He motioned her to be quiet.

"That's my twin brother! We were trying to get out of town when I was attacked in the alley. Why didn't you tell me he was alive?"

"I didn't know you knew each other," he said worriedly. "It seems he managed to escape."

Ailéas was drowning in emotions. A warmth was spreading through her chest while her heart skipped a beat. Fillan hadn't died in Berwick along with everyone else they'd known! The young woman almost leapt for joy at the old man's neck. She was no longer alone in the world.

"I have to find him!" she said with glistening eyes.

"I've thought long and hard during your recovery," he replied uneasily. "You're only really safe here."

"That makes no sense! You just said the English and the Lann Fala are collaborators, that everyone knows my description!"

"Has anyone ever come to attack you in this tent?"

No one had. Even when people had come to look after the other injured soldiers, no one had bothered her. Bradley had made sure of it.

"There's no better hiding place than under the enemy's nose," said the old commander in a professor-like tone.

"But I'm healed! I can't hide in this tent forever! Especially not if we're heading north!"

"I've thought about that too. I thought about making you my personal healer. Given we're in the middle of a military campaign and my age, it wouldn't seem so strange."

"Healer?"

"Do you have any idea what that involves? Do you know the basics and the herbs?"

"My master taught me, yes, but…"

"Well, it's perfect then. I'll teach you the rest, so the illusion will be perfect and you'll be safe."

Everything was moving too quickly. Ailéas felt panic taking over. She didn't want to stay among the English, following their trail of war and death. She wanted to find her brother. If the destiny she'd learned the day before was real, it could only be a good sign for their reunion.

"My brother… if I don't find him again…"

"It's too dangerous for the moment. Much too dangerous!"

"I don't care! I won't stay here doing nothing! You don't understand…"

"I understand perfectly, but think about it: you'll put yourself in danger, and if you're captured, you'll put him in danger too. The Lann Fala won't hesitate to use you to find him before they kill you both!"

"So, I just have to…"

"Wait it out. The war has only just begun. There's too much movement, too much foolish bravery."

"Wait?! For how long?"

He stared at her without replying, and the teenager understood that he didn't know himself.

Ailéas was comforted to know that her brother was alive,

but still felt defeated. What would become of him when he couldn't even hold a sword properly? She feared the worst.

"It's your turn to play," said Bradley, interrupting her thoughts.

He was trying to occupy her mind, that was clear. She felt a wave of tears building in her eyes and she threw the dice with such force that it hurt her fingers.

She wanted to scream.

13

UNCERTAINTY

The preparations for Bealltainn continued, and Dalkeith was covered in bright colors. Thanks to Deorsa's talent for lying, Sören's group was able to relax in comfort. He had presented them as distant cousins and convinced the innkeeper to kick out a few unfortunate souls. Despite their clear lack of physical likeness, he told the story so well that even Fillan found himself believing it. The teenager felt bad for the people that had been kicked out but couldn't help appreciating the lie: for the first time since he'd left Berwick, he could sleep in something that resembled a bed.

He was burning with questions for Deorsa, but the man left the town before dawn and only returned after nightfall each day. During his rare sightings, he was always busy and didn't pay the slightest bit of attention to Fillan. The only person that seemed worthy of his precious time was Sören, to whom he passed news of the region in hushed whispers.

That was how the teenager learnt, eavesdropping on their conversations, that King Edward's troops were advancing on the northern part of the Lowlands. The Graham clan, in alliance with the other Scottish chiefs, was planning to hold them at Dunbar.

Fillan could have pestered Sören for answers, but the Norwegian was always disappearing and seemed to be avoiding him, which annoyed him even more. The longer he didn't know what was going on, the harder it became to bear. Luckily, though, life in the town had the gift of calming him. Dalkeith was far from the bustling city of Berwick, but it still made him think fondly back to his old city and gave him the chance to join in with the daily routines of the residents.

The first night, Edan and Fergus had headed straight for one of the most infamous buildings in town, The Purple Thistle, which left no doubt as to the services it offered. Kyle insulted them and mocked their inability to seduce women except for with their money purses. She hated that they lowered themselves to that sort of business. Fillan shared her view. Alastair, as a man of honor and respect, had always pressed upon him that buying another's body with the power of money was revolting. Fergus was ashamed and didn't go back to the Thistle. Edan's little trips only lasted for two days before Kyle gave him a black eye for it.

Ever since Sören had agreed to take him to Scone, Fillan and Kyle had gotten closer. They talked a lot before, during and after their training. She was difficult to gauge and had a carefree nature. One minute she showed all the manners and grace of a lady of the court, and the next she was throwing out insults that were even more vulgar than Edan's, while physically throwing things too.

With such a curious mix of softness and brutality, she gave off a mysterious air. Despite all their talks, Fillan still knew barely anything about her as she always evaded questions and refused to talk about her past. If he pushed too hard, she'd spend the next two hours pretending he didn't exist.

On the fourth day, when the sun had not yet risen, Fillan finished his run around the town. Now that they had more time on their hands, Kyle had decided to make him work on his endurance before each session. When they arrived at their training patch in front of the inn, he was drowning in sweat while she had rosy cheeks. As they tried to catch their breath, Sören appeared and leaned against a log, cutting an apple with his dagger.

"Carry on!" he called with a chuckle. "Just pretend I'm not here!"

Fillan hated the feeling of being watched and missed a step, which Kyle punished with a smack. Then they got to work on a spear attack that would, she said, allow him to take out slower enemies with one strike. You just had to aim right.

He repeated the movements, once, twice, before correctly hitting her in the throat. Fillan felt like he was making progress and learning much faster. Kyle wasn't the type to sing and shout about his achievements and simply gave him a smile.

"Let me have a go!" called the Norwegian as he jogged over to join them.

"If you like," shrugged Kyle.

She took the last piece of apple out of his hands with a teasing stare and crunched on it as she turned and headed to join Moira, who was passing by.

"I hope she hasn't been too soft with you!" said Sören.

Fillan simply gestured toward his many cuts and bruises all over his arms.

"What, that? That's nothing! In the Highlands, those are tokens of affection!" Sören chuckled.

Fillan stayed still; he'd never seen the mercenary joke around like this.

"You're going to show me everything you've learned. We've got a long road ahead and I don't want you to be a dead weight if something goes wrong."

Like in Cranshaws, Fillan couldn't stop himself from thinking. Sören didn't say it, but his tone implied it.

"Did you ask Kyle to train me?"

"I would have done it once I found out we had to take you to Scone. But she decided to do it long before that. She's a smart one. Alright, *en garde*!"

They began to turn around each other, each trying not to be blinded by the sunlight that was rising above the horizon. The air was dry and humid, and smelt of earth and dried leaves. Their blades met, and Fillan felt the almighty strength of his opponent.

"What's Deorsa's role in the Brotherhood?" he asked, straining his muscles.

"You really don't have any idea?"

They broke apart and began circling again, face to face.

"Is he a… negotiator?"

"Worse. He's a spy!" said Sören as he attempted contact again.

Fillan had anticipated the trajectory of the sword and was able to turn and duck to avoid it. The mercenary approved with a grunt.

"You could move out of the way a little faster," he said.

"You don't seem to like him. Deorsa, I mean."

"You expect me to believe you want to hug him?"

"Only to strangle him."

The Norwegian burst into laughter, terrifying Fillan.

"Do you trust him?"

While he asked the question, Fillan tried a reverse attack that the mercenary blocked easily.

"Deorsa is the type of man I hate. He's used to looking for the slightest weakness, clue, or trail that can give the Brotherhood an advantage. But that's what he's like with everyone. It's in his nature. I don't know anyone who likes him. To him, every conversation is a battle of wills. He's a damn asshole."

"But…"

"But I have to deal with him. Despite his many faults, he's useful to the Brotherhood because he's very good at what he does."

The cry of a cockerel rung out in the distance as the sun rose above the forest. The sounds of nature began to mix with the noises of the townspeople waking up.

"This Brotherhood, what is it exactly?"

Sören's eyes traveled down to his dropped guard.

"Stay focused!"

"I don't know anything!" he protested. "And Deorsa is avoiding me!"

"I'm not the best one to talk to you about it."

"You're the only one who can!"

"The Brotherhood is a secret society," replied the mercenary after a long sigh. "Few know of their existence. Their full name is the Brotherhood of Assassins."

The teenager felt a shiver run down his spine. His sword hand shook.

"Assassins?"

"Specialists in concealment and elimination," agreed the Norwegian.

"But to what aim?"

"Don't you know the meaning of the word 'secret?' I can't tell you anything. Plus, even I don't know what they want with you."

Fillan suspected that wasn't wholly true. He'd seen Sören from his hiding corner as he talked with the spy and pointed to an imaginary mark on his wrist.

"Deorsa said that you were part of…"

"My god, you bleat like a sheep. You'd be better off focusing on your footwork," lectured the mercenary before he struck a blow from below.

Fillan barely blocked and almost fell backwards. He'd lost his rhythm and tripped over his feet. His opponent had lost all traces of humor in his face and stepped back, sword raised in the air. Fillan knew he had to choose his next question carefully, or Sören would close off.

"What's a Child of Fal?"

"Where did you hear that name?" asked Sören, his eyes bulging. "Did Deorsa tell you? Kyle?"

"Neither. I heard Cornavii questioning my master about it, just before he killed him."

"It's just an old fable. It doesn't matter."

Another lie, and the Norwegian now seemed very uneasy.

"And what is it about? Is there a link between the Lann Fala and the Brotherhood?"

When he looked into the mercenary's eyes, Fillan stepped back. Kyle would have stopped the fight there, but Sören jumped on him and dealt a series of devastating attacks. Fillan only stopped the first two, which made his muscles scream. With the third attack, his sword flew into the air and clattered to the ground. His warrior teacher would have been very disappointed, as she believed that being disarmed was the greatest dishonor.

"You talk too much," said Sören, his voice trembling. "You ask too many questions."

"Because I have so many questions to ask!"

"Shut up! You need to learn to concentrate, to control yourself and to stop acting like a child!"

Fillan didn't even try to pick up his sword, instead charging the Norwegian with a scream to try and hit him. His opponent easily stopped him and pushed him to the ground, and his knee pinned him on his back.

"But it's more than that," continued the warrior on top of him. "You're scared."

"That's not true!"

"But it is! You are afraid. Something in you is stopping you from being fully present in the fight."

"I'm telling you, that's not true!"

The Norwegian gave a doubtful murmur.

"I wish I could believe you, because there's no place for cowards in my group. Deorsa tells me that an English patrol has just set up not far from Dalkeith. I'm organizing a raid with Kyle and Edan to eliminate them. You're coming with us, and then we'll see what your fear is about."

He left without stooping to help him up.

Alone in the dirt, Fillan was trying to control himself, as he felt a wave of terror crushing his chest.

He had never fought for real.

But more pressingly, he'd never killed anyone.

14

RAID

"**Q**uietly," said Sören as he shortened his stride.

They had reached the woods where the English were based, about half a mile east of Dalkeith. Between the dark lines of the trees, red light from their campfires flickered up to the tree canopy. A column of smoke, which had led them here from the surrounding hills, billowed up towards the black sky. A breeze swept the ground, and only the sound of rustling branches interrupted the night's calm.

The group had waited until the town was asleep to move out. They hadn't wanted to raise any suspicion and got ready in Deorsa's room. Ever since he'd learned that Sören wanted to take Fillan with him, the spy seemed extremely stressed. He hadn't ceased trying to convince the mercenary chief against it, but was met with a wall of ice. Resigned to the fact, he could only pace around the room to the beat of Fergus's tunes while the group gathered their equipment.

For the occasion, the Norwegian had given Fillan a black gambeson padded jacket.

"It won't stop a direct stab," he'd explained, "but it might see off an attack from height. Anyway, it's better than that chiffon you're wearing. It'll let you keep your agility and discretion."

The young man, who had been wearing the same clothes since he'd left Berwick, thanked him timidly. Moira had seen to it that the padded armor fell perfectly on his shoulders and fit his form. She then gifted him the tartan she'd been lending him since the start of their journey. He slung it over and around his shoulder, above the rest of his clothes.

They were just about to leave when Deorsa tried one last time to reason with Sören, and Kyle pulled Fillan aside. She had pulled her hair up into a neat bun and wore leather armor which came up to her neck. Like all of them, she had covered her face in dark color. She should have looked terrifying, but Fillan thought it suited her.

"Here, this is for you," she said as she handed him a piece of cut bone hanging from a string.

"A pendant?"

"Yes. It's Ogme, the Celtic god."

Fillan stared at her silently, trying to figure out what it meant.

"You don't know much about religion, huh? Ogme is one of the *Tuatha Dé Danann*, the ancient gods. He's a warrior god, but also a great speaker. Legend says he could guide the souls of the dead to the Sidh with just one word."

"Why are you giving it to me?"

"You remind me of him a bit. You never stop talking. I thought I was going to murder you this afternoon."

After Sören had informed him he would be going on the raid, Fillan had bombarded them all—the Norwegian aside—with questions to try and understand what awaited him. He was full of apprehension. Kyle had humored him the most, but when he asked her the same question for the third time, she pushed him over.

"Don't look at me like that, I'm just messing with you. Talking is useful, sometimes, but other times you must know how to react. I'm giving it to you as a good luck charm, so he can watch over you tonight. And also so you remember, just like Ogme, that sometimes talking isn't enough: you have to fight."

Fillan felt torn, both touched by her gesture and worried about its deep meaning and what awaited him.

When Sören made them slow down in the darkness of the woods, Fillan took a moment to touch the pendant under his clothes. It made him feel like someone was watching over him as the air felt like it was closing in on him.

The camp was only about ten yards away when Sören

silently indicated for them to draw their swords. Then he told them to wait and disappeared into the shadows.

Whenever a leaf moved too quickly, Fillan feared seeing an English soldier—or worse, an antlered helmet—burst out of the trees. The moon was almost full, but its light could barely penetrate the trees which shifted sinisterly in the wind.

A moan rang through the night, but it was only a soldier yawning.

Sören came back from his scout and whispered a few words to Kyle and Edan. Then he firmly grasped Fillan's shoulder.

"Now is the time to prove you're not afraid, kid."

Fillan gritted his teeth.

"Kyle, Edan and I will take care of the English who've woken up. You head straight for the one asleep in that tent."

"Even a coward could handle that," said Edan. "Meal is already cooked."

Fillan could hardly see Kyle's eyes in the darkness, but he liked to think they were full of encouragement. They left him there and headed towards the camp, soon disappearing into the darkness of the foliage. He mustered up the courage to move. With every step he crept closer to the camp, he thought he could hear rumbling of horses' hooves, but it was only the rapid beating of his own heart in his chest. His legs and hands trembled lightly. He thought about Ailéas, who would surely not have faltered in such a situation. Instead of making him sad, this thought now gave him a burst of courage.

The voices of the English were getting clearer. They were gathered around a fire, and one of them was even singing a song while banging a beat on a tree stump. The sound was a relief for Fillan, who was worried he'd be discovered if he stepped on a twig. He moved forwards quickly and with flexibility, using the cover of the trees.

His heart almost exploded in fear as he knocked the tip of his sword against a rock. His body was instantly drenched in sweat as he dropped down, hiding. Unless any soldiers walked around the back of the camp, they couldn't see him, which was reassuring.

Unfortunately, that was exactly what happened.

A branch cracked behind him, and he waited for the shout to raise the alarm. One second, two seconds. He didn't dare breathe. Three seconds. Four seconds. A strange sense of calm remained in the air. Five seconds. Six seconds. Still holding his breath, Fillan slowly turned his head. One of the English stood less than a yard away from him with his back turned. He was urinating against a moss-covered tree trunk.

He knew the man would head back to camp if he turned right, and he couldn't miss the feeble glint of the man's sword. He would have to take a breath soon, and he thought about the arrow attack Kyle had taught him if the man discovered him. Luckily, the man turned to the left and disappeared out of sight.

He took deep breaths to calm down and waited, waving away Sören's signal to move in. His head was so sweaty that it slipped down his weapon. The chatter in the camp reverberated through the trees.

"I only went to piss, and you're finishing all the wine!" exclaimed the soldier who'd rejoined the others. "You're an asshole, Callum! Give me that!"

"Ugh, we're going to Dalkeith tomorrow anyway. We'll show off our swords to all those bumpkins in the town and take whatever we want."

"You're so sure of yourself," said a third with a Continental accent. "They don't seem to like us too much around here."

"Who cares? We'll get rid of a few."

"I can't wait until we leave this area. I'm not feeling it."

"Well, that's because all you can feel with your tiny dick, Frank, are the cheapest brothels."

They all burst into laughter.

"What were they thinking, sending us so far from the advance guard?"

"It's those damn Red Warriors!" said Callum in annoyance. "I don't understand why our good king even cares about them. All they're good for is wasting our time.

'Ere we are chasing shadows, and the military campaign is going on without us. I'm telling you: they must be traitors!"

"And I'm telling you, you'd do well to keep your mouth shut about it when we get back to camp," warned the Continental man. "These guys don't mess around. They cut down a guy who let the kid get away."

"And the commander let them do it?"

"You're so naïve, Frank! Do you think he had a choice? They've got their noses in everything! Did you hear the latest? They went back to the ashes of Berwick."

"What were they looking for there?" Callum interrupted and burped noisily. "The bodies of the kids?"

"Not even! Knick-knacks, weapons, cash, I don't know! But I bet it was for weapons."

"We're going to miss the best bits of this war with all their messing around."

A bird hooted nearby, but Fillan didn't pay it any attention. He was too absorbed in what the soldiers were saying.

"Look!" groaned Frank. "Barely a sip left!"

There was another hoot, and Fillan understood. As soon as he moved into the darkened tent, the noise outside became muffled. There were no screams, not even the sound of clashing weapons, just a succession of strangled gasps. Sören and the others killed the English without a fight.

Just like assassins, thought Fillan, remembering the discussion he'd had with the mercenary chief.

He approached the one he was supposed to take care of and found a boy barely older than him. He gripped his sword tightly and willed himself with all his might to spring into action. The wind was tinged with the smell of burning wood and blew through the tent, disturbing the tent flap. In the corner, he thought he saw Ailéas, staring at him with her green eyes, the scar on her forehead crumpled with a severe look.

The wind flapped the material again, he blinked, and the sight disappeared.

Something in Fillan was screaming at him to move, but his emotions paralyzed him. First terror of taking a life like that. Then shame too, of becoming a murderer. Like all the soldiers in Berwick.

Two hands grabbed his own. Fillan panicked but it was only Sören, who'd crept into the tent without a sound. The Norwegian's fingers squeezed tight. They were covered in blood. He glared at Fillan icily and pushed their hands to lower the blade. The tip pierced through the ribs of the soldier who awoke with a gasp of surprise.

His horror only lasted a second, as the mercenary hit his heart.

"*Fois dhut**," he whispered as the body gave a final spasm.

---

* 'Fois dhut' means 'rest in peace' in Scottish Gaelic.

Fillan tried to stop his trembling hands.

"You're afraid," said Sören, staring at him with wolflike eyes. "Something in you makes you doubt yourself." He traced a line of blood with his finger down Fillan's chest. "Right here. What is it?"

"I don't know," lied Fillan.

"Well, find it. And sort it out quickly, or you'll get yourself killed. Because of you, others could die too," he concluded and then headed out of the tent in silence.

Fillan pulled his sword out of the motionless body, and a drop of blood bubbled feebly.

Before he left the tent, he glanced over again at the corner where he thought he'd glimpsed Ailéas and saw nothing but shadows. His heart skipped a beat.

15

BEALLTAINN

Dalkeith had become an immense inferno with countless pyres that blazed under the stars. In this brilliant light, the fort seemed to be under attack by orange shimmers, flickering like unreal chimeras. Smoke billowed above the noisy city.

Midnight struck, May began, and the festival of Bealltainn was in full swing in honor of spring. The town had never been so full. Hundreds of people from the surrounding areas had traveled for the event. On every street corner, beer flowed in the euphoric atmosphere; not a second went by without someone bursting into laughter.

Everyone was dancing, singing, hugging, eating, and getting drunk in the firelight to the sound of the musicians playing rousing melodies on their clarsachs* and their lutes.

* The clarsach is a Celtic triangular harp dating from the eighth century, the time of the Picts (the Irish who populated Scotland).

Ever since the first fire was lit, Fergus had likewise lit up with joy, running through his entire repertoire and surprising the other players with his otherworldly musical experimentation.

Fillan had been wandering the streets, trying to enjoy the festivities. He had already drunk two beers, but he didn't feel any lighter, unable to lower his guard. All these flames awoke painful memories he tried to fend off. The permanent tension gripped him and prevented him from letting go.

For the second time, he found himself in the main square around a bonfire that was so big it almost seemed like the sunrise. Around twenty people held hands in a circle around it. A young redheaded girl asked Fillan to join them, but he blinked and turned on his heels.

He saw Deorsa heading towards him.

"Fillan! What a pleasure to see you here!"

He couldn't even pretend to smile.

"Such a shame we haven't gotten the chance to chat these last few days," lamented the spy. "I would have liked to exchange words with you!"

Judging by his slight wobble, the man was tipsy—though Fillan wondered if that might be an act, because he still had the usual glint in his eyes.

"I heard you killed a man during the raid?!" he whispered in his ear. "Well done, you, that's a big step!"

Fillan almost choked on his beer. Firstly, because he'd

never imagined he'd be congratulated for taking a life, and secondly, because the feeling of the sword slicing into the English soldier's body still gave him cold sweats.

"In many places," continued Deorsa, "it's a rite of passage to become a man. I'll always remember the first time I killed! Snake and dagger. The dagger was only because I'd forgotten to choose a poisonous snake," he said with a laugh that spilled his beer. "What, cat got your tongue?"

"Sören had to help me do it," admitted Fillan, even though he was sure the spy already knew.

"So what? You didn't run away or piss your pants. That's something."

They drank and silently observed a spark from the fire rising into the sky.

"What does the Brotherhood want with me?" asked Fillan, pretending like it was nothing.

"Not so loud," said the man, returning to stone, as though he'd never had a drop of alcohol. "This isn't the time or the place."

"You send me all over the place, and I'm not even allowed one question?"

"You're special to the Brotherhood, but I'm not permitted to tell you why."

"But…" started Fillan in annoyance.

"A bit of advice for you," interrupted Deorsa with a conspiratorial air. "If I were you, I'd get away from the mercenaries tonight. Enjoy the party and the beer, go dance, and empty your head a bit!"

He gave him a malicious smile before laughing as he walked away. Fillan hated him more than ever.

"What was that old snake telling you?" asked Kyle as she joined him.

She had traded her leather armor for simpler clothes, though they were still masculine. All around them, the women wore dresses and flower crowns. Kyle stood out, but it didn't seem to bother her in the slightest. The only thing she'd done was let down her hair, which tumbled down her back. Fillan thought she looked magnificent.

"To get away from you tonight," he said, trying to get a reaction from her.

"Sounds like something that old codger would say."

"You don't like him either?"

"The first time Sören introduced me to him, he called me 'honey.'"

Fillan grimaced as he pictured what must have happened to the spy after that.

"You get it. I kicked him in the nuts. Why do you think his voice is so high?"

They burst into laughter.

"Come on," continued Kyle as she took him by the arm. "I'm taking you to meet someone much nicer."

She led him with a skip to a cottage. Curious bones adorned

the walls, and the skull of an auroch was displayed in one of the windows. There were more garlands here than anywhere else, and the majority of those that wound around and through the village seemed to start from this specific point.

Fillan had spotted this strange building the day they arrived, but it had been closed up until tonight. The door was open now and a mountain of flowers were spread around the entrance. Inside sat an old woman in a dark dress embroidered with flowers.

"A druid?" asked Fillan in surprise,

"Shhh," replied Kyle, hitting him in the side.

The elder must have been more than fifty years old and was waving a wand around a cow held by a peasant with a string around its neck. She was saying indecipherable words with her eyes bulging. She finished her sermon and traced a symbol on the animal's forehead after dipping her finger in a bowl of blood. The cow gave a moo under the joyful eyes of its owner.

Fillan couldn't help but tut, throwing a look over at Kyle, who seemed fascinated.

"Tilda!" she cried once the peasant and cow had left.

"My little Kyle! And you brought someone with you!" enthused the old woman. "Get over here, you!"

He found himself a few inches away from her wrinkled face and had no time to utter a word before her milky eyes were taking in his features.

"I was wondering if you might take a little look into this mule boy's head."

"I would, it's just that I've got a crowd," she said, indicating the large queue of donkeys, horses, chickens, and pigs all accompanied by their owners. "Plus, I've got a feeling that your mule-headed friend doesn't align with the old ways. Am I right, tutting boy?"

Fillan nodded, annoyed. Unlike his sister—and Kyle, obviously—he didn't believe in all these superstitions.

"Oh, stop sulking," said Kyle. "It's Bealltainn!"

"So, what should I do?" said Tilda, wiggling her nose like a rabbit. "Look into him? Don't look into him? Other mules are waiting for me."

A donkey eeyored.

"Fine," grumbled Fillan as he met the insistent look of his friend.

"Just in time! All the rest of you can wait a little longer!" called Tilda down the line of peasants and beckoned the young people into the tent.

The inside was just one room and very surprising. Everywhere hung bones, jars, plants, and indescribable things. An old hay bale lay in a heap, which must have been the bed.

"The little one's not wrong," said Tilda as she invited them to sit around a table. "It's Bealltainn! A magical night where you can't help but believe."

She held the skeptical teenager's hands and stared into his eyes.

"This festival is more important to you than anyone, tutting boy," she whispered. "I can feel it. Do you know why we do all these rituals?"

"I don't think so," frowned Fillan.

"It's the end of the shadows!" the elder practically shouted. "Every year on this night, things become clearer, and the truth rises. In the fires of Bealltainn, the lies we tell ourselves burn along with the bouquets of flowers. What is it you tell yourself?"

Fillan tried to hold back from tutting again up against the druid's fervor.

"Yes, Bealltainn is important to you because there's a fire inside you. Do you feel it burning you up? That's because you're trying to run away from it. And the more you flee, the more it devours you."

His skepticism cracked a little. He felt a bubble of anguish in his chest.

"Guilt," concluded Tilda as she pressed her thumbs into his palms. "That's your fire. That's what makes you doubt yourself, and freezes you instead of letting you spring into action."

Fillan gave a furtive glance at Kyle, because she was the only one who knew how much he suffered from losing his sister.

"The little one didn't tell me anything! It's not hard to see in you," said the old woman, tapping on Fillan's face. "It's so clear, even if you don't want to see it. Don't look so shocked. You know I'm right: the urge to run away from your emotions is strong. You have to face them or you'll never grow up. But I sense that your guilt is double-edged. One part recent, and one older. You're just at the start of your path," concluded the druid, "but sooner or later you'll have to face your fire. And better sooner rather than later."

When they left the cottage, Fillan felt awful.

"Oh, come on…" said Kyle as she saw the look on his face. "Tilda really helped me a few years ago. I thought she could do the same for you."

Fillan shrugged and didn't respond.

"Damn," continued Kyle with her hand to her head, "I should have asked for a blessing for the ass you are! Let me know if you start to eeyore and I won't attack!"

He couldn't help but smile.

"See, that's better."

She drew him to a corner to drink the Bealltainn mead, a honey beer brewed with bees and their venom. Fillan found the nectar delicious, slightly bitter, sweet and terribly spicy. Once they'd finished their pints, they danced for more than an hour. Kyle even taught him a new jig and he wondered how the warrior knew how to dance so well. She was as graceful as a hawk.

It must have been past three in the morning when they finally made their way back to the training ground. Only a few dying fires remained as Dalkeith was lulled to sleep by ever-quieter music. Fillan breathed in the cool air that blew through his hair; he hadn't felt so alive in weeks. When Kyle grabbed him and kissed him, he was lost in himself, forgetting everything. After a few seconds, the warrior whispered in his ear.

"Remember what Tilda said: better sooner than later. Let go."

Fillan looked at her without understanding. He was about to kiss her back, but he was plunged into darkness as a hood suddenly covered his face.

"Kyle!" he yelled, afraid that something would happen to her.

Strong arms picked him up and dragged him to the ground. He tried in vain to fight. After several long minutes, he was thrown somewhere and hit his head. He heard the sound of a stone scraping another stone, then fainted.

16

RITE

When Fillan awoke, he found himself surrounded by icy darkness. He tugged off the canvas bag covering his head, but it didn't help him see any clearer.

"Kyle?!" he yelled, staggering to his feet.

Only the muffled echo of his voice answered. His eyes gradually adjusted to the darkness of wherever he'd been thrown, and he could make out four walls. Three of them consisted of a pile of uneven rocks that overlapped with incredible precision and towered a little over six feet. The fourth wall was the entrance, blocked by a huge smooth stone.

"Is anyone there?!" he shouted.

An oppressive and claustrophobic silence answered him. Above his head were other rocks, which formed a flat ceiling. A thin streak of light pushed through a tiny hole between two of them.

He realized that he'd been locked up in a dolmen, an ancient sepulchral chamber, a few ruins of which were dotted across Scotland. He'd had the opportunity to play in one around Mordington a few years ago. These ancient constructions comprised only one room and were built atop mounds and gigantic megaliths. This is where they once stored the bodies of the deceased for their eternal rest.

A grave, Fillan thought. *I've been buried alive.*

Panic gripped him. He threw himself against the smooth stone and nearly dislocated his shoulder. He tried twice more before frantically inspecting the rest of the burial chamber in search of an escape, to no avail. Realizing he couldn't get out, he screamed until his voice was hoarse. But no sound could pass through the strongly entangled stones. In sheer desperation, he hammered his fists against the rock prison, only to cut his skin on the sharp edges.

The narrow room began to sway, and he let himself slide to the ground, trembling. His head in his hands, he tried not to sob and did everything he could to master the fear thumping in his chest. Who'd locked him in here? And what for? And most importantly, what had happened to Kyle? Just thinking about it terrified him. Like a statue, he had no choice but to face it and believe that old Tilda might have glimpsed the future.

Sooner or later, she'd said, *you will have to face your fire.*

Fillan tried to subdue his emotions as a new wave of

anguish took his breath away, but a voice behind him startled him.

"Fillan," it said, "what are you doing here?"

A shiver ran down his spine and he turned slowly. He saw his twin in the sliver of moonlight. Ailéas stood in front of him with a blindfold that had slipped down and a mop of messy red hair. She watched him with her big green eyes. His sister, however, did not look any older than eight years old and there was no scar across her forehead.

He couldn't help but scream at the sight of the vision, backing up against the stones that cut into his back.

And better sooner than later, the voice echoed in his head.

"Fillan?" little Ailéas asked again.

He had fallen into the Sidh, the Other World. There was no other explanation. Or was it all the alcohol he had drunk? He gave another scream, closed his eyes, and shoved his fingers in his ears as he curled up in a ball.

Bealltainn, he remembered. It's Bealltainn, the magical night where everything is possible and everyone burns their own lies in the fire of bonfires. Was the elder with the milky eyes, and Kyle, correct? When he found the courage to reopen his eyes, the little girl was sat on the floor and watched him without moving, her head tilted to the side, like she used to during a conversation.

"Ailéas, is that you?" called Fillan in a trembling voice.

"Of course it's me! No need to shout, you almost broke my eardrums!"

He would have tried to touch her, to see if she was real, but he dared not make the slightest movement: he was terrified.

That damn fear that paralyzed him over and over again.

"Are you real?" he could only ask.

The child pouted and bit the corner of her mouth, twisting her face. It was the exact same expression she always wore when someone said something upsetting to her and she couldn't hide her pain. Over the years, she had learned to hide that expression, especially when Fillan tried to hurt her.

All the emotions Fillan had been trying to bury for weeks came flooding in, and he began to cry as if he were a little boy again himself.

"I'm so sorry, Ale," he said, using the pet name he hadn't used in so many years. "I didn't want to flee in Berwick. I didn't want to, but the flames…"

He choked on his own sob. All the anguish of his guilt flared up, and his heart was ripped into pieces before the emotionless glare of his sister.

"I left you," he moaned. "I'm so sorry."

"It's no use," replied the little one, continuing to watch him without showing the slightest hint of emotion.

"Why are you saying that?" he yelled in anger, his guilt fading at the idea that his twin would not forgive him.

In a blink of an eye, little Ailéas disappeared.

Fillan crawled to where she had been, feeling the air and running his hands along the ground, but there was nothing. He curled up like a newborn and cried long and hard beneath the beam of light.

The night passed, bringing an ever more biting cold across the dolmen. Eyes half-closed, Fillan observed the mist that escaped from his mouth with each of his exhales while his mind was tangled in thoughts and emotions.

Guilt, of having done nothing to find the body of his sister. Anger, at himself for running away like a coward. Loneliness, because of the loss of his other half, an orphan now even more orphaned. Guilt again, to have been so mean in recent years while Ailéas had done everything she could to reconcile their opposite characters. Doubt, because he did not understand why he had come to hate her. Sadness, to imagine that he would never hear her voice again. Anger again, towards the whole world, as if every person could be guilty of his own faults.

With each new emotion, the consuming fire in his chest grew bigger.

"There's no point in wanting me to forgive you," the little voice of his sister said, who had just reappeared in a corner of the tomb.

Fillan watched her without bothering to get up.

"It is you and only you who must forgive yourself," continued the child.

He felt stupid for getting so carried away.

"It's impossible," he replied, shaking his head. "You're dead…"

…*because of me,* he thought, unable to say the words aloud through his dry throat.

"You have to stop beating yourself up about it," little Ailéas continued. "There was nothing you could do."

"I can't."

"Yes, you can. You just have to want it, or the fire will continue to devour you. And the more you bury it, the more it devours you. It is what makes you doubt yourself and paralyzes you, instead of animating you!"

His twin had ended up with the voice of old Tilda.

"What good would it—" he whispered.

His hallucination shifted and flames ignited in the stones around him, without producing any heat. Ailéas was now covered in dust and blood.

"You have to survive," she said, pointing the birthmark on her wrist, which gleamed in the light of the blaze. "You must fulfill your destiny, Child of Fal. You are no longer the Fillan who simply hides."

While he was consumed by misunderstanding, the creaking of a beam rung through the small space of the burial chamber. Ghostly embers flew into the air and everything disappeared in the darkness, even the little girl.

After a few seconds, Fillan began to believe.

"Only I can forgive myself," he repeated in the silence of the dolmen.

As he stared at the stone walls, he felt something shift deep within him. A buried memory. It was a year ago, maybe two. His twin had just saved him from a group of Berwick bullies. "I won't always be there," she had lectured him, worried. "You have to learn to survive alone. Promise me."

He had promised, just to get her to leave him alone.

What would she think of him today? He couldn't talk of honoring her memory if he did not keep his promise; if he did not do everything to survive and fight like she would have done. It clicked, and the guilt that ignited everything in his body changed. The burden of his regrets did not disappear, but the fire—his fire—now became a catalyst of determination. He got up suddenly, determined to find a way to get out of there.

"Yes!" laughed the voice of little Ailéas, which echoed through the room. "Now you understand!"

Despite the cold numbing his fingers, he inspected each stone that made up the dolmen to see if one of them was loose. He tried again to move the large rock blocking the main entrance. He managed to unearth a broken femur that protruded near the bottom of a wall, in the ground he'd been walking on all this time. He considered using the bone as a lever to move the entrance stone, but it would not hold. He remembered a small gap he had noticed in the corner, as if a stone was missing. He had tried with a flat rock to get it out, but he hadn't been able to shift it enough to pull it out. Using the bone, he now succeeded with a cry of joy.

"You understand!" echoed his twin's voice.

Four more stones gave way as he pulled, and the cool night air hit him. A narrow passage came into view, which opened out under the stars. The teenager sprang out of the dolmen, taking in full breaths of air with the sudden urge to scream.

Bealltainn, he repeated in his head. It was the end of darkness, the buried fire that decided to burst forth. He understood why the old druid had spoken of rebirth. Coming out of the ground, motivated by a new determination, he felt he'd been born for the second time. He felt ready to do anything to survive. After all, that's what Ailéas would do without hesitation.

Sören was waiting for him at the foot of the mound, surrounded by a mist that seemed to come from the land of the dead. A smile twisted his white-blond beard.

17

LEITH

The Bealltainn rite of confinement was what Sören had subjected Fillan to during the night. As the sunrise bathed the dolmen in light and dissipated the morning mists, the Norwegian explained to him that it was a test passed down through the ages. The Brotherhood of Assassins in Scotland was the only group who still practiced it. It was a rare legacy of the intriguing organization that the mercenary followed, and which he had put each member of his group through.

Sören had congratulated him, but Fillan had simply given him a blank stare before heading to the training ground.

Kyle was waiting for him there with a firm stance, as if she hadn't doubted for a moment that he would pass the test. She tried to apologize, but he cut her off. He was angry with her because she tricked him. This rage had provoked a formidable ferocity which allowed him to hit her several times. Once the session was over, he left her there without a word, without a look, creating a wall of awkwardness between them.

Now that the festivities were over, Deorsa had advised them to leave Dalkeith shortly after noon to reach Leith, a port city near Edinburgh, as quickly as possible. There, they could cross the mouth of the Forth to reach Scone faster. The English were advancing, and the group had to maintain its lead.

It took a day, during which Fillan sulked ostensibly, before the first houses of the city suburbs came into view. Everyone pulled down their hoods, even Fillan, who had been given a coat by the leader of the mercenaries before leaving Dalkeith.

"Edinburgh is only a few miles away," said Sören, slowing them down for all to hear. "I wouldn't be surprised to find that every corner is crawling with English spies or Lann Fala, so let's stay cautious."

"What did the old snake say?" Kyle asked, speaking of Deorsa.

"He wasn't too sure, so let's avoid getting ourselves noticed too much."

"Why are you looking at me like that?!" Edan bellowed.

"Because you screwed up big time in Dalkeith," retorted the warrior in annoyance. "Seducing the baker's wife and blacksmith's wife at the same time, seriously?!"

"In his defense," Fergus said, "he didn't have much success with either of them."

"Oh, yeah, yeah, music man! Just because I'm not as good as you for…"

"That's enough," Sören interrupted. "Kyle is right. If Patrick de Graham's son hadn't intervened, you would have ended up rotting in a jail, so keep to yourself."

The throngs of refugees were growing, forcing their horses to tighten together in formation. Fillan and Kyle's knees touched, but they avoided each other's gaze.

"Once we enter the city," resumed Sören, "Edan, Fergus, and I will go to the docks to find someone who'll give us passage to cross. Moira, Kyle, and Fillan, you'll wait for us at the Shor'O'Forth inn. No need to make that face, Kyle. Better to go there than anywhere else. Either way, you'll have to stay on your toes."

He suspected that the Norwegian was misinterpreting Kyle's reaction. What bothered her was almost certainly getting stuck with Fillan, who was acting as if she didn't exist. The two groups separated shortly after passing the city gates. The young man, the druid and the warrior dismounted to progress through the main thoroughfare. The bustle of all merchant towns surrounded them. A ceaseless ballet of barges, merchants, travelers, and beggars jostling and shouting at each other surrounded them.

The clamor of Leith contrasted with the terse silence that fell over the trio.

"I'm feeling some tension here," said Moira, wedged between her two fellows.

"Oh, that?" Kyle said. "It's just Fillan the simpleton, who sulks at the entire Earth because of the rite, even at the woman he kissed during the night of Bealltainn!"

Fillan felt himself turning crimson.

"Well, look at that!" Moira laughed. "He does have some strange ways. But don't you worry, my boy, Kyle isn't just anyone."

As he caught the murderous look she shot him, he was convinced that he'd never find such a character like her again in any town.

"Don't hide behind your horse," teased the druid. "We know you're there!"

"I don't like people using my feelings to trick me, that's all," he replied, trying to be as cold as Sören might have been, but emotion shook his voice.

"Because you think I kissed you for fun, just to kill time before we stuffed your head in a bag?!" Kyle fumed, turning red with anger.

He didn't say anything.

"Don't move," she yelled, kicking him hard in the butt. "This will put you in your place! It's about time I give you a piece of my mind!"

"Stop it right now!" thundered Moira, noticing that passersby were watching them. "I don't want to put up with your bickering, just because you are both incapable of seeing what's so blatant to everyone else."

"Oh, yeah?" asked Kyle, playing smart. "And what's that, Miss know-it-all?"

"That you both desperately dream of repeating your nocturnal experience, but you prefer to behave like children."

This time, Kyle also turned crimson.

Satisfied with the effect, Moira led them inside the Shor' O'Forth, where the joyful and drunken tavern atmosphere was aplenty. There were so many people that no one paid them any attention. They sat in a corner of the room and ordered beers that they sipped to blend into the background.

A long time passed without any of them saying anything.

"I'm going to go…" began the druid, looking for an excuse she could use to escape the discomfort of the two young people, "…to the bar!"

"I'll come with you!" Kyle replied, jumping up.

"No, you stay there!" ordered her friend, before disappearing into the crowd.

Fat sailors began to sing horribly out of tune.

"Did you mean what you said earlier?" asked Fillan, trying to drown out the cacophony.

"When I said you were a simpleton? Absolutely!"

"I was talking about—"

"I know what you were talking about," spat the young woman furiously. "And you're a moron if you think I only kissed you to help Sören take you to the dolmen. I did it because I wanted to, that's all. Ask me a question like that again and I'll dump my beer all over you."

She hit him in the shoulder, and he pouted as he pulled a splinter from the table.

"What was Moira implying when she said that you weren't just anyone?"

"Nothing at all."

She was lying, just like every time he asked a question of her, but she had moved closer to him. Their knees were touching, and she stared at him less gloomily, as if waiting for something.

"I thought you would at least try to apologize for ignoring me since yesterday," she finally sighed. "I underestimated your stupidity."

"But I…"

"You are a simpleton," she concluded, getting up to go join the druid.

He followed her with a questioning gaze. Since when had he become so bad with women that he found himself sputtering like a kid? He swallowed his beer in one pull to forget his stupidity, and observed the regulars who drank and ate happily. Seamen raised their mugs and sang louder, and their high notes sounded just like suffering seagulls.

Someone told them to shut up by throwing a stool, which provoked an angry wail from the innkeeper.

Fillan let himself be lulled by the memory of the taverns of Berwick where the mood was not that different. Among the crowd, a movement of red hair caught his eye. He stood up suddenly when he recognized the way Ailéas walked and almost fell over his seat. The young woman left the establishment and he rushed after her without thinking.

The twilight breeze, laden with spray and the smells of the city washed over him. He spotted the long, tawny hair making its way through passersby to turn down a road adjoining the inn. Fillan felt his heart beating so fast it might burst as he ran to join his twin.

He caught up with her in the alley and tugged her arm, forcing her to turn around. In the middle of the hair, two frightened blue eyes appeared in the half-light. He hastened to let go, so she didn't start screaming. It was not his sister, he was wrong. He apologized profusely and let the young woman run away at full speed.

As he retraced his steps, he cursed himself internally. Ailéas was dead—he had to face it and move on. This was what Bealltainn had taught him.

Absorbed by his thoughts, he only saw the man walking towards him at the last moment, a red cape flapping in the darkness.

A Lann Fala! he thought, his body freezing.

He dodged the first arc of the dagger, then freed himself and looked for his sword, but discovered he had made a terrible mistake before the fight even began: he had left it inside the inn.

He leapt aside to dodge another attack before punching the warrior in the face. Bones in his knuckles cracked, and the man groaned. The Lann Fala struck another blow with his dagger, then another with the reverse, which Fillan dodged. With a nimble kick, he sent the blade flying in the air before grabbing it with his fingertips.

The man gave a frightened cry and tried to flee, but Fillan, whose very being cried out for blood and vengeance, stabbed him frantically. The Lann Fala collapsed with a frightened howl. Fillan struck, again and again, the memory of his sister's dim eyes popping up in his head with every stab he landed, with every trickle of blood that spurted out.

He only stopped when a hand prevented him from doing more.

"Have you lost your mind?" Sören growled.

Fillan did not understand, but when he got up and looked at the body, he almost collapsed. The man he'd taken for a Lann Fala was just a lousy robber.

Rage and fear had blinded him.

"He attacked me… I thought he was a Lann Fala…"

Someone yelled down the main thoroughfare to call for help.

"Edan," Sören said to the bald man standing at the end of the alley, "you leave with the others, and we meet at the docks! We're going over the rooftops!"

They climbed up before setting off at a demanding pace, disappearing in the black heights of the city. In front of them, the path opened towards the north and the dark mouth of the Forth, waiting for them like a dark maw. They'd only gotten one street away from the inn when the first guard sounded the alarm. The chaos spread below, and they doubled their pace, jumping from roof to roof.

They reached the port out of breath, and the rest of the band joined them with the horses and their belongings.

"We have to go!" yelled Edan. "The guards saw us leave; I wouldn't be surprised if they follow us!"

Without wasting a second, a man who looked more like a bandit than a boat captain invited them to board a holque*.

Once on board and leaning on the rail, Fillan tried to calm the thumping of his heart as the wind swelled the wide sails of the ship.

"Sören just told me what happened," said someone softly.

Kyle settled next to him.

"How do you feel?"

---

* A holque is a sailboat primarily used for river and sea travel. It is normally limited to coastal areas.

"Like someone who just killed a man!" He threw his arms in the air.

"That bandit would have killed you."

"Nope! I managed to disarm him, and he tried to run away! I was so sure it was one of Cornavii's men that I slaughtered him."

"Do you want to hear some advice?" asked Kyle calmly, grabbing Fillan's trembling fingers and gently wiping away the sticky blood that covered them.

"Do I have a choice?"

"Nope!" she retorted playfully. "Calm down and don't be so hard on yourself. It's the first time you weren't paralyzed by a fight, and you didn't kill an innocent."

"You don't understand! I acted like a rabid beast!"

"You did what you had to. Many others would have done the same. Do you imagine that Edan would have patted your bandit on the back? I myself have experienced times when anger blinded me."

"And what did you do?"

"I learned the balance between rage and reason," she explained, grabbing the carved bone hanging from Fillan's neck. "It's not for nothing that I gave you this. Ogme is a good example of this balance. For the moment, it's no use to torture yourself: what's done is done," she continued, before depositing a kiss on his cheek and leaving him to his thoughts.

He gazed for a long time at the dark waters of the Forth, which shone with the reflections of the moon. The further they sailed from shore, the more the lights of Leith shrank until they were no bigger than sparkling dots. A few gusts whistled through the masts, like a funeral oration. Fillan decided to clean his bloody hands, which had finally stopped shaking.

Something inside him screamed and demanded revenge he couldn't take. And this violence frightened him.

9

The nightmare becomes more tangible, only to blur again a moment later.

The huge stag moves slowly through the smoke and ash. His eyes glow at times, hotter than the flames that greedily devour the village.

The animal lets out beastly grunts that vibrate as loudly as thunderstorms.

When the wind blows away the black fumes, it looks like a hungry wolf on the trail of its prey.

The cries are less and less numerous, but more and more atrocious.

At the foot of a building eaten away by fire stands a small child. His clothes are stained with blood and soot and part of his red hair is burned. He cries silently.

He chews his lip with all his might to keep from screaming.

He knows what awaits him if he were to make noise.

The open eyes of the lifeless body lying before him keep reminding him.

He doesn't hear the crack above his head.

18

HOLD

"I can't take any more of this!" whispered Ailéas, distraught and giving up on the meadowsweet herbal tea she was preparing.

She wanted to scream, but restrained herself because they were in the camp.

"Following this army of death wherever it goes, knowing that you're slaughtering Scots—people like me—it makes me sick!"

Bradley watched her uncomfortably without answering. It was not the first time she had gotten herself into such a state. With each new stage, after each battle, she exploded.

"I know that face!" she fumed. "It's no use looking at me like that. What did you seriously expect? You don't think I hear the fighting? Or the screams of the women who your soldiers bring back? I even hear them laughing about their bloody exploits! All this makes me want to vomit, constantly."

He remained silent, but she was even more agitated than normal.

"You have nothing to say?!" she continued. "Where was your honor during all of that? You save me for your good conscience and yet you let it all happen?"

"You don't know what you're talking about," he finally decided to say in a calm voice.

"Oh, I see. And I'm way too stupid for you to bother to explain it to me!"

"Let's just say that, knowing you, you would not want to hear what I have to say."

"You don't know me."

The old commander nodded silently and checked that the surroundings of the tent were empty before inviting her to sit down. He served her a cup of wine which she accepted without thanking him.

"This war is necessary," he said simply.

"What?! Are you kidding me? How could it be necessary?!"

"You see, I do know you a little: you immediately go off on your high horse! Yes, some wars are required when they prevent much worse situations."

"What could be worse than these massacres?"

"The fracturing of Scotland into several clans and

lordships who would bicker eternally over a piece of land, as was the case until not so long ago. This campaign is the only way to unify the country, you understand?"

"By slaughtering its people and subjugating them? Great! That is some unification!"

The old man's mouth twitched.

"No, of course not. Alas, this is the inevitable collateral damage of such campaigns. What I'm trying to tell you is that Scotland needs England's help so as not to implode."

"You're seriously going to try and make me believe that your king does this out of the goodness of his heart?"

"That would be dishonest of me, because it's obvious that our king takes revenge. As you know, John Balliol chose to betray his word and his oath before fleeing. No one forced his hand."

"I know why the war broke out," Ailéas said in annoyance, rolling her eyes. "No need to lecture me! But go on, you were about to explain how killing thousands of innocent people is going to unite Scotland."

Bradley sighed and took a long sip of wine, staring at Ailéas.

"When King Alexander III of Scotland died ten years ago, a succession crisis erupted and nearly plunged the country into chaos. It was your own guardians," he said, pointing his fingers, "who called on our king to arbitrate the conflict and ensure the stability of the kingdom."

"I told you there was no need to lecture me," she grumbled.

"What I'm trying to get across to you is that this war is only the continuation of a long series of events. It's unfortunate, but that's how it is, and I'm convinced that it is a necessary evil to prevent your entire country from tearing itself apart. When Balliol abdicates, there will be discussions, negotiations."

"Ah, negotiations. You are so gifted in that area," she spat as she brought her face close to the old man's. "We could say that Berwick was an example of your negotiations! You should go tell that to everyone you've slaughtered there! It will give them a nice lesson! You can try to convince yourself all you want, but that is all just rubbish to sugarcoat your atrocious crimes!"

She turned on her heels and left the tent, enraged.

Several days passed with her giving him little more than a few words, which was not easy given that she had to follow him like his shadow through the entire camp. While she was still furious, she had no choice: she had to play her role as a healer, preparing herbal teas and inhalations to maintain the illusion. Enveloped in her silence, she never stopped thinking of Fillan, wondering where he might be and if he was okay.

She spoke again as they progressed further north, following the Chief Lieutenant and Earl of Surrey, John de

Warenne. King Edward had entrusted him with the mission of taking the town of Dunbar, an important stronghold and the last strategic milestone in the conquest of the Lowlands to Edinburgh. Shortly after setting up the new camp, she spotted the spectacular Scottish fort on the tip of a cliff which protruded into the sea like a claw.

She had only had the chance to go there once with Alastair, a few years before, and she remembered that the castle dominated the whole city with its splendor and its port below. But imagining the horrors that would soon unfold there, her heart sank.

Inside the command tent, which had been erected under pouring rain in the middle of the surrounding plains, Ailéas was preparing an infusion in a corner while Bradley hunched over a map, debating strategy with two of his men.

"We won't attack head on," he explained. "Marjory Comyn* requested help. Warenne wants us to focus on it."

"Who answered?" asked one of the soldiers.

"Part of Balliol's army will not delay much longer," replied the third. "But the king could not risk the trip. Sir Patrick de Graham has already arrived from Dalkeith. He has settled high in the west beyond Spott Burn Lake."

* Wife of Patrick IV of Dunbar, Count of March and English ally, who decided to support the Scots by handing over the fort to them before the arrival of the English.

"Another turncoat."

"I fought with Graham in France two years ago," Bradley replied. "He is a man of honor. Intelligent. He hasn't got the stomach to bear the massacres."

"Man of honor or not, he might run into us and take us from the rear with his cavalry. We must take care of him first."

All nodded.

A soldier burst into the tent.

"Sir, you said you didn't want to be disturbed, but…"

"Get out of the way," growled a man who didn't have the patience to wait to be introduced.

At the sight of him, Ailéas's blood froze. She almost dropped the jug of water she held in her hands. The warrior with the antlers, the murderer of her master, had just entered the tent with two of his men.

Lann Fala, Bloodied Blades, she thought, observing their red capes.

She managed to turn her back halfway to them, so that no one could make out her face.

"Lord Cornavii," Bradley said dryly.

"What is Warenne waiting for to launch the assault?" demanded the knight without any form of politeness in his ghostly voice.

"Because of the Scottish reinforcements. He wanted me to prepare a flawless strategy."

"Good. I'm sure King Edward will be delighted with this future victory. He also told me that he would come himself to take Dunbar's keys back from that whore Comyn," added the Lann Fala, spitting on the ground.

"Can we hope to see you on the battlefield?"

"Me and my men have more important things to do," he replied, staring at the old man with his piercing, haughty eyes.

"Is it about that boy and that girl I received reports of?"

"That and other matters, according to the will of the king."

"The king's will?" repeated the commander in a voice tinged with sarcasm.

He knew full well that the Order of the Templars pulled the strings on this subject.

The helmeted warrior approached slowly, his armor rattling with each step. He placed his two gloved fists on the map, and Ailéas saw the hilt of his gigantic sword sticking out.

"Be careful not to say words you might regret, old man. An accident in the middle of a military campaign can happen so quickly."

To Ailéas's amazement, Bradley bowed, though as stiff as a board and with clenched teeth.

The warrior's gaze suddenly fell on her, and her head felt like it was going to explode. Her heart raced, and she had to make a huge effort to look natural and stop her hands from trembling. The images of Berwick resurfaced, and terror forced its way into every inch of her body. Her entire soul cried out for revenge, and she thought of the dagger that Bradley had offered her, hidden in her boot. It was obvious that she would be dead before she could land even one blow.

The teenager absorbed herself in the mixture of St. John's wort leaves and raspberries, pretending to ignore the gaze that landed on her, afraid she'd be unmasked at any moment.

She panicked for another second, then noticed out of the corner of her eye that the Lann Fala observed the other occupants of the tent in the same manner.

"We have to talk alone," Cornavii announced to Bradley.

She sighed discreetly in relief, then left without rushing so as not to arouse suspicion, followed by English soldiers and the acolytes of the warrior with the helm.

"After Dunbar," said the Lann Fala once he found himself alone with the commander, "the army will move towards Edinburgh."

"I suspected that would be the case."

"That's because you're a smart man, and intelligent men can anticipate. That's why I wanted to speak with you."

Bradley said nothing and allowed the warrior to continue.

"As you know, King Edward is not only interested in the two fugitives. He is also searching for objects of importance."

"I heard of your research after the capture of Berwick. What is it about?"

"Do you seriously think I'm going to tell you?"

"So, what do you want me to anticipate?" asked the old man, ever the pragmatist.

"Thanks to an informant infiltrated within the enemy, we know where some of these items are. When we approach this place, I wish to ensure that you do not create any problems."

"Why would I?"

"Because I'll be in charge of operations from now on."

"And my men, too?"

Cornavii nodded, smirking. Bradley firmly crossed his arms. He struggled to not let his anger show but still began to wander around the tent.

"King's orders, of course," added the knight.

"Will it be in Edinburgh?"

"No, later, near Perth. At Scone. I wanted you to have time to make up your mind."

As he watched Cornavii, who took malicious pleasure in imposing his superiority with a crooked smile stretched under his helm, the old man couldn't help but think back to his argument with Ailéas.

England could help and save Scotland. He was sure of

that. But what about the presence of the Order and the Lann Fala?

The girl's words echoed in his ears. *It's all bullshit.*

A trace of doubt crept into his mind.

19

BROTHERHOOD

The further north they trekked, nature became wilder and more vibrant. Fillan, who did not remember having lived close to the Highlands, discovered breathtaking landscapes as if for the first time. Hillsides bordered plains of emerald, and mountains with groves intertwined and stretched as far as the eye could see. They sometimes rose so high that their unreachable peaks were surrounded by clouds. In other places they surrounded lochs whose still waters reflected the gray of the sky.

Their journey to Scone lasted two weeks and took place uneventfully, the English not having ventured so far. Sören had ordered them to set off as soon as they had landed in the port of Burnisland, after crossing the Firth of Forth. He wanted to widen the distance, again and again.

A heavy and monotonous rain covered each day, though Fillan eventually adjusted to the rhythm of travel. He was also happy to find that since Bealltainn, no one called him a 'kid' anymore or nicknamed him 'the maggot.'

The deluge stopped as soon as they arrived at Scone, as though it were welcoming them, and Fillan was surprised by what awaited them at the end of their long journey.

"An abbey?" he asked, when they stopped in front of a building attached to a church.

"Don't worry," the Norwegian laughed, "there are no plans to let them take you into the orders."

They dismounted as a procession of monks filed through the main entrance. Upon spotting someone, Sören abandoned them.

"Where is he going?" inquired Fillan.

"It's going to suck," Edan answered simply.

"Eh? Why?"

The leader of the mercenaries rushed straight at a monk to take him aside and strike up a conversation. It only took a few seconds for him to start visibly arguing.

"That's why!"

"Who is that?"

"He's Father Thomas de Balmerino," Moira replied. "He is the head of this abbey, and he's the one who made us do this entire journey from Berwick."

The man dressed in his cowl listened to Sören's yelling

with the greatest of calm. The afternoon sun made the top of his tonsure shine.

"He's from the Brotherhood?"

"You could even say that he is the brains of it in Scotland," explained Fergus. "With all this mission's problems, it's no wonder Sören has a few choice words to say to him."

"What can he possibly want from me?"

"We don't know," replied the bald man.

He'd answered too quickly for it to be the truth.

"Come on, we've arrived at our destination: I have the right to know!" complained Fillan.

Edan was energetically picking his nose, Fergus decided suddenly to tune his lute and Moira adjusted the bit of her horse. Only Kyle returned his gaze, pinching her lips, as if dying to tell him what she knew.

"Why don't you tell me anything?" he practically yelled.

"Because we don't know anything," replied the druid without even looking at him.

"You all suck!" he spat, turning on his heels.

Deep down, he felt hurt. During the last few weeks, he had gotten the impression of being part of their gang, of having managed to integrate, but some barriers apparently remained.

He did not see Kyle, who attempted to join him, nor Moira who held her back. He contented himself with walking away to do a tour around the abbey.

He knew he had lost his temper too quickly. The secrets and the misunderstandings were a large part of it, but there was something else.

It was this place.

Over the past few weeks, he had seen and passed through many places, but this was the first time he felt so out of place. The impressive architecture of the building, the stained-glass windows, the monks who swung their rosaries with each of their steps—all this reminded him of only one thing: he had killed in cold blood.

Fillan had never been religious, but he knew one thing, which Alastair had reminded him of from the first moments after he took him in: killing was a sin. He now felt like an intruder, imagining that everyone looked at him as if they knew.

His conscience kept nagging at him.

"You arrived a few days early!" shouted a voice behind him, which he immediately recognized.

"Deorsa," he said by way of greeting.

"What a horrible face you're pulling! What were you thinking about?"

Fillan fell silent, leaving it to the spy to make the conversation.

"Could it be because of the little outburst I just heard?"

"I'm sick of not knowing what I'm doing here."

"A little birdy tells me," continued the spy, ignoring him, "that you killed a man in Leith. Is it true, this time? Yes, I see it in your face. No, it wasn't any of the group who told me about it. I figured it out by myself, thanks to the description of the murderer circulating. Let's just say that in wanting to make you unrecognizable to the Lann Fala with this scar, I'm afraid Sören has made your face more… memorable."

"And Cornavii…?"

"Doesn't seem to have made the connection, fortunately. But he will perhaps remember that he met a kid at Cranshaws matching the same description, if ever this one reached his ears. Anyway, it goes without saying that killing this man was unwise."

"Shut up!" shouted Fillan, starting to raise his fist.

"Such anger! Who'd have believed that you were cut from the same cloth as Sören?"

"Deorsa!" growled a voice. "Don't you have anything better to do than annoying that boy? Perhaps ensuring that we have all the information we need and that you didn't miss anything?"

Fillan turned to look at who had come to save the spy's nose from getting fractured. It was a gigantic man in his thirties, taller than even Sören. His thick muscles protruded from his tartan, and he had the build of a giant. Behind his head, long brown hair was bound up above the handle of a claymore.* Everything pointed to him being a native of the Highlands.

"No information ever escapes me, William," Deorsa retorted, narrowing his eyes before walking away.

Fillan then found himself alone with the mountain of muscles.

"He can be really hateful sometimes. Hello to you, Fillan."

"Definitely. But everyone knows me even before they meet me; I don't know anyone."

"Forgive me, my name is William Wallace," said the Highlander, squeezing his forearm vigorously.

"Are you also part of the Brotherhood?"

"It's been a few years, yes."

They began to walk, continuing the tour around the abbey that Fillan had started.

"I don't even know what we're really talking about," he continued, annoyed. "No one's told me anything since I left Berwick. All I know is it's your Brotherhood of Assassins who dealt with the Guild, and that you wanted to get us back, my sister and me."

---

* A claymore is a very large, broad-bladed sword that is usually used with two hands. While the full-size version did not appear until the late fourteenth century, smaller versions (also known as hand-and-a-half swords) were used by the Highlander Scottish warriors from the end of the thirteenth century.

"I'm sincerely sorry about her."

Fillan eyed Wallace from the corner of his eye. Underneath his rock-like build and his rough-hewn features, his face was adorned with a real pain, the kind that only those who have been through a similar ordeal can spot.

"I understand your frustration. I've been there, too. Discretion, secrets, riddles: all this is part of the Brotherhood's methods. It's their only way to survive."

"So, you're an… Assassin?"

The colossus nodded.

"I joined the Brotherhood thanks to Sören. After the death of my father, he was the one who took me in and raised me, so to say. He didn't explain anything to you?"

"He's not a very talkative person."

"I know that well! He always kept a close bond with the Brotherhood, even after leaving it. But his independence matters more than anything to him. Knowing him, he must have felt that it was not his place to reveal anything to you. We've asked for a lot of patience, and I can only imagine how hard it must have been, given all the hardships that you faced before you got here. But the answers will come. We'll hold a meeting with the other members, and we will explain everything to you. Absolutely everything."

"You're going to want me to join your organization," guessed the young man.

"You are smart. I expected no less from you, with what Alastair told me about your character."

"Did you know my master?" gasped Fillan, astonishment stretching his features.

"Many of us knew him. Alastair has always been one of our collaborators, even though he never joined the Brotherhood. It is not for nothing that we entrusted you both to him after the disappearance of your clan. His loss will leave a great void. He was an exceptional person."

Fillan knew how true that was.

As they continued on their way, they found themselves facing a large, flat stone that rested on two feet of granite. Two monks guaranteed that the rock was perfectly aligned and in no danger of falling with infinite precautions.

"It's the Stone of Destiny," William explained, observing the questioning look of the teenager, who had stopped.

"What's so special about this pebble?"

"Don't repeat that too loudly or, despite their vows, these monks will come and kick your ass."

"Legend says that it was the Tuatha Dé Danann who brought it when they came from Ireland, it and four other stones. Does the Tuatha Dé Dannan mean anything to you?"

"Vaguely," replied Fillan, pulling the pendant out. "Kyle gave this to me before my first real fight."

"Ogme, I see," the warrior said, smiling. "You're lucky that Kyle likes you; she is an incredible young woman."

Fillan blushed, sensing that there were surely implications in those words.

"Anyway, the stone was said to have powers. When the Gaels, the first men, progressed through the country, the gods returned to Sidh and left it behind. Our ancestors seized it and established the tradition of coronation. Every man called to be King of Scotland, the guardian of the country, must stand guard over it on the day of his enthronement. It would even appear that the stone has the ability to speak."

Seeing how William venerated the badly cut pendant Fillan wore, he suspected that this rock would be of capital importance to Kyle.

A fine drizzle began to fall, and the pleasant smell of damp grass and wet stone seeped into the air. Their task accomplished, the monks bowed while pronouncing the same sentence several times.

"What are they saying?" asked Fillan, who didn't understand their words.

"*Lia Fàil* is the Gaelic name for the Stone of Destiny. It is also called the Stone of Fal."

It took Fillan a few seconds to make the connection, then he opened his mouth wide.

"Does it have anything to do with the Children of Fal?" he asked.

"Tonight, we'll explain everything to you," William answered with a benevolent smile.

He refrained from retorting that he wanted to know everything, now. After all, he wasn't entirely sure he was a Child of Fal, whatever that meant.

20

CHILD OF FAL

Sören strode briskly through the transept, followed closely by Fillan. Their boots clacked against the stone, disturbing the nocturnal silence in the church of Scone. They advanced using the light of the candles, which were placed at the foot of the pillars in the aisles, unevenly dispelling the darkness. Above their heads, the stained-glass windows of the second floor were only blackness and they could barely make out the ribbed patterns.

"Hurry up, I said!" said the Norwegian impatiently. "They're waiting for us!"

Even though Fillan knew that the council of the Brotherhood was to be held that evening, no one had told him exactly when. Exhausted by the journey, he had dozed off in the makeshift camp that they had set up in the forest a few feet from the cloister. Sören had shaken him awake shortly after midnight.

"There's nobody here," noted Fillan as they reached the choir pews opposite where they'd entered.

"They're down below," Sören replied, as if it were obvious.

"Below?"

The mercenary approached a semi-circular bas-relief which adorned the apse and drew a curious inverted V-shape amid the abundant engraved thistles. He lit two torches as the ground shook and a series of slabs disappeared to reveal a spiral staircase that descended underground.

"Are you coming too?"

"Just this once."

Deep down, Fillan was relieved. Even though Sören was colder than ever, his presence reassured him.

After an initial flight of steps made of stone blocks, a second flight appeared, larger and carved out of the rock. In a descent that seemed to go on forever, the stairs led them into the depths of Scone.

When Fillan arrived at the bottom of the stairs, a long corridor with smooth walls opened out. He thought he was entering the Other World. His footsteps were muffled, and the torch he held at arm's length made the walls around him shimmer. He had no clue what material these walls were built with, but they didn't seem to be made of stone or metal.

"What is this place?" he asked in a whisper, as if afraid

to wake someone—or something. "It's nothing like the architecture of the abbey."

Like nothing I've ever seen in my life, he thought.

"That's because it was here before," the mercenary explained.

"Before?"

"Yes, long before. Would you believe me if I told you that it was not men who built it?"

Was he implying that the gods themselves had fashioned this place? It was absurd, and Fillan resented him for playing games with him.

By the light of his torch, Fillan suddenly discovered that the corridor led to a bridge overhanging an abyss. He let out a curse of surprise.

"Oh, yeah, I should have warned you," Sören breathed, with a hint of a chuckle in his voice.

"Is it deep?"

"Enough that I don't recommend you try to check it out yourself. Keep going, and watch where you step."

The narrow structure stretched above the darkness. Thin wisps of mist floated here and there, blown by a faint breeze. Several drips echoed in the distance, producing curious echoes that reverberated off walls concealed by darkness.

Fillan advanced slowly, his legs trembling. Every two strides he couldn't help but check that the stone was holding his weight, though every look he cast into the impenetrable darkness on either side of his feet made him shiver.

As he progressed, he continued to wonder about where he was. He had never seen a bridge of such artistry, cut several feet long in one long block. He was beginning to doubt that the Norwegian had been joking. There was definitely something supernatural in this place.

He sighed in relief and mopped his brow when he reached a new corridor, at the end of which flickered a light. He found himself surrounded once more by the same shimmering walls, but these were engraved with countless symbols that he had never seen before, either.

After a few strides, the corridor opened into a large, circular room bathed in an orange light. Large candles gave off a gentle warmth and showed a glimpse of very high walls rising towards a ceiling of darkness.

For furniture, there were only five wooden armchairs that clashed so much with the rest of the room that he realized they must have been brought there.

"Fillan!" rejoiced Thomas de Balmerino, seated in the largest of the armchairs. "Welcome! Sören, thank you for joining us. We saved you a seat."

"I'd rather stay standing," he replied, grumbling.

"As you please."

With a wave of his hand, the abbot invited Fillan to the center of the circle he formed with three other people.

"You already know Deorsa," said the abbot, "and I understand that you talked to William Wallace soon after you got here. This woman is named Amy, of the Comyn clan. As for me, I am Thomas de Balmerino, Abbot of Scone."

Fillan took in the woman, who had every trait of a northern warrior. In her thirties, she had blonde hair trimmed to the length of her muscular shoulders. The scar that cut into her chin and part of her left cheek made her look fierce.

"We know everything that's happened to you since you left Berwick, but you—what do you know, my boy?"

Fillan did not like the way the monk called him 'my boy.' It sounded like 'kid' from Sören or Edan's 'maggot.'

"Not much," he replied simply. "I have been told hardly anything. All I know is that you call yourselves the Brotherhood of Assassins."

He glanced sideways at Sören, not wishing to embarrass him in front of the Brotherhood.

"The reason is simple: those who brought you here knew almost nothing."

The monk turned his head towards the mercenary.

"And we are sincerely sorry. It seems like someone betrayed us in the south, as soon as the English crossed the border. We couldn't do anything else."

"The past belongs to the past," replied the mercenary.

"That's a wise reaction."

Fillan held back a giggle. He recalled the Norwegian shouting at Deorsa in Dalkeith and yelling at the abbot as soon as they arrived in Scone. He was far from wise.

"Since we are talking about the past," continued Thomas, "that is where we must begin, so that you understand why you are here. The history of the Brotherhood reaches back several centuries. We have always opposed an entity of which you have already become acquainted through the Lann Fala. It is the Order of the Templars."

All listened calmly to the abbot's presentation except for Sören, who carelessly picked his fingernails with his dagger, his mouth twisted into an evil grin.

"What differentiates Assassins from Templars?"

"It's a vast subject, which we could discuss with you for hours! The Templars are convinced that the only way to achieve a harmonious and orderly society is by controlling the population. According to them, people's self-reliance leads to chaos because of the nature of man."

"And the Assassins don't believe that? So, what? You yearn for… disorder?"

The monk smiled, watching him.

"No, everything is not always so black or white. We believe that nothing matters more than free will. And that when a handful of people have all the power and rule over all the others, it is the door to injustice—because this, too, is the nature of man."

"And you can be sure that we hate injustice above all," added William.

"What actually happens? Do you fight?"

"Direct confrontations are not common, although we always seek to cut off the heads of the most dangerous snakes. You see, members of the Order covet powerful artifacts that they hope to use to control the masses. We do everything we can to thwart their plans so that these objects do not fall into their hands."

"Artifacts?"

"Like the Stone of Destiny," William explained.

"Aren't these just old symbols from legends? What's so special about them?"

Thomas, William, and Amy looked at him benevolently as Deorsa chuckled.

"Many are symbols," said the woman slowly, "but they are also more than that. They have a real power."

"A power? You mean, like magic?"

"So some might call it; others speak of a gift from the gods. Tell me, my boy, do you believe that such a thing can exist?"

Fillan shook his head: it was more unlikely than old Tilda's rantings, more implausible even than to believe that the place where they stood could have been built by gods.

And yet, he thought.

"And yet," continued Thomas, "it is. Sören denied our Brotherhood; he can confirm it for you."

Fillan quickly turned to the Norwegian, who nodded.

"What do I have to do with this?" he asked.

"Have you got any ideas?" called William.

"Is this about the Children of Fal?"

"That's right," agreed Thomas. "The Brotherhood, the Children of Fal, the Lann Fala, the Order of the Templars: everything is intertwined in an intricate web woven with the needle of fate. Long ago, the Tuatha Dé Danann walked these lands and bequeathed the artifacts we spoke of, but not only that. They also left behind the Children of Fal. They are very precious beings, because they carry the heritage of Tuatha in their blood. Like objects of power, the Brotherhood has protected these children in Scotland for hundreds of years."

"From what? The Order?"

"Among other things," replied the abbot. "Every Child of Fal is destined to join the Brotherhood to help protect the heritage of his ancestors. It has always been so, and it is why the Templars keep hunting them down and killing them. Ten years ago, the Order took advantage of the political instability caused by the death of the king and attempted to permanently annihilate the Brotherhood and the Children of Fal. They wanted to kill two birds with one stone. They succeeded, in part, and all of us here have paid the price of their rage. Your clan has always been linked to the Brotherhood; that's why they were slaughtered."

"And I would be one of those Children?"

In the light of what Thomas revealed to him, the question that had been nagging him for weeks now frightened him.

"Yes, you bear the mark."

Fillan instinctively raised his wrist to observe his birthmark. He finally understood Sören's reaction upon discovering it after they fled Cranshaws.

"You got it," Amy Comyn proclaimed. "That brand designates you as a Child of Fal from your birth. You were but an infant when the druid of your clan entered a trance and received confirmation that you were indeed born under the shadows of providence."

"You have always been destined to join the Brotherhood," Deorsa explained in a honeyed voice.

Fillan thought he heard Sören grumble. The mercenary appeared more and more annoyed as the members of the Brotherhood continued talking.

"For the moment," continued Deorsa, "you are only a target who we had to hide. But you can become something else."

An Assassin, Fillan thought.

"Come a little closer," William called, drawing a sword from behind his chair. "This is Claidheamh Fal, the legacy of your clan, Fillan. It means 'Sword of Fal.' Nobody other than you can handle it and be worthy of it."

Fillan grabbed the blade. It was incredibly light, and he noticed a strange, inverted V engraved on the pommel. The handle, covered with dark straps, was quite long: he could grab it with both hands. On both sides, the hilt ended in ornate Celtic tracery. He pulled the weapon halfway out of its laced leather scabbard and discovered a dazzling blade with a deep gutter that hinted that the core metal was different from its surface metal. The cutting edge was thinner than parchment.

"It is a weapon that has seen many battles," Thomas explained. "Just like its twin."

William grabbed a second, identical sword, which he kept in a tartan.

"This one should have gone to Ailéas," the old man explained. "The Children of Fal are always twins. Most importantly, the birthmark you have on your wrist means 'two' in the lost language of the Tuatha."

Fillan remained silent, allowing a moment for his emotions to run through him. He felt overwhelmed.

"Do I have a choice?" he finally asked in a shy voice.

"Of course," William replied. "In your veins flows the legacy of those who forged Scotland and who fought the Order, but it is up to you to embrace this destiny."

"Or write another one," Amy added.

"I would even add," said Deorsa, "that nothing good ever comes from coercion and we will not force you into anything."

Fillan took a moment of consideration as he tightened the scabbards of leather between his fingers.

"For the moment, my only desire is to make Cornavii pay for what he did."

"Revenge is an excellent motivator," explained Thomas. "But in the long term, you will have to move beyond it to serve a greater cause. The cause of the Brotherhood."

He wasn't sure what that meant, but he saw the opportunity to survive longer, as Ailéas would have wanted.

"What will happen if I accept?"

"We will train you, and you will become a fully-fledged member of the Brotherhood," said the monk, clasping his hands.

"For eight years, we have been trying to rebuild what was destroyed by the Lann Fala. With their return and the progression of the English, your help would be invaluable."

"And could I change my mind, later?"

They all cast meaningful glances at Sören.

"It's quite possible," agreed Amy, enunciating each word.

"You don't have to decide immediately," added William. "We will have a second meeting tomorrow evening, which leaves you some time to reflect on all we have said."

Fillan caught the blue gaze of the Norwegian and stared

at him for a long time, watching for a movement, a grin, a hitch in his breathing—anything that could help him decide.

But the mercenary looked away, troubled, and left the room without a word.

21

APPRENTICE

Fillan had a difficult time closing his eyes. All night, curled up around the two swords, he went over and over the revelations made by the Brotherhood. He felt reassured to still have a future despite the death of Ailéas, Alastair and the collapse of all his dreams, but it also terrified him.

Did he have what it took to become an Assassin? He, the handsome tailor-talker who had only just learned to hold a sword?

No matter how angry he was with those who called him a child, that was exactly how he felt, deep down. Like a kid with a sword. A kid that had been thrown into the middle of a conflict that was beyond him.

One question bothered him more than the others. Why had Sören disowned the Brotherhood? If he hated this organization so much, why didn't he dissuade Fillan from joining? To get rid of him? It didn't make any sense now that he had led him here.

However, the mercenary, who kept working for the Assassins, was no longer a paradox.

Fillan woke up around noon. He isolated himself and even Kyle, despite her morbid curiosity, left him alone.

She just let him know she was there if he needed it. He bumped into her several times in spite of himself and felt his heart split in two, every time. Whether or not he agreed to join the Brotherhood, they would be soon separated.

The sun was at its zenith as he wandered around the abbey. A voice startled him:

"Hey! You're the new one!"

Turning around, he discovered a young man barely older than him, with short, messy brown hair and a round, cheerful face.

Fillan observed him silently, wondering how he had managed not to hear or feel his approach.

"Are you okay, Fillan?"

He nodded his head.

"My name is James de Crannach. I am master Thomas's apprentice," he said, revealing a leather armband with the V reversed.

An apprentice Assassin, thought Fillan. This explained why he hadn't heard him coming.

Faced with the enthusiasm that James brought into their

conversation, the barriers quickly fell between them. Fillan asked him many questions that he had not considered posing the day before and so learned about the role of an apprentice within the Brotherhood.

"Master Thomas has been teaching me the role of an Assassin for a year," James explained. "He trains me to act in the shadows, to collect information and to analyze complex situations. To kill, also, when there are no other means. I am like one blade, discreet and deadly, which acts at the right time. It's not simple; it requires great mental strength."

"So you think it's a glorious mission, right?"

"It is rather, yes. But I always keep in mind what my father, rest his soul, always used to say: 'glory in death is not glory, it is only an illusion written in blood.' There is nothing glorious in killing. I take no pleasure in it, but sometimes it's essential and you have to do your best with it, otherwise you risk dying yourself."

Three years, four at the most, separated them and yet Fillan felt a chasm of maturity between them. He thought back to what had happened in Leith and his assailant, and these words relieved him, a little.

When he expressed surprise at not seeing the apprentice during the council the night before, the man burst out laughing.

"An apprentice like me, at a meeting like that?! Never in my life! These meetings are rare. You're the only one not from the Brotherhood, apart from Sören, who's had the chance to attend in years. Lucky you!"

Fillan felt that the conversation struck a chord with him. James was patient, caring, and despite the implausibility of their topic of discussion, their laughs and their astonishments had the taste of simplicity. They chatted the rest of the afternoon, and the wait until the second council meeting seemed shorter.

Around midnight, Sören took him again to the depths of the abbey.

"Aren't you going to give me any advice?" Fillan asked, annoyed, turning towards the mercenary as they progressed over the bridge surrounded by darkness.

"Here's some: listen to your heart and act accordingly. No one can decide for you. And stop looking at me with those eyes, like a beaten puppy—it makes me want to push you into the void."

The members of the Brotherhood waited in the room with the candles, as if they hadn't moved since the night before.

Once greetings were exchanged, they again invited Fillan to face them.

"Fillan," began Thomas de Balmerino in a low, solemn voice, "you know the question we are going to ask you. We revealed your origins and the destiny of those who, like you, were born under the shadow of providence."

His heart began to gallop, and he held himself as upright as possible.

"Would you like to join the Brotherhood?" Wallace asked.

Fillan felt terror seize him. He had the impression that a weight had fallen on him, and his eyes moved around, seeking an escape route, before crossing those of Sören. The two irises of the Norwegian's blue eyes stared at him intently and, remembering his words, Fillan probed his heart one last time.

Ailéas, he thought, looking at the mark on his wrist.

Since Berwick, he'd wondered what she would do in his place. Deep down, he knew. He had understood it as soon as the link between the Brotherhood and the Children of Fal appeared. His twin had always nourished the visceral desire to reconnect with their origins.

And those origins were the Brotherhood.

This thought comforted him. He relived the image of Little Ailéas who had spoken to him on the night of Bealltainn.

To survive.

"A few years ago," he said finally, "I promised my sister to survive at all costs. Today, I feel it is by your side that I will best be able to hold this promise."

He took a deep breath, and time stood still.

The wide flames of the braziers also seemed to freeze.

"I agree to join your Brotherhood."

Sören had no reaction, scowling at best.

The others, meanwhile, nodded with a smile.

"Perfect!" Thomas clapped, slapping the flat of his palm on the arm of his chair. "I think you made a sensible decision."

"And we'll make sure to prove it to you," William added. "Please, sit down."

Fillan sat down in the fifth seat, the one that Sören disdained, surprised at being able to remain, remembering his discussion with James.

"We would like your presence again this evening," began the abbot, turning to Sören, "for us to make amends. We will discuss the situation of our country, so it is important to us that you can take advantage of our information."

"I don't care," growled the man.

"Easy for you to say," Thomas said, his mouth pinched. "Deorsa, would you mind?"

"With great pleasure!" replied the spy, rubbing his hands together. "I think I speak without exaggeration when I say that the situation in Scotland is critical. After sacking Berwick, King Edward progressed along the coast. An uprising took place at Dunbar but was crushed. The Earls of Ross, Atholl and Mentheith were taken prisoner. Patrick de Graham died during the battle. His troops might have had the advantage because they were posted on the hills, but when their first charge was pushed back, it was a stampede: all the Scots fled. Graham and a handful of his followers left nothing to chance, but they were massacred by the cavalry."

William Wallace let out a curse.

"I couldn't have said it better myself," Deorsa said, watching him. "The Graham clan could have been a base in the south, but now… Subsequently, Roxburgh, Jedburgh and Umfraville surrendered, like so many other towns. Edinburgh was taken only days after you passed Leith, by the way," he told Sören. "John Balliol, who took refuge in Perth, has just accepted Edward's peace proposal."

"Scotland is finished," Sören concluded.

"For the time being, its independence and stability are compromised," retorted the spy.

"A curse on the Order," Amy spat.

"You're not thinking far enough," continued Deorsa. "With the abdication of Balliol, I imagine they're on their way to seize the Royal Archives, the True Cross, the Crown Jewels here, but above all…"

"The Stone of Destiny," Wallace added darkly.

"Fortunately," said Thomas, "we did what we had to do."

Fillan didn't understand what that meant, because he had seen the stone in the abbey garden just this afternoon.

"There is the question of the next few months. Between the clans that would like to oppose England but do not have the strength, and those that submit unconditionally for the sole purpose of keeping their titles and their lands, there is too much instability. I recommend that we let the winter pass. Sören, that's also what we advise to you."

"I'm old enough to know what to do, Thomas."

"There's no need to put on your airs," teased Amy. "You intend to retire to your clan at Loch Ericht, do you not?"

The mercenary pouted to indicate she was correct, as though she'd screamed "damn you!" at him.

"This brings us to a tricky question concerning Fillan," said the monk. "To be a part of the Brotherhood, he needs to be trained, and I think it would be good if he became your apprentice, Sören."

"What?!" exploded Deorsa, whose eyes—though doubled in size—still remained tiny. "Sören is no longer part of the Brotherhood! Leave him out of this. We know the success of the last mission entrusted to him: he only brought back one of the Children! Don't look at me like that, Sören, it's the truth!"

Fillan wanted to draw his sword and cut his throat.

"Anyway," growled Sören, "what makes you believe I would accept? You don't change! Still deciding everything for others, assuming that they will bend to your whims. You never take your eyes off me!"

"Money…" began Amy.

"Has its limits," the mercenary cut her off.

"Then it's settled!" rejoiced Deorsa. "I will take care of it!"

Fillan never imagined for a moment that this man could become his master. Spending the next few months tugging on his cloak? He'd rather throw himself into the abyss from the bridge outside.

"Wait a minute," Wallace said. "Sören, we do not wish to impose on you. The Brotherhood knows the price you've already had to pay in its service. But I also know it's best that the boy learns a lot from you. Of everyone present in this room, you're the best fighter, the only one who can teach him how to wield Fal's sword."

Deorsa was about to protest, but the abbot silenced him with a raised hand.

"Your former apprentice is not wrong, Sören. Plus, this way Fillan would be out of reach from the Order at Loch Ericht with you, during his training."

The mercenary glared at them with undisguised rage.

"That's what you had in mind from the start, isn't it? You didn't invite me here to tell me about the recent news."

The spy looked outraged and raised both hands to feign that his comrades had taken him by surprise too.

"This kind of method is what I loathe about you," continued Sören.

A leaden silence, disturbed only by the crackling of the braziers, fell over the room. Fillan felt Sören's gaze land on him, and he saw something he had seen only once before, on the morning of the Berwick Massacre.

The shadow of empathy.

"I'm going to accept your proposal," he said in a voice that could shake mountains.

"As for the price…"

"There will be no price. I'm not doing it for you, but for Fillan. He doesn't know what he's gotten himself into, and I want to make sure that he has all the weapons and knowledge to come out of it alive. And I know he won't get that with this obsequious ass," he said, pointing at Deorsa with a contemptuous glare.

The spy flushed with anger.

"I will take Fillan to my clan this winter. I will teach him what he must know. When he's ready, you will never ask for anything again. This is my 'price.'"

All the Assassins exchanged a look before agreeing.

All except Deorsa. But the majority had spoken.

On the way back to camp, Sören revealed to Fillan that they would leave for the Highlands as early as the following day.

Kyle was watching and waiting for him. She dragged him into the woods on the edge of the domain of the abbey so he could tell her what happened. All he managed to say was that Sören had agreed to train him as an Assassin.

Kyle did not seem to believe it, then when she understood what that meant, she began to smile.

"What's so funny?" he asked.

"I was afraid that you… Nothing at all, forget it," she said to him, hugging his neck.

Quickly, as if afraid of being pushed back, she planted a kiss on his lips. Fillan was surprised at first, but then seized the young woman's neck in turn and let his fingers run through the roots of her hair. He breathed in the smell of heather and mint that came from it, each touch electrifying his body.

"Nothing at all," Kyle repeated, pulling him down into the moss that carpeted the forest floor.

The night's cool breeze, the trees whose leaves crisscrossed with a gentle rustling, and the cry of a bird in the distance all disappeared amidst a cloud of sensations and shivers.

22

WOOD

Fillan woke up in the middle of the night, his eyes widening. A hand covered his mouth. He panicked and struggled, but a body astride him held him still. All his being quivered, and his pulse quickened. In the dark, Kyle's face came closer, putting a finger to his mouth.

He became aware of a clamor from the direction of the abbey, sounding like a mix of shouts and brutal orders.

"What's happening?" he asked when Kyle withdrew her hand.

"The English, or worse," she replied, helping him to his feet.

"Deorsa said they wouldn't be here for several days!"

"That filthy eel has screwed up. It wouldn't be the first time. Let's go find the others!"

They ran through the woods. Fillan caught a glimpse of

the flames that were starting to spread through the domain as he looked through tree trunks to his right.

The group was on high alert.

"What the hell were you doing?" Edan shouted.

"Mind your own business!" Kyle retorted.

The bald man looked them each up and down with a smirk. He was about to launch into a lewd comment, but Sören stopped him.

"You two," he said to Kyle and Fillan, "flee through the woods and away from the fighting."

"Without horses?!"

"No choice," Moira replied. "Ours are in the stable at the abbey."

"Fuck that!"

"Well said!" Edan called.

"Oh, you, shut up! What about the rest of you?"

"We'll wait to see what happens," Sören explained. "Once you get out of the woods, follow the road to the north. If we don't catch up to you before the Tay, cross the river and wait for us at Luncarty."

Kyle nodded.

"I want to fight!" interjected Fillan, who boiled with desire for revenge.

"No," Sören cut in categorically. "We don't even know what's happening."

"But if the Stone of Fal…"

"I said no! It's not your job to take care of that yet, and the Brotherhood has surely already found a way to keep it safe. Have you already forgot the obedience an apprentice owes to his master?"

Fillan's eyes flashed.

"Good. Watch out for each other, and no messing around!"

They grasped each other's forearm before parting ways. Fillan felt something was changing between him and Sören. He hastily packed his things, girding one of the swords of Fal to his waist, wedging the other in the straps of his bag. The group had already disappeared into the tangle of trunks when they began to run.

The sound of their footsteps was muffled by the forest carpet. Fillan could barely see: a branch slashed his face, leaving a red welt on his cheek, but he ran faster still. If he slowed down for even a moment, he would lose sight of Kyle.

Torches suddenly appeared in front of them. They were swinging between the trunks, forming a flaming wall that was headed in their direction.

"Oh shit!" Kyle cursed. "They're searching the whole forest."

"Get up into the trees!"

"Eh?"

"The woods are dense and dark. They won't see us up there. Do you think you can manage?"

"What do you take me for?" she retorted before grabbing

onto the first branch within reach. "You'll see if I can manage."

She disappeared among the branches. He copied her, and a man brandished a torch right beneath their feet less than a minute later. It was definitely an English soldier.

"Do you see anything?" he barked in an authoritative voice.

"Nothing," replied another. "Are we sure they're here?"

"Yes, the orders were clear: they're somewhere in this forest! So move your ass and find them!"

Fillan hugged Kyle a little closer.

"Are they looking for us?" he whispered.

"If so, that's very bad."

"It'd mean the Brotherhood has been betrayed again…" said Fillan in comprehension.

She nodded gravely.

Preceded by the sound of his regular and rapid footsteps, a scout came running to speak to the man standing under the tree.

"The fire from the abbey has reached the forest!" he announced in a shrill voice.

"Is this a joke? What a bunch of incompetents! You others, you inspect every inch of this forest before everything starts to burn! Move!"

The English resumed their mission, searching thickets meticulously.

"Follow me," Kyle whispered in Fillan's ear.

"What are you doing?!"

"You want to stay here and wait for the fire to cook us like bread? We need to move from tree to tree; the branches are solid enough."

Just before leaping onto the adjoining oak tree, she suddenly kissed him. When she pulled back, Fillan thought he could see fear in her eyes, but he convinced himself that he was mistaken. Kyle was fearless.

They progressed just as slowly in one direction as the English did in the other, because they had to make sure that each new branch would not creak or break. Sometimes a torch loomed a few yards beneath their feet and they forced themselves to slow down, even to stop, clinging to the trunks like squirrels.

Around them the leaves were rustling, and an owl hooted every now and then, but they were mostly enveloped in an oppressive silence. The slightest noise in this quiet, however small, would sign their death warrant.

In her haste, however, Kyle slipped on a branch and a sinister creak resembling a doom chime rung out as she barely caught herself.

"Did you hear that?" yelled a soldier at the foot of the tree adjacent to theirs.

Kyle straightened up so as not to fall, but the wood cracked even more.

"Holy shit! They're in the trees!"

"Shoot those bastards down!"

Fillan only understood what he meant once the arrows started flying. He helped Kyle find solid footing and they fled faster, no longer caring if the wood creaked. Hissing whooshed in their ears, interspersed with the dull sound of iron spikes digging into the trunks.

"You can't see anything up there," bellowed an Englishman. "I have an idea!"

A flaming arrow grazed Fillan's arm.

"What are you doing?!" came a shocked voice. "A fiery arrow in the middle of the forest? You're crazy!"

"It's burning down anyway!"

Most of the arrows turned into streaks of fire. They flew at full speed, illuminating the night with ephemeral lightning. Arrows that didn't hit the trees fell into the undergrowth where they sparked new blazes.

Amid the shouts of the laughing soldiers, a clanking of metal burst through. Then another.

"They're attacking us!" shouted a soldier. "At arms! At arms!"

Sören's voice boomed above the hubbub. "Kyle, Fillan, get the hell out of here!"

They obeyed without thinking and jumped from branch to branch. They were scratched and almost twisted an ankle several times. Despite the confrontation that was taking place not far away, the arrows kept whistling by.

Several trees had turned into gigantic candles and the fire began to pursue them.

"This damn forest goes on forever!" yelled Kyle.

Fillan was about to answer her, but pain slammed into his shoulder and he howled in spite of himself.

"Fillan!" she cried after turning around.

A deep terror seized her at the sight of the body falling out of the tree, slowed by a few branches that it hit on the way down. She distinctly heard the tail of the arrow that broke when it hit the ground, and the gasp of pain that accompanied it.

"I got one!" shouted an Englishman. "Get over here!"

Fillan got up, stunned, and instinctively drew his sword despite the pain that tore through his shoulder. Luckily, it wasn't his dominant arm that had been hit. He blocked the soldier's first attack, but the pain that spread through his whole body brought him to his knees. The soldier raised his blade to deliver a killing blow, but a glittering spike shot through his chest.

Kyle had tumbled down the tree at top speed to rescue him. She tore her blade from the twitching body and turned to face another soldier.

Throughout the forest, the flames spread more and more quickly, illuminating the night and revealing many silhouettes.

"Come and get me!" screamed Kyle with all her might, dodging an attack while two other English soldiers rushed at her.

"Sören!"

She twirled nimbly, her weapon whistling through the air, and slaughtered two of her assailants with a controlled sweep. Fillan was terrified to see her get killed and tried to get up, but he had lost too much blood.

The nearest oaks were ablaze, and tongues of fire flickered all around. Then he saw him, moving through the embers.

Cornavii.

Soon the metallic antlers of his helmet loomed over him, and Fillan felt a hand grab his throat. Kyle, who was struggling with three infantrymen, could do nothing more than scream, her face bleeding.

"I figured it was you in Cranshaws," the tracker said in his ghostly voice. "That awful wound nearly fooled me, but not now that I've seen this."

He grabbed the boy's wrist and lifted it into the flamelight. Fillan tried to struggle, but the Lann Fala slapped him brutally with a gloved hand.

"I've been looking for you for eight years. Eight long years after letting a mere child escape. I can't wait to see if you'll squeal just like your mother."

Hooves pounded the ground.

"Cornavii!" thundered the voice of Sören, who jumped from his horse.

The rest of the gang following him rushed to help Kyle face the English.

"You were in Cranshaws, too," recalled the Lann Fala, straightening to face the Norwegian. "Your face is vaguely familiar to me. But then, there are so many dirty faces north of the Tweed."

"Shut up and come face me instead!"

"In such a hurry to die!" sneered the red warrior.

Through his blurred vision, Fillan saw Cornavii attack with rapidity, brandishing his huge sword in a vertical attack. Sören sidestepped it and the blade stuck into the ground with a muffled sound. Sören returned his attack, but Cornavii's great sword vibrated again in the air, forcing him to slip away.

"You are nimble, Assassin!"

Sören squinted and braced himself, the blade leaning over his face in a posture of power. He tried two high attacks before approaching the Lann Fala in a twirl to strike his helm with the pommel.

Far from being destabilized, his adversary gave him a gash on the back of his thigh as he retreated.

They circled each other for a few moments, attacking and blocking, both failing to hit. Sören blocked an attack with both hands diagonally. As Moira pulled Fillan up onto her horse, he saw the mercenary free himself by turning fully around and activating the blade under his wrist. He used it to attack the back of one of Cornavii's leg straps.

The Lann Fala grunted as he staggered and pushed away Sören, who returned to attack but failed to block a thrust that sent a shoulder guard flying and slashed his shoulder.

Cornavii looked around. He saw that some of his men were dead and the others had fled. He considered the blaze at his back before attacking with a devastating blow, screaming, and nearly breaking Sören's blade.

Destabilized, Sören watched Cornavii disappear among the flames without having the time to react. Foaming with rage, he took a first step, wanting to pursue him.

Moira's voice brought him back to reality.

"Sören!"

Fergus brought him his horse and they rode off, hounded by the raging fire. At their backs, the flames had reached unimaginable heights. Trees were creaking and collapsing with a crunch, blowing unbearable heat into their path.

Stuck against the body of the druid, Fillan felt himself slipping into darkness with every jolt. Cornavii's words about his mother rung in his ears.

In the sky, less than a mile above the flames, he could have sworn that a crow was following them, flying in wide circles.

He closed his eyes and sank into the abyss.

9

The nightmarish loop is nearing its end.

Black shapes, piles of soot and blood, crawl on the ground and leave trails in their wake that gleam by the light of the flames.

The last cries turn into moans. They ring out one after another in a final gasp of horror.

The beam has just given way, taking with it part of the frame. For a moment the sky lights up, full of new stars—embers that vanish silently.

The stag continues to wander with its slow, rattling step. It doesn't stop its roaring, spitting hatred and bloodlust.

Beneath a cart devoured by fire, a child firmly holds their mouth with both hands to keep from moaning.

The heat from the fire gnaws at their back, but they don't move. They stay stuck there, petrified, despite what it was costing them.

Despite this beam that they keep staring at.

23

ORDER

"You take yourself for a turkey, perhaps?" Bradley teased, to provoke her.

Ailéas angrily blew out a strand of hair that fell across her face.

"This turkey will give you a good beating!" she sputtered.

"To do that, it would have to stop waddling and shaking. What are you looking to do, gobble up flies? Must I come and take your feathers off myself?"

The teen's fingers crunched on the leather of her sword.

She leapt up in two large strides and attempted a backhand attack while leaning, striking a blow that was faster than it was powerful, to create surprise.

"I'm not—"

The old commander blocked with one hand, and the

metal clunked. She didn't lose balance and arched her body by tilting forward to slide her blade closer. She wanted to hit him with its tip to take advantage of their proximity.

"—a turkey!" she cried, pushing with all her might against his blade.

Her opponent pivoted and freed himself by twisting the hilt of his weapon. Carried by her own momentum, Ailéas fell headfirst onto the ground.

"Yes," Bradley said, scratching his beard. "You have to put more strength into your attacks."

That was easy for him to say: his arms were almost as wide as her head.

"Mhm," Ailéas growled, getting up.

Pieces of straw had become stuck in her disheveled hair.

"That's the same expression as from the bad days. Don't take the turkey joke to heart; it's meant to motivate you!"

"Well, it failed. It only pisses me off!"

"Exactly! Use that rage and go on the offensive! You must not give up and let yourself be destabilized, otherwise you're blinded and you won't think properly anymore. But your sequence wasn't so bad."

He casually patted the top of her head, like he would have done to flatter a mare for learning a trick. She freed herself, fulminating with anger, and understood once she saw his smirk that he had done it on purpose to provoke her once again.

"It's all very well to look mean," he warned her, "but don't give up the advantage, and attack!"

She stormed off with a cry of rage.

At the end of July, a month before, she had yelled at him in yet another outburst of anger and thrown a concoction of plants at him because she felt herself wasting away, like an animal in a cage. She could no longer bear to see the strength and fervor that was such a part of her be left to weaken.

So, when he came to find her the next day (still smelling of the camphor that had seeped into his clothes) to offer to train her in combat, she wasn't fooled. She immediately realized that he was trying to occupy her mind.

Torn between the desire to get the hell out of there for good and to be as cautious as he kept telling her to be, she had accepted. He was giving her an outlet for her frustrations, and she was convinced that she could surprise him and show him what she was capable of.

After all, she was far from a bad fighter. The years spent at Berwick had given her the opportunity to fight, and it wasn't just from Alastair's teachings.

Between the boys who pursued her too enthusiastically, unable to understand that she did not give a damn about them, and all the trouble her brother got into, she'd dealt out multiple thrashings and had carved herself a solid reputation across the whole city. It also earned her the nickname 'the Red Terror.'

As it turned out, fighting in an alley with the strength of her fists or with an old walking stick was nothing like facing a trained soldier. On the first day, it only took two minutes for her confidence to crumble. Despite his age, Bradley was a formidable opponent. She could have given up, fully embraced the horrible passivity that stretched out before her, but something inside her screamed loud enough to bring out her fighting spirit.

To his men, Bradley was a bit eccentric, and the fact that he wanted to have a healer capable of defending themselves at his side seemed logical to them. However, they always made sure to move away from the camp for their fights, just in case.

Ailéas trained as often as she could. She had stopped believing that she knew everything, and she was actually learning, convinced that when the time came for her to stand on her own two feet, she would be unbeatable.

Bradley was about to deliver a brutal blow, lengthening his leg. She shifted, felt the blade brush against her shoulder, and blocked her opponent's shin before initiating a lock, holding his two-handed weapon by the blade and aiming at the groin.

"Now that's better!" rejoiced the old man. "But don't forget, never take your opponent's power for granted."

He brought his foot firmly towards himself and unbalanced her effortlessly. She couldn't finish her move and fell upside down before she collapsed again in the grass.

Red Terror bites the dust, she thought, convinced that would have made a few people laugh.

She sat up and settled into a cross-legged position, catching her breath. They had been training for over an hour.

The old commander came closer and stared at her, his brow furrowed with concern.

"What else did the turkey do wrong?" she sighed in exasperation.

He continued to stare at her, hesitating.

"Go on, what else?!"

"I wanted to apologize for last night."

He didn't dare sit down next to her.

She stared back at him, raising her head and wrinkling her eyes against the sun's glare. She had refrained from questioning him since he had come to fetch her for training, preferring to focus on the fight.

She'd seen him enter the tent walking heavily and wobblly.

Bradley was not very fond of alcohol. She'd quickly noticed that on their certain evenings off, a large number of his men got drunk and yet Bradley would only accept one cup, two at most, to always keep a cool head.

The day before, she knew immediately that he had deviated from his usual path. And it wasn't just the sight of him: he reeked of alcohol.

"Oh, sorry," he said. "I didn't want to wake you up."

"You burped so hard at the entrance to the tent that you'd have to be deaf to not hear anything."

He smiled, embarrassed, watching her with small eyes.

"Are you angry with me?" he asked.

"No, why would I be?"

"Oh, good, good. That's nice. It's good that you're not angry. I don't like it when you're angry."

"And here I thought you don't care."

"Don't say that!"

He had hiccupped, then burped again, before sitting in a chair with his arms swinging at his sides.

"I'm sorry, you know. So sorry…"

She had given him a sideways stare, expecting him to start crying. She had known her share of alcoholics in Berwick who were whiny drunks, which she couldn't stand, and it always made her want to give them a good punch. That a man was unable to control his emotions horrified her, and when he then gave a long lament it was a hundred times worse.

But despite a trembling voice, the old commander had kept his composure.

"This is not what I wanted for you. You deserve better than… all this. You're a smart one, you know. Don't make that face! I'm afraid you were right from the start…"

"About what?"

"All of it! No, don't get up. I know, I know, I'm lowering

my voice. You were right about everything. Too many deaths! Too much hate! Blood, always blood."

She didn't say anything, waiting for him to continue.

"And all this for what? Eh!?" he spat with a grimace, leaning towards her after glancing everywhere, as if he was afraid of being overheard. "For a handful of treacherous and power-hungry manipulators. What a fool I am."

He shook his head silently and fell asleep on his armchair, where he snored like an asthmatic bear.

Now he towered over her, sword in hand, trying to hide his shame. That decided it.

"What did you mean?"

"I think I drank too much, and I don't remember anything," he replied gloomily and turned his head away.

"Others might believe that. But I'm getting to know you and I'm sure you remember everything, down to every word."

He sighed, planted his sword in the ground, and stood quietly.

"During all our discussions," she continued, "you have always been sure of yourself, of what you think about England and Scotland. I wanted to hit you the first time you spoke about unification. Why this change of heart?"

Another sigh.

"It's the Order, isn't it?"

She was getting to know him better and better, that was for sure. Upon seeing his morose attitude, she had immediately made the connection with the visit he had received in the morning from the Lann Fala.

Since the crushing and successive English victories that had punctuated the summer, and since the abdication of King Balliol in Stracathro at the beginning of July, the Templars were becoming increasingly present and commanding. Bradley tried to hide his anger, but Scone had changed something.

She didn't know exactly what had happened there, but she had got wind of some rumors. They said the Lann Fala had very harshly punished some of Bradley's men, despite protests from the commander, and that had pissed him off.

"It's the Order," she agreed for him. "But why now? Why change your mind overnight? They've been here from the start!"

"It doesn't just happen overnight," he retorted, finally coming to life. "Let's say, rather, that it's a bit like a small stone that you roll from the top of a hill. It begins by bumping into another stone of identical size. Then together, they lead to another, bigger one, and before you realize it, you end up with a gigantic landslide."

"Wait, the Order, is that the little stone?"

"I never said I was good at metaphors; I'm a soldier."

"Lucky you didn't say that!" she joked. "It doesn't make any sense."

"At the beginning of the war, the Templars didn't take up too much room, at least on the surface. They whispered in King Edward's ear, but I was convinced that it was only to obtain privilege and first-hand information. With Scotland defeated, I deluded myself into thinking they would fade away, but it's been the opposite. I didn't see the landslide coming."

"What do they want then, if not victory over Scotland?"

"Chaos. They use political issues, disputes between Scottish clans and allegiances to each other to divide and conquer. The disunity of Scotland is useful to them, because they can act more freely and with impunity."

"To find Fillan and me?"

"Not only, no. Your descriptions are still circulating, but I have come to understand that Cornavii is the one who wants you the most. It is believed that he is trying to wash away some affront that you've done to him. No, the group is more concerned with looking for an object, which they thought they'd found in Scone."

"The Stone of Destiny?"

The old commander sat up, looking at her with his eyebrows raised.

"No need to look at me like that!" she defended herself. "What do you think I do all day? I'm bored in this damn camp. I had to find hobbies other than being a turkey in the dust. Eavesdropping is one such hobby."

"If you get caught…" he began, worried.

"I'm not stupid and I'm not a child anymore. The last

guy who asked me what I was doing, I told him that I'd found a fungus capable of solving impotence. You can't imagine how well that worked."

He laughed.

"Anyway, you're right, that's what they're looking for. The Stone was brought back to Westminster, but there was a problem. Maybe it was a fake or it ultimately wasn't what they were looking for. The war should be over, but I get the feeling we're going to keep marching for most of the autumn before we settle somewhere."

"And what about me, in all of this? What you said yesterday was right: I deserve better than all this, and I won't be able to follow along forever…"

The old commander sat down at last, staring uncomfortably at his leather boots.

"You knew this was going to happen eventually, right?" she said. "And then, given what you say, the danger of Lann Fala will still be there, anyway."

"I didn't offer to train you to fight for no reason. I know the day will come when I won't be there to defend you. To be honest, I've often wondered why you haven't already packed up and left."

"I just told you, I'm not a kid. You've explained the issues, and I kept them in mind. But if the situation is at a stalemate, I have to go and find Fillan."

"Yes," he said gravely.

"But when?"

She delivered the question she'd frequently been asking herself in a low voice with a hint of apprehension. She was dying to get on the road, to look for her twin, but where to start? Left to her own devices, her chances of survival and finding her brother were very slim.

"After the winter," he replied.

It was not advice or a possibility. To the old man, it sounded like a no-brainer. For Ailéas, it sounded like the death knell of eternity.

"Don't get upset," he said when he saw her fidgeting. "I know it may seem long, but trust me. The cold freezes everything—flowers, lakes, and rivers, but also military campaigns. You will be safe until the end of winter, just before the various army corps return to motion. And when the time comes, I promise to help you find your brother."

She knew how stubbornly he kept his promises, and the anger that was about to explode in her chest subsided.

An end to this ordeal was finally taking shape. And with it came hope.

She squeezed the leather cuff that covered her wrist.

The prospect of one day being able to find Fillan, even up against many dangers, warmed her heart.

Her sword whistled through the air as she stood and drew it. She swore to herself to train with all the ferocity she could muster.

24

BEINN EALLAIR

The cart slid into a pothole and went over a bump. Fillan woke up abruptly and moaned as he felt a piercing pain radiate through his shoulder.

The raven was long gone from the sky, where clouds were scattered in shades of white and gray.

He felt horribly ill, as if a swarm had beaten him before dancing the jig inside his head. He felt like he was extricating himself with difficulty from a long nightmare, which he risked plunging into again at any moment.

He fidgeted feebly, his body covered in sweat, and tried unsuccessfully to spit out something that filled his mouth.

"Calm down, don't move; let me take that off," said Kyle softly as he coughed and choked.

She removed a cloth tied around his head and he realized that they'd gagged him.

"What's the matter with you?" he said indignantly, massaging his jaw.

He was trying to look angry but didn't have the strength.

"We had no choice. You had a fever and you started to rave and scream. Sören ordered that we put this on you so as not to attract attention from all the villagers in every place we passed by. Moira and I protested."

"Of course I protested," exclaimed the druid, sat alone at the front of the cart, reins in hand. "You gag prisoners, not the wounded. But Sören would hear none of it."

Fillan did not doubt it for a moment.

Kyle helped him to drink. He coughed, drooled, choked, and drooled even more, but what little cool liquid he did not spill on his chin or on the warrior's jacket did his dry throat a lot of good.

"Besides, it really put us in danger," added Kyle. "We could only move you by cart, which forced us to take the main roads."

He wiped his stuck-together eyes, trying to put his mind in order. Everything was just a confused heap that made the distinction between reality and dreams difficult.

"What happened?" he asked. "All I remember is Moira healing my wound… After that, it's just a blank void."

"And then some!" laughed the druid. "Your blank void occurred while I tended to your wound. When I removed the head of the arrow, your eyes rolled up into the back of your head and you started drooling on Kyle's hands."

"Oh, yeah! Just like a little slug!"

Fillan looked at her with eyes wide in shame.

"I'm kidding, you simpleton," she said, patting him on the leg with a flirtatious smile. "Given what you've been through, you had every right to drool a little…"

Fleeting moments, shreds of memory, came back to him. A hand holding his arm covered in blood, swinging in the rain. Kyle jamming a piece of wood between his teeth and caressing his cheek, telling him "Bite!" An unbearable pain like lightning, which made him scream. And in the middle of the pain, a gaping pit of darkness sweeping him away.

Of what followed, he only had vague, dreadful impressions. A succession of unbearable awakenings where his whole being was reduced to nothing but suffering. These were interspersed with nightmares, which he could never retain any memory of, but he knew were terrifying. He kept sinking, deeper and deeper, not imagining for a moment that the abysses might have a grounding in reality.

With his good arm he groped at the wood of the cart, seeking out Kyle's hand. When he found her, he didn't even have the strength to squeeze it, but clung to it as best he could.

"What happened to me?" he asked in a weak voice.

"The wound got infected," Kyle explained. "We hit bad weather right after leaving Scone. We really thought you'd have to stay there."

"And we didn't get far," Moira added. "After removing the arrow, I couldn't cauterize your wound. The fever didn't take long to arrive. It took me several days to find the herbs needed to help your body fight the infection. Believe me, most would have joined the Sidh, but you held on. You're tough, Fillan. After a few days of struggle, the fever finally came down."

"Several days?! How long have I been in this state?"

"Almost two weeks," announced the druid.

Fillan felt like he had just been knocked out.

"And am I okay? I mean, is my arm…"

"You'll recover. The worst is over. Neither the bones nor the ligaments were affected. And that, I can assure you, is a miracle given that the arrow broke when you fell. However…"

He felt dread creeping into his heart.

"… you will have consequences."

"What kind of consequences?"

"For starters, a nice scar. But above all, some reduced mobility. With the infection, it was inevitable."

His jaw clenched at the thought of becoming crippled as he had only just joined the Brotherhood. He tried to pull his arm closer to him, but it hung limply.

"No! Don't try to move it yet! Kyle, do me a favor and

smack this invalid over the head! Harder than that, so he stops moving around! You call that hitting? That's a hug! Let me show you."

She bent over herself, at the risk of falling out of the seat, and slapped him on the back of the head.

"Ouch!"

"There's no need to make that face; you won't get sympathy out of me. You deserved it! With the scare you gave us, it's out of the question that you reopen your wound or that you exhaust the little strength you have. You must let your arm heal."

"I just want to get up," he moaned. "Kyle, help me, please."

"Gently!" ordered the druid. "Or I drug one of you with my plants and I thrash the other!"

Leaning against the wood of the cart, Fillan discovered that they were in the middle of nowhere. A dazzlingly beautiful nowhere. He observed a primal Scotland unfolding like a sparkling emerald being unwrapped from its case, which the centuries had polished and few had had the chance to look upon. The rolling views of the Lowlands seemed almost insignificant in comparison to the heights that broke up the horizon with incomparable green, beveled edges.

Fillan imagined the giant who, several millennia before the first man set foot on these lands, had these carved out these hills with a gigantic swordfish, sculpting the valleys and creating the lochs from his footprints. He even pictured him stretching out once his work was done to fall asleep eternally, eventually becoming nothing more than a hill covered with grass and moss.

The few houses he saw seemed to be drowning in the middle of the opulent greenness, as though they were intruders that the natural beauty was trying to swallow up, little by little, in a fierce struggle.

They were in the heart of the Highlands.

"It's beautiful, isn't it?" rejoiced Kyle, her eyes roaming all around.

"Truly magnificent. Ailéas would have loved it."

Kyle tried to press herself against him, forgetting about his wound and provoking a loud yelp from him.

"Kyle, if you hurt my patient, I'll kick you out of my cart with my stick!"

The warrior stuck out her tongue, but the druid turned around and looked at her in dismay.

"How old are you, girl?"

They laughed heartily, and Fillan savored this moment of serenity.

A hammering of hooves drowned out the noise of the wind.

"So, lovebirds, is everything to your satisfaction?" Edan teased as he drew level with the cart.

"Shut up!" retorted Kyle.

"And here I thought you weren't one for tasting the forbidden fruit…"

There was a thud, followed closely by the neigh of a horse. Kyle had straightened up suddenly to throw a punch at the bald man's face. Taken by surprise, he was almost unseated and narrowly caught the mane of his mount.

"Oh, you filthy little devil!" he yelled, holding his nose.

"Edan," said Fergus who had also just arrived and now tried to reason with him. "Why do you always have to bug Kyle?"

"No I don't—"

"Yes, you do," Moira cut him off. "What's the matter? Are you jealous?"

"But… I… No way! She could be my damn daughter!"

"That's the worst part," explained the warrior who knew him best. "He pisses for the sole pleasure of pissing. Without ulterior motives. It must be amazing to be such a pain in the ass!"

"You're all ganging up on me!" Edan screeched as he closed the flask of brandy he'd just taken a sip of courage from.

"No, we gang up against your stupidity," retorted the druid, massaging her temple with one hand. "Learn to behave yourself a little, especially with young women."

Edan just burped and stared.

"Anyway, glad to see you're better," Fergus said with a big smile at Fillan.

The musician also seemed genuinely worried about him. Fillan now truly believed he was one of the band, and it did him a world of good.

Sören's absence made the image of the forest of flames and Cornavii came crashing back to him.

"Is Sören okay?" he asked, worried.

"Stop fidgeting!" Moira lectured him. "Otherwise, I'll give you some herbs to make you rest. There, that's better. Sören's fine, he went ahead to make sure everything was in order at Beinn Eallair."

"Beinn Eallair?"

"His clan's stronghold," Kyle clarified.

"And Cornavii, is he...?"

"We don't know," Kyle continued. "We ran away as if we had the devil on our asses."

"He practically was," Edan said. "The whole forest burned down; we came close to being roasted like chickens. That's what helped us outrun the English without too much difficulty."

"But Sören..." Fillan recalled. "I saw him wound Cornavii!"

"That coward tracker was the first to bail out!" Kyle spat. "If you ask me, he'll recover from his injury. I bet he has more lives than a cat."

She looked worried.

"What's that look for?" he asked her. "It's a good thing that we know Sören is a match for him, right?"

"I don't know. The Lann Fala are obsessive warriors, Cornavii more so than any other. For him, it's a new failure, and that might make him even more dangerous."

"And the rest of the Brotherhood? Thomas, Wallace, and the others? What happened to them?"

"Sören got word when we passed by Kinloch Ranoch yesterday. Everyone is okay. Scone was ransacked, though."

Fillan thought of the Stone of Destiny. He hoped that the Brotherhood had actually found a way to get it to safety.

"Aren't you afraid the Lann Fala are following us?"

"No chance," Fergus said calmly. "They're not going to risk the Highlands right away. They are strong, but the clans would gladly beat them to a pulp. Even though Scotland is defeated, they have much less power up here than in the south. Don't worry, you have nothing to fear. By the way, this is Loch Ericht."

Fillan leaned over the cart and saw a vast loch whose clear waters were like a mirror. Immense mountains stretched on for miles, immaculate cones that went on for eternity. They walked alongside the water, then followed a branch of the river that led to a narrow gorge. The regular noise of the cartwheels mingled with that of the river, echoing against the cliffs that surrounded them. The road turned, passing under a rock overhang that looked like a frozen wave. The fort of Beinn Eallair gradually came into Fillan's view.

"Close your mouth," Kyle chuckled, "or you're going to swallow a fly!"

Fillan had seen several forts since Alastair took him in. Scotland had dozens, all more impressive than the last. But he had never seen one like this before.

Beinn Eallair was not particularly tall. It was medium in size, compared to others. It stood, however, on the side of the cliff, nestled into the mountain, as if it had been hewn out of the rock by the giant he had imagined earlier. Four towers soared to different heights and the main dungeon was so massive that it gave the impression of being only a ridge in the mountain that surrounded it with its arms.

They followed a road that led them upwards and crossed a drawbridge over a deep chasm where water flowed. When they passed the main enclosure, Fillan opened his mouth wide again in surprise.

Almost everything seemed deserted and abandoned. He felt like he had just entered a ruin. The fortress seemed to have been attacked decades prior and kept the memory of it everywhere. For some strange reason, the fort seemed more magnificent still in its emptiness.

Sören, who had traded his leather armor for dark and

simple clothes, came to meet them as they crossed the courtyard.

"Fillan," he began, approaching the cart, "I'm glad to see you're doing better. You gave us all a scare, as well as breaking our eardrums."

"Is it… only you?" Fillan couldn't help but ask, looking around.

"Almost," replied Sören. "Some people take care of the maintenance of Beinn Eallair throughout the year, when we're on the move."

"But your clan…"

"Was decimated years ago by the Templars. There was a great battle here once, but fortunately for us, no member of the Order who had seen this place is still alive to show others how to reach it."

Fillan stared at the nicks streaking the walls. There was even part of a rampart that seemed to have exploded.

"They are my clan now," continued Sören, indicating the entire group.

For the first time, Fillan saw Sören as a human being capable of feelings, and not just as a brute. He understood that the Norwegian must have gone through trials like his own, and he wondered if they might have something else in common that he had not yet discovered.

25

ASSASSIN

Beinn Eallair was a strange and mysterious place. Given the scarred and decrepit façades, Fillan had expected to live among ruins overgrown with rubble and cobwebs, but he was amazed to find a luxurious and well-maintained interior. The great hall was so huge that it could have accommodated a battalion of warriors without anyone having to squeeze around the long wooden tables lined up there. Several logs blazed permanently in the huge hearth, illuminating the high walls dressed with gorgeous curtains. The kitchens, the armory, and even the former guardhouse—now converted into a study—were just as impeccable.

However, some parts had not survived the damage of time and had collapsed, making them inaccessible.

On many levels, Beinn Eallair was no comparison to

many other Scottish clan strongholds. A curious aura enveloped her, like a mystical breath from times long gone, which gave the impression that each stone contained a secret, an enigma or a clue.

The week of his arrival, Fillan harassed Sören so much that he finally told him the history of the fortress. It was very old. The most widespread legend said that it was built by the Gaels as a stronghold as they continued their conquest of Scotland with the aim of expanding Dál Riata*, their kingdom.

Beinn Eallair had long been Assassin territory.

That was why the Norwegian had joined them: his clan had been linked to the Brotherhood since it had begun in the wild lands of the north. The castle had always been thought of as a considerable strategic asset, and only a chosen few knew of its existence. In the flourishing era of the Scottish Brotherhood, a few decades earlier, this place had been the nerve center where the men and the information that helped fight against the Templars passed through, under the greatest secrecy.

But after relentless searching, the Templars managed to find the location of the fort.

The Order alone was not powerful enough to act directly.

---

* Dál Riata was the name of the Gaelic kingdom of the sixth century, which stretched from modern-day Argyll in Scotland all the way to Northern Ireland.

They could only stir up animosity among the clans while they hid in the mountains, pushing the most belligerent to go to war under the same banner, that of blood and hatred.

A great battle took place, which lasted for many days. The bones of the countless dead still lined the bottom of the river.

Sören was not there at the time of the attack and, upon his return, his relatives had all been massacred. Along with what was left of the Brotherhood, he set out to kill all those who knew the existence of the fortress, so that it became a secret once more.

Since then, Beinn Eallair was only a shadow of its former glory, now lost forever.

The Assassins had given it to Sören because it was all that remained of his clan.

Apart from the stones and their marks, no traces remained of that era except for an old couple: Mairead and Ruadh. They maintained Beinn Eallair throughout the year and allowed Sören, whenever he decided to return, to come back to a warm home.

The first weeks at the castle enabled Fillan to gain his bearings and adapt to a slower pace of life than anything he had known before. Moira kept an eye on his shoulder injury to ensure it healed as well as possible.

He took advantage of his convalescence to explore every corner of the fortress with Kyle. The times spent strolling through the darkened corridors were precious to him. He was obsessed with her charm and personality.

One day she led him to the flooded areas of the castle, in the cellars.

"It was once a network of tunnels running through the mountain," she explained. "There was one collapse too many and the water broke through to flood the caves."

"The Brotherhood's network?"

"That's right! I guess that's where they had meetings like those you attended in Scone. Sören told me that there was something else too, even older."

He remembered Scone and imagined similar, mysterious rooms unfolding under Beinn Eallair, now prisoners submerged under the water.

A part of the Tuatha Dé Danann heritage lost forever.

"Do you want me to show you a secret?" asked Kyle, her eyes sparkling with mischief.

He nodded and watched, amazed, as she dived into a pool of dark water before inviting him to join her. His recovering shoulder shivered in contact with the icy liquid. She set off, dragging him by the hand, and they swam through a submerged corridor that led them into an adjoining room. Thin streaks of light seeped through multiple cracks, revealing a floating platform on which there was an impressive statue. They pulled themselves out of the water, dripping.

"Who is this?" asked Fillan, touching the cut stone fingertips of the statue.

"Must be an Assassin."

He nodded, noticing the mark of the Brotherhood. The man or woman—it was impossible to tell—was depicted in a noble posture, their hand resting on a claymore broadsword. Perched on their other stone wrist was a royal eagle about to take flight. The animal seemed alive and stared at them, as if sizing them up to assess whether they were worthy of dwelling there.

"I get the feeling that you didn't lead me here just to show me that," he said, noticing the way she looked at him.

"Not just for that. You may be less stupid than you look, after all."

She kissed him, pressing him against the stone, and they abandoned themselves underneath the sculpture, under the empty eyes of the eagle who enveloped them in the shadow of his wings.

Their relationship, however, did not get any easier.

Kyle valued her independence and hated the thought of being owned. She kept repeating that she was content to do what pleased her, with the sole aim of enjoying life, nothing more, nothing less.

Fillan was not surprised by such an attitude. It was how he'd behaved in Berwick, where he had notched up conquests, sometimes accumulating them without anyone suffering and not caring that the girls he frolicked with could also go look somewhere else. He'd had nothing like a romantic relationship, and it helped him to enjoy life, too.

So he was surprised to notice an unhealthy jealousy like which he had never known to arise and worsen as the weeks passed. The more distant Kyle became, the more he wanted to cling to her. It was suffocating.

He was quick to notice that, of the gang, Fergus was the one she was closest to and he got it into his head that there was some past dalliance between them. Every laugh, every look, the slightest proximity between them became an intolerable torture.

Towards the end of September, he risked asking Kyle about it, even admitting to having questioned Moira about it. The druid hadn't revealed anything to him and had given him a lecture, anyway.

"You did WHAT?!"

It only took a second for Kyle's face to become enraged.

"I…"

"Shut up! I can't even believe that you dared to do that! I hate snoopers! What are you looking to do? Stir up shit in the gang? And all this for what? Because you're jealous?"

She was screaming now. The whole castle had to hear it.

"What could possibly be going through your head? Isn't it enough that I sleep with you? What more do you want from me, you moron?! I'm free to do whatever I want!

If you can't control your emotions, buy yourself a goat and go to hell!"

She could have given him a disgusted look, even slapped him, but she just stared at him instead, her eyes bathed in pain. She turned on her heels, left Beinn Eallair, and vanished. When Fillan worried over the following days that she had not returned, Edan explained that she was known to go and lose herself in nature every now and then. With a knowing wink, he advised Fillan to be patient with her mood.

He quickly realized his stupidity, and not just because he missed her terribly. Kyle was right. She couldn't give him anything more; nothing could erase the fear that he felt rising each time he had to be apart from her. The fear of losing her, like everything he had already lost. He had to push away this thought thousands of times, and thousands of times it would resurface.

He had to accept it.

Moira decreed that he was recovered. To the great astonishment of the healer, he had regained almost all range of movement, and only a few gestures brought a grimace to his face. Sören wasted no time and immediately began his training.

If Fillan thought Kyle severe during their training, it was nothing compared to the Norwegian, who was ruthless. He forced him to get fit again, because his convalescence and infection had undermined much of his strength. He climbed the tallest tower of the fortress twice a day, from where he could see the snowcapped mountains sticking out of the steep gorge. He also had to swim in the icy waters of Loch Ericht after running there. Every evening, he fell exhausted into his room, with no remaining strength to even change his clothes.

Once he was fit, the mercenary taught him the way of the Assassins.

The first lessons were about discretion, since Fillan currently moved with as much delicacy as an ox. Sören showed him how to anticipate his every step, in slow motion, to move as nimbly and with as much stealth as a cat. One of his favorite training exercises was to steal food from old Mairead's kitchen while she was there, without her noticing.

He also had to learn to disappear into the shadows, to take advantage of darkness and dodge the light. Under the inquisitive gaze of his mentor, he devoted himself, within the fortress and in its surroundings, to hide-and-seek games during which one or several members of the band were to find him or perish under his imaginary blows. Moira often spotted him, Fergus always heard him coming, and Edan swore regardless of whether he won or lost.

Of all his teachings, the one Sören valued most was combat.

"In the end," he explained, "it's the last resort to save the day. So you must be the sharpest blade there is."

Although Fillan had developed his sword-wielding skills with Kyle, he still had much to learn. Sören spent several hours a day, along with the rest of the training, teaching him all kinds of techniques. He made him practice new guards and attacks, then repeat them over again until they became automatic.

Over time, the relationship between apprentice and mentor changed. Sören was as gruff as ever, but an indefinable link was forged between them. Fillan had already known that link with Alastair, whose work and skills he had long admired, and he'd been driven first by the desire to match them, then to surpass them. It was a mixture of respect and competition, fear and reverence. Fillan, however, felt that something brought them even closer, without understanding what that could be. He soon realized that the mercenary seemed have some of the same emotions and fears as him.

By the beginning of October, and after five weeks of suffering, stiffness, and bruises, he had made great progress. He felt stronger and surer of his body, almost forgetting that he had been shot in the shoulder. On the other hand, he was not stupid: he expected that everything would be much more difficult in real life and that on the day he'd have to kill again, he would need to keep Ogme's balance in mind.

As if the thought alone could summon her, Kyle finally

decided to resurface. Fillan decided not to find out what she had been doing all this time. He hoped to prove to her that he had understood the lesson and that he respected her independence.

Happy to see him, Kyle celebrated their reunion by confronting him with her sword in order to see the progress he had made and to finally bury their argument. She won the high ground and drew a line under the past with a kiss.

The autumn passed, between the tenderness of the moments they spent together and the harshness of Sören's training, which pushed his limits further than ever before.

Fillan picked up a habit he never told anyone about. The secret of a moment that belonged to him alone.

Every week, he went to the submerged room that Kyle had shown him. He settled on the stone, dripping, and stared at the statue of the Assassin, feeling the weight of the destiny the Brotherhood had spoken of. This remnant of a forgotten time, lost and buried under the rubble of failure, screamed to him about the responsibilities that were now his thanks to his heritage.

He kept wondering if he would ever live up to what was expected of him.

As winter approached and the entire landscape was covered with a mother-of-pearl veil, one morning he took the stairs that led to the cellars and discovered that the underwater passage had frozen over.

He sat down facing the frozen surface.

"So that's where you hide every week," said a voice from behind him, after about ten minutes.

Fillan jumped when he recognized Sören's voice, having heard no sound to indicate his approach.

I would have lost at hide and seek, he thought. After all, his mentor was unbeatable and showed a discretion close to invisibility.

"Kyle suspected it, but she wouldn't tell me. It's quite a feat to have gained her trust. What do you do down there?"

Fillan shrugged, not sure himself.

"It's hard to say."

"Try anyway," insisted the Norwegian, sitting down beside him.

"Looking at the Assassin statue, I think of my sister and the Brotherhood. This story of destiny, I know Ailéas would have liked it a lot, but it scares the crap out of me."

"How come?"

"What if I'm not worthy? And what if, in the end, whatever I do, I disappoint the expectations that Thomas and the others placed on me?"

The mercenary said nothing, his face calm and benevolent.

"You think I'm right and shouldn't have agreed to join the Brotherhood?"

"I think you're going about this wrong and not asking yourself the right questions. Instead of wondering whether you're worthy, do everything you can to be worthy by imagining that there will always be a better version of yourself to achieve. All that really matters are your actions and your will, and whether these allow you to survive. You must learn to trust yourself."

"And the question I should ask myself?"

"Eventually, you will have to ask yourself if the Brotherhood is worthy of you, because it isn't more important than you are."

Sören patted him on the back and walked away, his leather boots echoing on the stone steps.

Fillan stared at the frozen water, imagining the Assassin standing in the other room, and realized that all his life he had never had so little confidence in himself.

My actions and my will, he thought, and he got up to go to practice.

26

DESTINIES

As winter progressed, Beinn Eallair and Loch Ericht became trapped in the ice.

An impenetrable blanket of snow fell on the mountains and the surrounding valleys. The landscape turned into a frozen picture of white hills that blended with a milky sky. The valley was so full of white snow and sparkling stalactites that it became impassable.

Far from slowing down, Fillan's learning accelerated.

In the middle of December, he found himself running through a fierce storm that thundered over the castle. Sören had led him into the hills before abandoning him without any explanation. Fillan wandered for many hours, struggling against the waist-deep snow while the wind, laden with raging flakes, lashed at his body. He managed to find his way back to the fortress, cold but proud of his success. The Norwegian believed that his resistance to the harsh conditions of the north was essential in building his character and his fighting spirit, and he was not wrong.

Fillan had changed enormously.

Not only in his body, where his muscles now stuck out almost as much as Sören's. Nor just because of his skills in combat that he had honed with such relentlessness that they now made him an equal match against most of the group, his mentor aside.

No, the change was due to his attitude, which had evolved profoundly as he learned to trust himself.

Through his training, he shaped his inner rage, channeled his desire for revenge, and became calmer and more thoughtful. It could even be seen in the way he walked, catlike and purposeful.

Each of the tests Sören put him through instilled a philosophy of overcoming weakness within himself. Failure was just a chance to do better next time.

Sometimes the mercenary's anger toward the Assassins subsided and his words about them became tinged with hints of nostalgia. It never lasted long, though, and was soon replaced with a frown.

The enigma surrounding the strange relationship Sören had with the organization persisted until the night he came to shake Fillan awake and ordered him to follow him.

Not knowing where they were going, Fillan complied without taking the trouble to dress properly, which he regretted when he realized that they were headed to the top of the highest tower of the fortress.

Freezing cold and swirling snowflakes smothered him.

"I'll be frank with you," Sören said after silently contemplating the darkness that gripped the mountain for a few moments. "You really surprised me. Who would have imagined that the boy I picked up in Berwick last spring could endure such training and become a warrior?"

If someone had told him that a year ago, Fillan wouldn't have believed it himself.

Sometimes, he reflected on the journey he'd been on. He pictured the old Fillan, for whom only money, glory, and his future as a tailor mattered. A vague feeling of contempt washed over him. He wanted to slap this old version of himself: he was so egocentric, incapable of the slightest action, and locked in a straitjacket of fears.

"Yet that's what you did. You found the strength you needed to surpass your limits."

He thought back to his vision of Ailéas and of the second sword of Fal that currently rested against the wall of his room.

The wind whistled like whispering voices.

"A final test awaits you, perhaps one of the most difficult. Normally, apprentices take longer before they must face it.

But you have progressed quickly, and the times are far from normal."

"Will my training be over after this?"

"Let's just say you'll have taken another step. In the way of the Assassins, nothing is ever fully accomplished. It's always possible to improve."

Fillan waited stoically, amid the blizzard, until his mentor told him what to do. He had learned to stay quiet and in his place, eager to prove himself.

"You have earned my respect, my boy," said the Norwegian, squinting his eyes slightly. "Very few people can say that."

A wave of pride washed over him.

"That's why I think you have a right to know the reason that led me to leave the Brotherhood. I owe it to you, as proof of my trust."

"Isn't it because of what happened here?" asked Fillan in surprise.

"Not only. After the Templars pushed the clan rivals to slaughter everyone in the fortress, I remained within the Brotherhood for some time. The Order had been hit very hard and there was a lot to do, a lot to rebuild. It was a godsend."

"A godsend? What do you mean?"

"To think about something else," Sören said gravely.

Fillan recalled channeling all his energy into his workouts with Kyle, trying to forget his grief.

"But after a while," continued Sören, "I started to hate what I was becoming. The death of my kin had opened my eyes to the flaws of the Brotherhood and its contradictions."

"What kind of contradictions?"

"The Assassins aspire to the freedom of all men. But it is rather paradoxical to note that they themselves are not free, altogether. They conform to many principles, carry out orders, and kill to counter the Templars, even if deep inside themselves they wish for something else. The problem is, it's a never-ending struggle. The more time passed, the more I felt like I was dissolving into the Brotherhood. My free will was slipping through my fingers."

"So you left," Fillan concluded.

"I had given too much. Lost too much."

"How did the others react?"

"Pretty badly," replied the Norwegian, grimacing. "Thomas, to whom only the Brotherhood matters, took it very badly. It got worse when the Lann Fala formed and the Order sought to finish what they started here in Beinn Eallair, hunting down all the Assassins. I helped them, but many clans, including yours, were decimated. For a while, Thomas and Deorsa thought what was happening was my fault, that the Assassins could have prevented all this if I hadn't turned my back on them."

He heaved a deep sigh.

"But no one can know for sure."

"And then," ventured Fillan, "it's hard to fathom that the choice of a single person can have such consequences."

A chilly atmosphere crept between them.

"Not in their eyes, because to them, we're the same, you and me."

"You mean that I'll get to grow that big beard soon?" chuckled Fillan, who felt the need to lighten the mood.

A smile tugged at Sören's lips, and then he removed the armband that covered his forearm, the very band that Fillan had seen a blade emerge from as he'd confronted Cornavii at Scone. On his wrist, the scar of a burn stretched into a brownish stain.

"I don't understand," said Fillan.

"I think you do."

Fillan brought his left hand to his own wrist and couldn't speak as a deep thought crept into his mind. He stared stupidly at the Norwegian without daring to say anything.

"I, too, am a Child of Fal. Or at least, I was."

Fillan's mouth dropped open.

"You're a… But suddenly… But why are you…?"

"Calm down. I'm sure you must be shocked."

It wasn't exactly the word for what was going on in Fillan's mind. It was more like his mind was completely blown.

"Just like you, I was destined from birth to become an Assassin, because of this mark and because a druid had announced that it must be so. Thomas and Deorsa especially resented me for leaving because the Children of Fal are so rare. But along with everything else, I couldn't bear the feeling that everything was written in advance."

He continued to stare at the scar on his arm, where the birthmark was no longer visible at all.

"When I left the Brotherhood, I burned it, like I wanted to stop myself from looking back. But what is quite ironic," he continued, putting his armband back on, "is that every step brings me back to the Assassins. I've almost come to believe that whatever I do, it's impossible to escape destiny. When I saw the mark on your wrist, just after Cranshaws, I understood what I'd gotten myself into, and I felt like fate was laughing at me."

"Why are you telling me all this now?" started Fillan, almost angry.

"You look like someone who thinks they've been lied to," Sören observed.

"If you had told me all this before I decided to join the Brotherhood—"

"What would you have done?" he cut him off. "Made your decision based on my history and my choices? I already told you: all that matters is listening to your heart. And I'm telling you now not to take me as an example. I am not one. We are alike in certain respects, but we are also very different. All I want is that you don't forget that your free will matters more than anything—despite that mark on your wrist, despite what the Assassins might tell you, and despite what I might tell you."

Fillan watched the snowflakes twirl around him, soaking the fabric of his clothes just as his mentor's wise words soaked into his mind.

"What happened to…?"

"To my twin?" finished Sören, guessing what Fillan was going to ask. "He died right here, during the massacre. I cried for him for a long time."

He spoke calmly, without emotion. Fillan wondered if he would one day be able to do the same about Ailéas, because every time he thought of her or invoked her name, his heart sank terribly.

They observed the dark decor in silence, leaning on the stone. Suddenly, Sören came to life and climbed the ledge to stand above the void.

"You survived the rite of confinement: you became a better version of yourself, stronger, more determined. You have gained self-confidence, but today you must find faith. A much deeper, unshakable faith, which will make you capable of anything. Turn your gaze inside yourself, without fear, and dive! This is the ultimate test."

He crouched before stretching suddenly into a leap into the void.

Fillan's eyes almost popped out of their sockets. His

mentor had already disappeared, caught up in the darkness that stretched below the tower. His fingers tightly gripped the frost-covered stone.

"Leap of faith!" shouted the Norwegian's voice, echoing in the storm. "You must not hesitate!"

The teenager couldn't believe it; it was suicide.

He placed his first foot on the ledge, felt his leg tremble, then climbed. Without the shelter of the parapet, the gusts doubled in intensity.

Staring into the darkness, he expected to feel a terror unlike anything he had experienced during that year. But the apprenticeship had done its work, and an icy calm came over him.

He was composed, determined.

He opened his arms, closed his eyes, and jumped into the void.

As he fell, he thought he heard the cry of a crow, but maybe it was just the wind whistling in his ears.

27

REVOLT

"Go screw yourself, Deorsa!"

"All I'm saying is I expected a little more comfort. It is a fortress, after all. From the time of its great era…"

"I already hate the idea of you staying here," Sören cut him off, "so don't even dream about being treated like a prince. This room will be perfect for you."

The spy had arrived at the end of the afternoon, an hour earlier. This had plunged the Norwegian into a terrible mood. Fillan was the only one who'd agreed to accompany them through the corridors of the castle, the rest of the band having fled at the first blows of their verbal fights.

"Something just brushed against me! Just there! Come see with your torches! Sören, if it's a rat and it bites me in my sleep…"

"You might wake up a little less stupid."

Deorsa's mouth froze in a pout, his eyes narrowed.

"And it's not a rat, it's a bit of your frozen cape. Such a moron. You'll be no worse than anyone else. Stop complaining or I'll put you in the dungeon. There's a whole bunch of rodents down there, as well as an icy cold that will make them want to snuggle up against your body!"

"You wouldn't dare..."

Sören raised his eyebrows slightly, ready to accept the challenge, but the spy groaned, intertwining his fingers.

"Here will do fine," he said, passing the alcove to sit on the bed, which released a cloud of dust.

"I imagine that with a log in the hearth and a curtain or two, it will be more... bearable. And a mirror, maybe."

Sören gave an exasperated sigh, and Fillan restrained himself from bursting out in laughter. He had just seen a rat, about the size of an otter with shiny eyes, slipping discreetly under the bed just behind the feet of the spy.

"Because you plan to stay long?" grumbled Sören with his rocky voice.

"Don't you like having visitors?"

"I don't like having parasites. When you're around, I feel itchy all over. And I get rid of whatever itches me."

"You have some very curious thoughts, Sören. I imagine we'll never be able to get along, given your attitude. Me, so helpful, gracious, well-meaning—and you, a thick bully and—Ah! Let go of my jacket, you'll wrinkle it!"

"You didn't answer my question. How long are you planning to stay here?"

"That's going to be up to you, really."

"Who invited you, again?"

"I had barely crossed the threshold of Beinn Eallair when you jumped down my throat without letting me explain what I was doing here. What possessed you to welcome me with a bucket of urine, anyway?"

"It had to be emptied somewhere!"

"You're lucky it only got on my boots! In short, Thomas asked me to come to make sure Fillan's training was going well."

"I find that hard to believe," said Sören, wrinkling his nose. "Thomas knows there's no love lost between us, but my word is unbreakable. I would never mess up the job. I know you, and I bet it was more your idea. You still can't get over that it was entrusted to me rather than to you, and you've worn down the dear abbot, who gave in as one does with a child."

"What a poor image of me you have. When will you understand that I am not your enemy?"

"You're not my friend either, damn it!"

"Clearly. In any case, judging from the stature and the attitude of the boy since I arrived, I get the feeling that everything is going well. He's gained muscle and he has a keen eye for details. We will have the opportunity to talk about it more later."

Fillan was dying to speak, so he could show Deorsa, who tried to treat him like a child who was not in the room, how much he had changed. He clenched his teeth and his fists, just watching and listening. Now that he was part of the Brotherhood, he had to show the spy respect.

"Thomas wasn't the only one who wanted me to come here," continued Deorsa. "Wallace asked me, too. There's no need to look at me like that, Sören; unlike you, your former protégé likes me."

Fillan remembered the few words he and the Highlander had shared in Scone and doubted that very much.

"He wanted me to give you the news and a favor from him, but… you see, I haven't eaten since yesterday and I bet I'd feel much more talkative over a bowl of something tasty, with a piece of bread in one hand and a beer in the other."

"As if you need that to rant for hours," the Norwegian blurted, rolling his eyes.

⁂

It was not late, barely eight o'clock, when they gathered in the great hall with beers, a little bread, and cheese while they waited for dinner to be served. The huge hearth chased away the evening frosts and gave off a sweet warmth with the smell of burnt wood.

Deorsa had had time to change and make himself

comfortable in his new quarters. Before that, he passed on a message to Fillan from James de Crannach, who hoped that his training was going well. The other apprentice of the Brotherhood told him he was looking forward to comparing their techniques and hopefully participating in missions together soon.

Deorsa, Sören and Fillan were gathered around the same table while the rest of the gang shunned them like the plague. Kyle, who hated the spy more than anyone, led the group in trying to make as much noise as possible. A beer in each hand, she had even started a burping contest that kept provoking exasperated looks from the representative of the Brotherhood.

"I'm surprised that Edward didn't try to push farther north during the autumn," Sören said before taking a sip. "Given how well they've established themselves in the south."

"I didn't say that," Deorsa said. "He has definitely tried, but his influence is not worth much, north of the Tay and the Clyde. Some clans conducted a few shows of force, to make him understand that he couldn't venture so easily into the Highlands. In any case, strongholds in strategic places were more interesting to him: Berwick, Edinburgh, Dunbar, Glasgow, and so on. When winter came, he was forced to break up his army and distribute it through several garrisons throughout the south."

Fillan swirled his beer in his wooden tankard, splashing

the foam. He listened attentively to the discussion. During his training, his mentor had explained the importance of remembering every word. This was also what being an Assassin was: knowing how to be content to listen and have a memory that retained everything that was said.

"And the Order?"

"It's mainly the Lann Fala who are still active. The Templars didn't take long to figure out that the Stone of Destiny they had brought back from Scone to Westminster was a fake."

"I suspected you'd been up to something with it," Sören said, staring at his apprentice with a meaningful look.

"Damn it!" squeaked the spy, biting into his bread before hitting it on the table. "This loaf is harder than a brick! Anyway, the Order…"

He was interrupted by the old governess of the fortress, who placed a steaming pot between them.

"Oh, good evening, Mairead! Long time, no see! How are…?"

The old woman spat at his feet and glared at him through eyes milky with cataracts.

"What could you possibly have been telling that serving woman?" Deorsa asked after she was gone. "She used to love me in the old days!"

"Me?" said Sören, displaying an innocent face and the hint of a smile. "It's not my fault. You're the ungrateful pig that just criticized her bread. She may be old, but she has good hearing and doesn't tolerate fools with no manners."

"Damned old age," the spy cursed. "One of the few things that make a person so touchy. Or is it senility?"

"Be careful that she doesn't hear you again, or the next time she might spit in your soup."

The spy glanced around furtively, then dunked his entire piece of bread into the hot liquid they'd just been served to soften it before biting into it.

"What is this favor that Wallace wanted you to ask me?"

"He gave me a letter for you," Deorsa said, pulling a piece of parchment from the folds of his clothes.

"Knowing you, you are already aware of what it says."

"He would like you to join him not far from Lanark in three weeks, when spring begins. First, to bring him Fillan, who'll be able to cut his teeth during the raid he's preparing, but also for you to support him. I believe he has already forgotten the promise he made to you at Scone to no longer involve you in Brotherhood matters."

"And you haven't?"

"The way you treat me, the less I see you, the better. I look after myself. I finally realized that we don't need you, even if Thomas can't see that."

The Norwegian remained impassive. He swallowed his mouthful of stew noisily.

"A raid on Lanark? Why there?" he asked.

"William moved often during the winter to ensure that no one would follow the Stone's trail. The Lann Fala didn't make it easy for him. Fortunately, the cold and the frost helped him, but they also hindered us from getting the artifact to its destination. That's what we're going to have to undertake with the first thaws."

"Let me guess: knowing William's character, he wants to get ahead of the English and bring the first attack to them."

"You know him well, that's for sure. He's heading for Lanark because there's a garrison there and there's already a lot of tension. He wants—and here, I quote him, 'to kindle the fire of revolt throughout Scotland', from the southern English borders to the remotest clans of the Northern Hebrides. Once he wins his raid, he hopes the clans of the region will rally together and the rebellion will grow."

"I sense you're skeptical," Sören said.

"Perhaps your former apprentice is a little too optimistic. Certainly, such a revolt would serve the interests of the Brotherhood. It would occupy Edward for a while, and thereby slow down the Templars while we move the Stone. Wallace's action in Lanark is sensible and welcome. On the other hand, for it to keep going, that's another matter. Some clans have been at war for years and will not come together so easily, not even to face the English."

Sören listened to him while biting into a huge slice of bread, from which juice and meat fat dripped.

"And if I decline the invitation?" he asked, glancing in Fillan's direction.

"Then I'll be the one to take Fillan over there, and you can do whatever you want."

Fillan stared at his bowl thoughtfully. He felt divided between his desire to prove himself within the Brotherhood and wanting to stay with the group. He felt like he still had things to learn from his mentor, but above all, there was Kyle. Watching her perched on a bench, mocking Deorsa's gait and making Edan and Fergus laugh out loud, he realized how difficult it would be for him to be apart from her.

For a few moments, only the sounds of the spy chewing and scraping his bowl mingled with the festive din of mercenaries. Fillan felt the Norwegian's eyes on him, and then he stirred with a grunt.

"You guys come over here a minute," Sören said to the gang.

Kyle eyed them suspiciously. Fillan was amused to see her dragging her feet and grumbling as she joined them. Once they were all seated, Sören explained the situation.

"You know how I work," he said once he'd finished his explanation. "I am in favor of debate and communal decisions. I plan to accompany Fillan and I can go alone, but I want you to have your say."

"I'm in," Kyle said, staring at Fillan. "Last time I saw those fuckers, they almost killed me. I've been looking forward to returning the favor."

"If this event is to be a great moment in Scotland's history," added Fergus, "the bard in me can't miss such a legend."

"Well said!" Edan exclaimed. "You can tell of how I killed them all by myself and forged my legend. Why don't you ever sing about my exploits, anyway?"

"Your last feat was burping for ten seconds," teased the warrior. "What song do you want to compose about that?"

"Uh…"

"And you, Moira?"

"It's not even a question. Where you go, I go. If something happened to you and I wasn't there to treat you—or end your suffering if it was too serious—I'd regret it all my life!"

Fillan thought she was being funny, but she was extremely serious. Druids had a strange relationship with death.

"Well, that's wonderful!" rejoiced Deorsa, who had just stolen the bread from the Norwegian's plate and begun dipping it right into the pot. "We will all leave together in a week!"

The leader of the mercenaries fixed him with an icy and penetrating glare.

"I mean…" stammered the spy. "We'll leave… whenever you want."

"That sounds better."

They then spent a good part of the evening drinking and laughing. Fillan was slightly drunk when he headed back to his room. Sören's voice stopped him in the hallway.

"Fillan? Do you have a minute? I just wanted to remind you: don't forget what I told you in the tower. Wallace has summoned you, but remember that you are free to choose."

"Why are you repeating that to me?"

"Because he didn't invite you to Lanark for no reason. I know the methods of the Brotherhood, and he has a plan for you."

"What?"

"Your first assassination. You have to be perfectly sure of yourself so you don't fail the Brotherhood in its plans."

He searched his heart.

The embers of rage that were born on Bealltainn were strong and nourished a flawless determination.

He was no longer afraid.

9

It's all over.

There is only fire, the smell of ashes and blood in the ruined village. The night is getting lighter and the sun will soon rise.

The deer walks away, howling one last time.

A hooded man pulls the child from under the cart and tries to calm his tremors. He whispers a few words of comfort in his ear, without success.

The little one doesn't say anything, doesn't struggle and doesn't cry anymore. His eyes are empty and his mouth hangs open, in the middle of his sooty face.

He clings to the shoulder of his savior as he sees a charred rag doll lying on the floor.

He wants to speak, shout even, but his lungs are on fire and his throat is so dry.

So he clings on tighter and, with his little finger, points to the collapsed beam.

28

HOPE

Ailéas awoke with a start, her forehead covered in sweat. For some time, the nightmares had been less frequent, as if the demons of her past had finally decided to slow their chase. Sometimes they rebounded, more real than ever, and horror tore her from sleep with brutality. She found herself in her bed, trembling and frightened, with the horrible feeling that she was eight years old again, more vulnerable than ever.

She stared for a long time at the canvas ceiling of the tent, trying to calm her breathing and anchor herself back in the present. Between the stitches of the fabric, the day was beginning to dawn with slivers of sunrays.

Bradley's hoarse cough rung out and made her jump. She rose quickly and dressed in a few seconds before joining him.

The old commander was sitting in his bed, his nose buried in a pile of documents. He paid no attention to her as she fussed around her worktable, chopping herbs that she mixed with dried apple before throwing them all into the water she was boiling.

"Hello," she finally said, approaching the old man and touching his forehead.

He didn't have a fever, but he didn't look so good. He hadn't slept or slept very little. The bags under his eyes had grown heavy, and his features seemed more drawn than ever.

"Ah! Hello, Ailéas. I didn't see you there. Damn winter," he grumbled into his unkempt beard. "It almost makes me miss the French military campaign from a few years ago. Could you make me a…"

She handed him the herbal tea she'd just infused.

"Thank you, my throat is killing me."

"If you had covered yourself last night with more blankets…"

"Pooh, I'm tougher than that!"

He sipped the beverage, was seized by another fit of coughing, then swallowed it all in one gulp.

"Oh, that feels good!" he exclaimed. "Come on, hop, it's time to do our tour around the camp. Afterwards, we'll go for a walk in the forest; I have to talk to you."

"Are you sure you're well enough?"

"What do you take me for, an invalid? Leave me be! I can

get up on my own, for goodness' sake! Instead of fussing, go put on your wool, it's freezing this morning."

She brought him her fur coat.

"You act like I've got one foot in the grave," he cursed, frowning.

Ailéas said nothing and looked annoyed. She had grown to love the frank optimism and stubbornness of the old man. But it could also get on her nerves, especially when he thought himself invincible and was convinced that everything would work out for the best.

Especially when that was certainly not the case this time.

He had been coughing up his lungs for some time now. The winter had been particularly harsh and, over the last few months, the Lann Fala had forced them to trudge from the county of Fife to Argyll. Bradley had grown weaker, though no one else had noticed. Only Ailéas had her suspicions, which were confirmed over the weeks.

The day before, he had coughed up a thin trickle of blood, barely wider than a lock of hair. She watched with wide eyes, but he had just shrugged his shoulders.

"Stop making that funereal face," he insisted, putting on his jacket.

This attitude frustrated her endlessly.

Didn't he understand that until she found Fillan, he was all she had in the world? She couldn't imagine what would happen if he died.

They left the tent, and an icy breeze greeted them.

Some rare remnants of snow that the cold had long since turned to ice lingered in some places.

The old commander cracked his back with a sweeping movement, clapped his hands and headed forwards.

"Let's go, men! Everything must be shinier than our king's crown!" he yelled.

The morning inspection that he carried out two to three times a week was one of his favorite activities. That and the battle reports, a few days after having had time to mourn the dead and heal those who were not yet dead. He explained to Ailéas that this was what brought him closer to his men while constantly reminding them of his authority—an essential part of life in a garrison, where time passed more slowly.

Ailéas admired his natural charisma. As Bradley's sickness became more and more apparent, for the first time she feared that one of the men would use it to undermine their superior. Instead, they were united in a completely different emotion. Everyone deeply respected Bradley. During the last few days, she had even seen a look of sorrow identical to hers on many faces, as if some soldiers also feared that their world was about to crumble.

"I know of nothing better than a well-kept and orderly garrison to boost your morale," enthused the commander after a few minutes of perambulations and greetings.

I could think of plenty of things, thought Ailéas, who didn't appreciate the rigor of the military camp.

"There's no denying it: when the Lann Fala leave us alone, we're a well-oiled machine, and all is well."

It had been some time since they had seen Cornavii and his men, which greatly pleased the old warrior as he no longer had his authority taken away from him.

"Do you think we'll see them again?"

Whenever one of the men in the red capes appeared, she was afraid of being unmasked.

"I can't promise anything, but I hope not! They have other fish to fry and must certainly be bothering a commander in the north. Let them stay there and let them rot!"

They left the camp behind, which would soon wake into the monotony of everyday life. The sun rose higher and higher, shining its rays through the mist in the countryside.

As they walked down the forest path, Bradley accepted the arm that she held out to him, trying not to use it too much for support.

"Winter is coming to an end," said Ailéas, passing a beech tree and spotting the first buds.

This simple sentence seemed innocuous, but it meant a lot. She had not forgotten the old man's promise. Quite the contrary.

"You're right, and spring will do me good. No need to

stare at me like that; I haven't forgotten the conversation we had, or all the ones after it. Nor have I forgotten what I promised you. It's time for you to stand on your own two feet."

"But to go where?" she asked, feeling her heart jump. "I still don't know where Fillan is."

"Let's sit down for a moment, shall we? I told you that we had things to discuss, and that's exactly what we'll do. That big stump right there will do nicely."

He was out of breath and took a long sip from the bottle that Ailéas had made sure to fill with a fresh infusion.

"I conducted a little investigation on my side, in total secrecy."

"What? But how? When?"

"In total secrecy, I said! I did not wish to attract attention. And then, I wanted to be sure before telling you anything and give you false hope."

She waited for him to continue, hanging on to his every word.

"I made contact with a member of the Brotherhood of Assassins."

"I don't know them."

"It's not surprising, given that they are extremely discreet."

"The Brotherhood of Assassins…" repeated Ailéas. "Are they murderers?"

"If you're wondering whether they kill people, just like England, Scotland or me, yes, they are murderers. But they don't kill for fun, or at least as far as I can tell."

"What does that have to do with Fillan?"

He took another sip, then wiped his beard.

"To find your brother's trail, I had to think long and hard. Scotland is huge, and it was like looking for a needle in a haystack. And then I remembered one thing: the Assassins are the sworn enemies of the Templars."

"How do you know that?"

"Do you remember when I told you about that mark on your wrist and about what happened to me in the Highlands when I was younger?"

She nodded.

"The clan in question had ties to the Brotherhood. By spending time with them, I was able to learn a little more about them and even made some connections. Of course, they didn't reveal anything essential to me, except that they were fighting a long and fierce battle with the Templars. By remembering that, I had my first clue."

"I don't understand."

"It's simple: ever since Berwick, the Lann Fala have made it a point of honor to find you and your brother, and they are far from hiding it. As the Assassins have always sought to thwart the Order's plans, I wondered if they were perhaps looking for you too, or even better: if they knew where Fillan was. So I tried to contact them. But those I had known were either dead or disappeared."

Ailéas felt her heartbeat quicken in her chest.

"Through sheer perseverance, I was able to get in touch with one of them. Someone I trust recommended him to me."

"And he knows where Fillan is?" she asked, her voice trembling.

"He knows almost everything."

She felt like she was going to explode.

"Your twin has joined the Brotherhood," said the old commander, looking serious.

Fillan, an Assassin? She couldn't believe her ears. He barely knew what a weapon was, let alone how to hold one.

"Are you sure we're talking about the same person?"

"Given what you've told me about him," Bradley went on, "I confess that this also surprised me. But it's him. The Assassin gave me information on your twin's whereabouts before winter which corroborated certain information, including what the Lann Fala knew. I even learned that the Merchants Guild made a deal with the Brotherhood to help you escape, that infamous night in Berwick."

"Who is this person who gave you this information?" she asked suspiciously. "Are you sure we trust him?"

"Trust? No, I wouldn't say that," retorted Bradley. "I don't know his name. All I did was tell him who I was and that I knew where you were. I had no choice; in this kind of situation, it's necessary to reciprocally exchange information to gain the other's confidence."

"If you don't trust him, how can you be sure that this isn't a trap from the Order?"

"Impossible to be sure, but it's a risk that I had to take to find your brother. There was no other trail."

"But it's a risk that concerns us both," she continued, trying to keep her calm. "You should have told me about it."

"I wanted to surprise you," he said, scratching his head. "I'm sorry, you're right."

Ailéas was lost in her thoughts for a moment. She felt torn between the fear of being exposed, which the old soldier himself had prevented for months, and the possibility of finding Fillan.

"Very well," she said finally, standing up with sudden determination. "What do we do? What's next?"

Bradley smiled at her reaction. He loved her ability to bounce back, in any situation.

"For now, nothing at all," he replied.

"What?! This is such a habit with you! You want to do nothing? You must have been a fern in another life. This is crazy!"

He laughed softly, so as not to arouse his cough.

"This time it's not my doing. The man of the Brotherhood

asked me to wait. It won't take long for him to reach out to me again."

She had a terrible sense of foreboding but chose to ignore it.

"Thank you, Bradley," she said simply, putting a hand on his thick arm.

The old man smiled before starting to cough again. Clumsily, he tried to hide the trickle of blood that had dripped into his beard.

29

IGNITION

Once their decision was made, Sören's group wasted no time in leaving Beinn Eallair. The road to Lanark was long, and they would have to cross the regions occupied by the English in the south.

Fortunately, the Brotherhood were correct: Edward's forces were confined to their garrisons and had not yet gone on the march. Luckily, they didn't come across any more Lann Fala, either.

It took two weeks for them to reach the meeting point, in the heart of an impenetrable forest of Lanarkshire. Dawn had barely broken when they entered a hidden, makeshift camp.

All around, men were busy in eager, continuous movements. Some sharpened weapons, cut arrows, or checked armor while others perfected their combat techniques.

Every single one was preparing for battle and the tension was palpable on their faces.

"Sören!" rejoiced William Wallace as he saw them dismount their horses. "I'm glad you accepted my invitation. You'll see, a great battle awaits us, and therefore a great victory, I can assure you."

By way of greeting, the Norwegian grumbled.

"I mostly just came to ensure that my apprentice fulfills his role, and fulfills it well, before I hand him over to you."

Fillan shook the Highlander's hand.

"My word, Fillan! I don't need to fight you to know that Sören has accomplished his mission. I'm happy to see it. And glad to see you survived his training. What I'm planning for Lanark is going to test everything you learned over the winter."

"I'm ready," announced Fillan, putting a hand on the pommel of Fal's sword strapped to his belt.

"But what's all this?" asked William, seeing the bound and gagged person strapped across a donkey. "Is that... *Deorsa*?!"

"Yup," agreed Sören. "What you see there is the result of a democratic vote. He annoyed everyone so much, it was the only way to avoid a bloody tragedy befalling him. Right, Kyle?"

She growled.

Fillan was the only one who openly opposed it, more to

look good than anything else, not wanting the Brotherhood to hold it against him afterwards.

Wallace rushed to the mule to free Deorsa.

"And the donkey, was that the result of a democratic vote, too?"

"No, that was just what we had."

"Damn it, Sören, I know you hate each other, but you could have made an effort…"

"An effort?!" the spy began to bellow as William removed his gag. "The only effort he's capable of is reckless violence!"

"Oh, shut up! Give it a rest," retorted Sören with an evil look. "I could have abandoned you somewhere and I didn't."

"So what?! I'm supposed to be grateful?"

"Maybe…"

Fillan left them to their argument and headed over to greet James de Crannach, who was studying a map of the region.

"Fillan!" he exclaimed once he noticed him. "I'm happy to see you. Did you get my message?"

"Yeah, that was very kind of you. Why didn't you come with Deorsa?"

"And have to put up with him the whole way? You're crazy!"

They burst out laughing.

"Besides, I had other things to do, and Sören would

never have allowed me to go to his fortress: so few people know where it is," he added, giving Fillan an envious look. "But tell me instead how your training went!"

Fillan told him in detail about the winter he had spent at Beinn Eallair, explaining his progress.

"Have you taken the Leap of Faith yet?" prodded James.

"In the middle of the night, in the middle of a storm; I thought I was going to freeze there."

He saw himself jump from the top of the tower, surrounded by darkness, and land in a body of water beside the fortress.

"You've progressed so fast, it's amazing! This must be one of the peculiarities of the Children of Fal."

Fillan smiled, torn between pride and embarrassment, and they continued to chat for quite a while. Thomas's apprentice was eager to get in on the action at Lanark, just like Fillan. Everyone was eager to prove themselves, and a touch of competition ended up in their discussion.

An hour later they were reunited with the mercenaries, gathered around Wallace as he explained his plan.

"There are two targets. The first is the town sheriff of Lanark, William Heselrig. He is an odious and ruthless Englishman, put in place by Edward to rule the city and its suburbs with an iron fist."

"Is he a Templar?" asked Fillan.

"Not directly, no. But it's no coincidence that the king

chose him. He assisted the Lann Fala after the massacre of Berwick. He is a close collaborator of the Order. James and I will take care of eradicating him. With the death of Heselrig, the garrison of the city will be in chaos. That's what the population is waiting for to rise up and confront the English."

"You mentioned a second objective," Sören said.

"In addition to the garrison in town, a camp has been set up not far away, in the woods. Its leader is Commander Dacre. He is the second target, and I would like Fillan to take care of this one."

He puffed out his chest and looked determined.

"I can do it," he announced calmly.

"Two assassinations and a revolt," said Sören pensively. "Aren't you afraid that something so dramatic will attract the attention of the Order and set them on our trail?"

"That's the risk, of course. But if we coordinate, we hope that the Templars will be fooled into thinking that the death of the sheriff and the commander are only consequences of the revolt, not their point of origin."

"It's a dangerous game, but it just might work," approved Sören.

"Especially if, as I hope, the revolt then spreads to all of Lanarkshire. I'm in contact with many people among the population, and they are just waiting for the right time to take action."

"It's an ingenious plan," Deorsa observed. "I've already told you that. It has every chance of working. When are you planning to launch the attack?"

"Today," the Highlander said.

"What?!" gasped Deorsa.

Fillan wasn't expecting to have to take action so soon either.

"There's no time to lose. With or without us, the people will rise up. Better to let it be on our signal. If we wait and the revolt is nipped in the bud, we will no longer be able to take advantage of the situation."

"But I wish I had time to do my scouting in the area!" Deorsa sputtered in annoyance. "To make sure that we are in no danger of setbacks, or worse, that the Lann Fala aren't waiting for the right moment to spring their trap."

"That too is a risk worth taking."

"Wallace is right," his former mentor added. "Better to use the element of surprise. We strike fast, like lightning, and we disappear as soon as the revolt has taken hold."

"Since when do you use 'we' again?" asked the spy with a haughty and contemptuous air.

"Rest assured that it has nothing to do with you," retorted Sören, stepping threateningly towards him. "I'd rather die than be associated with a wart like you."

William sat up, folded his arms, and interrupted them in a thundering voice.

"We don't have time for these petty quarrels," he raged. "The success of this operation hangs by a thread. It only takes one error, a hesitation, or a disagreement to make it fail— and then the fire won't catch. If you have nothing better to do but argue, you can leave this camp right away."

Sören stared calmly at his former apprentice and leaned his head aside, as a sign of appeasement. Deorsa folded his arms and scowled.

"Everyone knows what they have to do," resumed the Highlander to conclude the meeting. "James, Fillan: we have to act in broad daylight, which will not make it easy for you. You must not be spotted. Don't waste time, come on. Prepare yourselves and analyze the terrain."

Everyone dispersed.

When Fillan found himself at the top of a tree, not far from the English garrison, the sun was at its zenith. The sun's rays scorched his shoulders as he observed the comings and goings of soldiers in their tents and the different possible entries. The camp had been pitched in a valley, which was not to his advantage, but with the onset of spring, the vegetation was growing all around and offered plenty of cover.

He climbed back down and took the opportunity to exercise his shoulder to make sure there was no chance of it seizing up. It was stiff and tense, but it was bearable. Sören waited for him, leant against the trunk.

"Did you find out how you're going to get into the camp?" he asked.

"There's a gap in the palisade to the east."

"Keep calm," his mentor advised him. "And everything will be well."

Fillan was calm. Terribly quiet. Impatient, too. Not just to prove his abilities, but because that first blood would taste like the vengeance he had long dreamed of satisfying.

They clasped each other's hands tightly, and then he rushed forward.

Barely out of the shelter of the forest, he squatted down in the high weeds so the sentries wouldn't spot him and moved forward quickly, discreetly.

He felt like everything inside him was colder than the inside of a dolmen. The terror that once paralyzed him was gone. He saw the wooden palisade erected all around the camp, as well as the entrance gate where two men were climbing the watchtower. It was far too risky an approach, so he wasn't going that way.

He skirted to the left, hoping to take advantage of the shade projected by the wooden wall.

After a few steps, he heard a branch crack behind him and sensed a movement.

"Who's there?" called out a voice.

It was a patrolman.

Fillan did not give him time to sound the alarm and

silently cut his throat in one leap, without asking a single question. Without questioning how he felt about it.

The time would come for emotion.

Later.

He hid the body in the tall grass and continued on his path with extra caution, nearing the wooden logs that rose high into the air and that were squeezed so tightly together that one might think they made up a single, gigantic tree.

It didn't take him long to locate the irregularity that had made him try this approach. With the thaw, a log of wood had dropped out of place, leaving a thin passage at its base.

He listened.

Not a sound.

A peek through the gap revealed the back of a tent. He couldn't have wished for a better way to conceal his entrance and went in head-first. At the exact moment he twisted and got his belt stuck, a soldier emerged from beside the tent door.

If he turns around, I'm dead, Fillan thought, freezing.

An ounce of fear crept into him and started to crack the ice of his emotions. He was afraid of being spotted, stuck so stupidly, without even being able to reach the commander's tent. What a terrible and shameful end.

He breathed a sigh of relief when he saw the Englishman stretch and walk away.

He managed to free himself as he took a deep breath out and completely emptied his lungs.

Still crouching low to be less visible, he approached the tent and mentally reviewed the entire camp. Once he was certain of the right direction, he slipped away, taking advantage of the shadows of the tents or the palisade, depending on the orientation of the sun. Every time he had to break cover, he cast a quick look around before running like the wind, carefully measuring each of his steps and controlling his breathing.

Once in front of the correct tent, he stopped, holding his ear to the fabric.

A man sneezed inside.

It was Dacre, his target. Fillan had seen him return to his tent while he'd watched from his treetop perch. Before slipping between the pieces of fabric that he took care to cut with the utmost discretion, Fillan felt for Ogme's pendant against his chest and briefly clasped it in his hand.

Determination. Lucidity. Balance.

He entered silently to a subdued atmosphere. He noticed a bed overflowing with blankets, and the smell of camphor that permeated the air invaded his nostrils. A man stood leaning over a table with his back to Fillan, a little further away from the bed. He spotted armor propped against a chest, and its cape reminded him of something, but he couldn't remember what.

Just as he was about to jump, a soldier burst through the entrance in front of him, forcing him to flatten himself on the ground.

"Commander, Pete hasn't returned from his patrol."

"That lazy ass must have fallen asleep at the foot of a tree trunk after sipping too much wine again. Find him for me! No rations for him tonight!"

Fillan felt his confidence crack a little more.

If the body of the man he was about to kill was discovered, the alarm would be sounded and the whole operation might fail. He must do it very quickly.

No sooner had the soldier left the tent than Fillan silently climbed over the blankets and approached, sword drawn.

Judging by the grayness of his hair, Dacre was an old man, and he walked over to a chest of drawers on his left to grab a glass as a coughing fit shook his shoulders.

It was curious. Fillan had a sense of déjà vu. This build and gait meant something to him.

Berwick.

The word popped into his mind.

It's the cape and the build of the man I saw in the alley in Berwick.

Petrified by this dreadful observation, the image of his sister with her vacant eyes flooding his mind, he missed the perfect moment to strike. The commander turned and stared at him, dropping the documents and the cup he was holding.

"You... You're..." he stammered, holding back his cough.

Fal's sword pierced his chest, quickly, and it was quite dry when it came out.

The body of the old soldier fell to the ground, accompanied by Fillan's arm.

A spasm shook one of his legs.

"You are Fillan..." he breathed as blood began to appear at the corners of his lips. "You... You have her eyes."

Fillan did not have time to wonder what that meant before pain burst on the side of his skull and he dropped his weapon. A soldier who had just entered the tent rushed at him and immobilized him on the floor. A first blow flew at the level of his groin, a second to the liver, then a third to the temple.

Fillan was forced to shield his face, deflecting a new blow before he heard the shrill sound of a blade being drawn from its sheath. He barely stopped the dagger, an inch from his face, blocking the arm of his assailant.

Using a technique Kyle had taught him, he flipped his position by twisting his opponent's wrist to seize the weapon.

With a flick of his hips, he rocked his entire body and pulled the warrior over, who rolled in the blood of the old commander. With a measured, precise gesture, he stuck the short blade to their throat.

Ogme was pressed against his chest, as though to remind him of moderation, restraint. He was about to slide his blade across the fair skin when the warrior stopped struggling.

"Fi… Fillan?" they said in a low voice, full of emotion.

He stared into the eyes of the person under the hood.

Two eyes identical to his.

30

MIRROR

Everything around them disappeared.

The tent, the smell of camphor, the body of Bradley Dacre, the iron smell of his blood, the clamor of the army that spread through the entrance of the camp. Even the beating of their hearts seemed to stop.

There was only them in the world. They just kept staring at each other, almost forgetting to breathe, unable to believe their reunion was real.

Ailéas, with her mouth trembling.

Fillan, with his eyebrows raised and wrinkled.

They remained frozen for several seconds, not daring to move, as if the slightest commotion could break this suspended moment in time and make them disappear.

A breeze rustled through the layers of tent fabric. Fillan became aware that he was on the verge of slaughtering his twin and a red droplet had appeared from her neck, so he withdrew the blade and let it fall to the ground without a sound.

She pulled away, and they sat face to face.

"I thought I'd never see you again," she gasped, with tears in her eyes.

"And I thought that you were dead."

They embraced, and after all the ordeals they had been through, the hug felt like a return to their days of complementing each other.

The mirror image of one another, Fillan thought.

He couldn't believe it, convinced he was dealing with an illusion just like that of the night of Bealltainn. He stroked his twin's cheek, as if all the hits she had landed and their hug had been only physical manifestations of his imagination.

Yet she was there. She was real.

Ailéas could not believe it either and expected to wake up at any moment. The discussion she'd had with Bradley was only a few days ago and she didn't think she'd see her brother again for weeks, perhaps longer, with or without the help of the Brotherhood.

Happy and relieved, she tipped her head forward, touching their foreheads together. The nearing clank of armor joined the tumult that rose through the camp, but they did not hear it, too concentrated on the reassuring thought that was germinating deep within them: they would never be alone again. With this simple contact, they leaned against each other, accentuating the symmetry of their faces and tangling strands of their hair.

"There you are!" a voice exclaimed from the entrance of the tent.

The twins turned in one motion and saw a warrior dressed in armor with a red cape. He held a long, shimmering sword in his hand.

"Two for the price of one! For once, our information was right," rejoiced the Lann Fala before pointing at the body of the commander lying on the ground. "Besides, you saved me half the job."

Fillan was almost relieved to find that the man was not Cornavii, but he was still at the soldier's mercy. His Fal sword lay farther to his right, where Ailéas had knocked it. He'd be dead before he could seize the dagger he'd just dropped.

"Stand up! And no tricks, or I'll cut your throat."

He turned his blade towards Fillan, apparently having judged him to be more threatening because of his outfit and the empty scabbard hanging at his side.

Ailéas took the opportunity to pirouette aside and use the momentum to plant the dagger she had picked up deep into the warrior's neck, just above his throat.

There was barely a drop of blood or a sound of the blade, just a slight clink against the metal of the armor. The man's face twitched into a grin of surprise and pain. He tried to inhale a trickle of air and spat out blood, then collapsed to the ground with a muffled sound of metal and of fabric.

Fillan felt a strange, unpleasant emotion.

His twin had reacted with incredible speed, saving both their lives. An old instinct resurfaced, however: one he thought he had left behind while buried in the darkness of the Dalkeith dolmen.

The sudden, irrational urge to push her away and yell at her.

The shouts of the approaching battle helped him to ignore the unease that invaded him. His sister leaned over the body of the old commander, a hand resting on his crimson-turned chest. She whispered a few words that Fillan could not hear, then she chased away a stifled sob that shook her shoulders.

"Ailéas!" he whispered, picking up Fal's sword. "We have to go!"

He was angry with himself for interrupting her, but they couldn't wait in case another Lann Fala or English soldier came upon them. Gently, he grabbed his sister's hand and led her away. Just before leaving the tent, she kissed goodbye to the life she'd had during these past months and gazed at the workbench and the old fur coat that Bradley had given her.

One last time, her eyes rested on the body of her friend on the ground. She had dreamed many times of leaving all this, even raging and screaming, but she never could have imagined that it would be in such sadness and heartbreak.

Outside, the suffocating smell of smoke gripped them by the throat. The camp had descended into chaos. The ringing of weapons, the raging howls of the warriors, and the wails of the dying were everywhere.

"It's strange," Ailéas said, approaching the palisade. "We find ourselves in a similar situation to the one that separated us."

Fate sometimes brings strange surprises, her brother thought, and nodded.

They slipped through the gap to leave the camp, then ran at full speed through the tall grass. The twins didn't turn around until they reached the edge of the woods. The smoke from the garrison had turned into an imposing blaze above the valley, looming over the cries that could still be heard, even at this distance.

In the heart of the forest, Wallace's camp was totally deserted.

They settled down next to each other on a fallen tree trunk. As they examined each other, they realized that almost a year had passed since the tragedy of Berwick.

Both had changed a lot.

"Nice scar," Ailéas said after a short silence, pointing at his face. "Are you trying to look like me?"

"It was to avoid being recognized, just after Berwick."

"It suits you," she added. "It gives you a wild side that dissuades people from coming to annoy you."

Fillan observed her in turn.

She too had changed. The features of her face were refined, and she had lost weight. However, she seemed just as strong as before and had even gained an inch in height. His hair, which was no longer perfectly red like hers, sat above his shoulders.

They could not have said precisely how, but each felt how much the other had suffered.

"What happened at Berwick? I saw you on the shoulder of an English soldier and... I was sure you were dead."

She took a deep breath, enjoying the spring breeze and listening to the birdsong that mingled with the rustling of the trees. Then she began to explain everything.

How Bradley saved her life in the alley, the care that he had lavished upon her, the lengths he had gone through to keep her hidden.

"Without him, I'd have been dead a long time ago," she explained in a low voice.

Her face was painted with grief, and Fillan felt his heart sink as he was racked with guilt. He had followed orders and accomplished the mission of the Brotherhood, but in doing so he had killed his sister's savior and protector.

"I'm really sorry, Ale."

She twisted her hands and looked up at him with two

misty eyes, smiling in spite of herself upon hearing her nickname.

"He didn't have long to live, anyway."

Over the past two days, the condition of the old commander had significantly worsened. Ailéas was not a real healer, but she knew the undeniable signs: fever, cough, and lots of blood. Bradley wouldn't have survived more than a week.

This observation did not soothe the weight she felt in her chest.

"Why did you kill him?" she asked.

"It's complicated."

"Were you sent by the Brotherhood of Assassins to find me?"

"How did you…?" he breathed, frowning, surprised that she was aware of the existence of the organization and that she knew he was involved with them.

"Bradley told me about it. He managed to get in touch with an Assassin. To help me find you."

"I didn't even know you were alive. My mission was to kill Dacre."

"But then…"

Hurried footsteps interrupted them. Fillan rose, drawing his sword and then sighing in relief. It was only Sören, the rest of the band, and Deorsa. All were healthy and safe.

"Good job, Fillan," the Norwegian said. "The revolt has

spread throughout the city and the outer garrison will soon be reduced to a pile of ashes."

He froze when he saw the young woman.

"But that's…"

"My sister, Ailéas."

She stood up too, embarrassed.

"These are the ones who were supposed to help us get out of Berwick," Fillan explained to his twin before introducing her to each member of the troupe, one after the other, as well as Deorsa.

"Well," Moira said, nudging Sören with her elbow. "For someone who never wants to believe in destiny and keeps rejecting it, you have to admit that it does sometimes play some funny tricks."

Sören ignored her.

"What is she doing here?" he asked sternly.

"She was in the English camp."

"The English?!" Edan said, clutching his axe.

"Calm down and listen to us!"

It only took them a few minutes to sum up the situation.

"You say that commander wanted to help you find Fillan, but how?" Sören asked.

"He was in contact with a member of your Brotherhood."

"I'm not from the Brotherhood."

"I, on the other hand, am a proud member," Deorsa interjected, stepping forward and performing the bow he was accustomed to doing when meeting new people. "I deal with a great amount of information, and I have never heard of a commander we'd be working with. Are you sure you didn't make a mistake? Or that this Dacre wasn't lying to you?"

He had only opened his mouth for a few seconds, but hearing the insinuations in his voice about Bradley, she felt like slamming her fist down on him.

"No," she said curtly. "It was definitely one of yours. Bradley showed me a letter with a strange seal."

"This one?" asked her brother, showing her the pommel of Fal's sword.

She nodded.

The spy began to pace in thought, puzzled.

"Why are you pacing into the ground like that?" Sören asked irritably.

"You know I have a good memory, and I never forget anything."

"So you say."

"Dacre's name means nothing to me. However, I remember that a certain Sir Bradley was close to the Brotherhood some time ago."

"He did tell me that a clan of the Brotherhood had saved him in the past," explained Ailéas.

"Could it be the same person?" Fillan called out.

"Possibly."

Deorsa continued to walk in circles, visibly agitated.

"Wonderful!" laughed Sören. "You assassinated a potential ally in the enemy camp."

"You go ahead and have a good laugh, Sören. I seem to remember you were the first to side with Wallace when I asked that you allow me time to investigate. I could have discovered this kind of information!"

"No need to turn it on me!" exploded the Norwegian. "You better start wondering, because I get the sense that someone is playing double bluff in your damn Brotherhood, right under your nose."

"He's right, Deorsa," Fillan added. "After I killed Bradley Dacre, a Lann Fala entered the tent. He knew that Ailéas and I would be there, and he planned to kill the commander himself."

The spy sank again into silence.

"If you keep pacing like that, you'll end up in the Sidh!" Sören growled.

"We've suspected the presence of a traitor in our ranks for some time. We thought the leaks came from the south, after the advance of the English and some of our men got captured. But at Scone, the English knew where to find you, where to find Fillan."

Fillan met Kyle's gaze. Fiery arrows passed before their eyes.

"You killed the Lann Fala?" asked Deorsa in a tone of reproach.

"He was going to kill us; what did you want us to do?" retorted Ailéas. "Give him a pat on the back and ask him nicely to let us go?"

Kyle laughed, enjoying seeing Fillan's twin stand up to the spy.

"No, of course not, but the Lann Fala seldom act alone. We'd better get out of here as soon as possible."

"What's next in the plan?" asked Fillan.

"Wallace convinced Sören to accompany us, you and me, along with several clans to the border of the Highlands," explained the spy, "in order to spread the news of the revolt and push the people to rally."

They all bustled about, preparing for departure.

Fillan approached his sister.

"I have a mountain of things to tell you and explain to you. I can't promise you there won't be any danger, but…"

"What are you going on about?" she exclaimed without hesitation, grabbing the horse's reins as he held them out to her. "I'm not afraid of danger and I'm dying to see the Highlands."

She climbed up and galloped off, feeling the coolness of the forest whipping at her face as her entire being cried out for freedom.

31

PERIL

An arrow grazed the neck of his horse, which neighed in fear and nearly took off in a swerve. Fillan tightened the reins and shouted a command. He turned his head to the side and saw them posted at the edge of the wood to their right like a long, winding arm. He recognized the colors of the tabards.

"The English are attacking from the east!" he yelled at Sören.

He spurred on his mount to get closer to Ailéas, as if her mere presence at his side had the power to protect them from the new assault of arrows that descended upon them.

"Dunstaffnage Fort isn't far off!" yelled the Norwegian, at the head of the group of horsemen. "Push your horses hard to get them moving!"

They increased the pace, bellowing, and spurring on their

mounts. After one last shower of arrows became lost in the tall grass, they gained enough distance to be out of range.

Fillan cast another glance in the direction of the soldiers who had stopped bending their longbows into arches and were shrinking to the point that they could no longer be seen among the twisted trunks. Suddenly, a cloud of glimmers appeared under the rays of a sun still half-veiled by scattered clouds. It was a horde of horsemen who galloped at full speed in pursuit.

The valley became the terrain of a panting cavalcade, flooded with the thunder of hooves.

Out of the corner of his eye, Fillan saw that his sister had a look of determination, her hair blowing in the wind. She was wholly focused on her horse, glued to his black coat, no trace of fear controlling her emotions.

She knew everything.

It had been two weeks since they reunited and Fillan had explained everything to her. The Brotherhood, the Assassins, the Order, the Templars, the Lann Fala, their fight across the centuries, the link with their clan, the Children of Fal and their role at the heart of it all.

She hadn't seemed surprised, because what he told her had coincided with what she had felt within her for years. The fleeting, nebulous impression that her destiny had to be played out elsewhere. She had always suspected that Berwick was not that place.

With the approval of Deorsa, the only representative of the Brotherhood since their departure from Lanark, Fillan had entrusted her with the second sword of Fal.

Her hands shook as she took it.

"I often dream of this sword," she confessed with a stammer.

As she held her clan's legacy, Deorsa explained that it would also be possible for her to join the Brotherhood, if she so desired. The prospect of uniting in a common cause with her brother had made her happy. And then it was time to embrace hope for a future.

All this had forged a fresh determination deep within her.

"We're going around the river to the west!" yelled the Norwegian.

Behind them, the soldiers were getting dangerously close, to the point where the breaths of their steeds could be heard. Their animals were fresher, more alert, and much better trained.

"Is it still far away, this accursed castle?" Edan complained. "It won't be long before they're poking our asses with their spears!"

"Behind that hill!" Kyle shouted, pointing to a peak. "They won't dare come too close to the ramparts."

"Are you sure about that?"

"No, but it's better that the scouts recognize us, or they'll gut us like pheasants."

The bald man spat, dropping a slew of insults.

Each drew their swords as they sped in unison as a united cohort.

Dunstaffnage Fort was the penultimate stage of their journey. It was Clan MacDougall's fort, the clan to which Fergus belonged. Since they left Lanark, they had traveled at full speed towards the north-west, with a destination of the Highlands. The plan devised by Wallace was simple: he and James would lead the fire of the rebellion to Scone, which they would liberate from the English's tyranny before attacking several of their strongholds to occupy them. Deorsa, Fillan, and Sören's group were to rally several clan leaders.

In the south, the meetings had been secret. Many feared the "hammer" of the English, as they nicknamed the wrath of King Edward. Once they had passed the Clyde, on the other hand, they found many more sympathizers. The events at Lanark revived the hope of a free Scotland for some, and they were quick to send reinforcements to Wallace.

"To the left!" Fergus sang out, using his powerful voice.

A grove disappeared to reveal a wide beach, like a cove. A ship with an English flag was anchored not far away, and several men had already disembarked.

"It's not possible; how many of these idiots are there?" howled Edan. "Sören, are you sure you want to go that way? We'll end up stuck again!"

Dunstaffnage Fort stood at the tip of a peninsula jutting out into Ardmucknish Bay, off the mouth of Loch Etive. The path they took was the only one that allowed access from the mainland.

"The first archers we met were not an isolated group. We're already stuck. The English have invaded the region. Dunstaffnage is our best option!"

"Ah, damn it, what if they've already taken the fort?"

"Don't underestimate Clan MacDougall," Kyle retorted. "They're tough."

The bald man was about to spit a flood of insults, but the arrows began to fly again. A battalion of archers, posted above the sandbanks, had seen them coming from afar. The horsemen who were pursuing them slowed to avoid being riddled with arrows, too.

The first arrowshot was too long and flew over the group, which gave them the chance to gallop even harder. They were nearly out of reach when the tip of a new arrow found its target.

The horse whinnied horribly and collapsed, the saddle covered in blood. The fall unseated its rider, who landed heavily in the grass and lay motionless.

"Edan!" cried Moira.

"I'll take care of it," shouted Fillan, pulling on his reins.

The druid joined the others, who continued their sprint as the teenager turned around.

"Edan?!" he yelled.

The bald man was sat in the grass and shook his head, dumbfounded.

"Ready to go?" called Fillan, approaching quickly.

He couldn't stop completely; that would sign both their death warrants. Soldiers were already on their way to finish off the mercenary.

"I was born ready… Ah, damn!"

A shaft pierced his thigh.

"Sons of dogs!" he yelled, breaking the arrow. "Band of mangy bastards! I'll make you eat your c…"

"Edan!" hollered Fillan, now coming up to his level.

Because of Edan's injury, Fillan was forced to slow his ride to help his comrade climb onto the mount. Fillan grabbed his arm and, at the same time, an Englishman equipped with a pike rushed towards them. His intention was clear: kill the horse to prevent them from running away. Fillan saw the metal point approaching and felt his heart racing.

Then the assailant's head flew through the air, spreading a net of sticky blood.

Ailéas had joined them at full speed, ignoring the danger, and swung her sword of Fal through the air.

"Bunch of sickos!" Edan bellowed. "We can say for sure that you've got some pair of balls! Let's split up, there's more coming!"

They rode away, only avoiding the arrows falling from the skies by chance.

The English ended their pursuit as they approached Dunstaffnage. The building seemed like it was hewn from a single block of stone, imposing, impregnable. Its walls rose high and its surroundings bustled with activity. The clan warriors were preparing for war.

The group dismounted, and Sören and Deorsa approached one of the Highlanders to exchange a few words.

"How do you feel?" asked Sören to the bald man as he headed back towards them.

"Like a boar that they've tried to gut."

"Well, that allegory works out nicely for you," Kyle laughed. "You already have the looks and temperament of a boar, even when you're not injured."

"Dirty little pest... Ah, be careful!" he grumbled at Moira, who was already tending to his injury.

He noticed the disgusted look Ailéas gave his bloody wound.

"Do you want to give me a little kiss better?" he asked with a mischievous look.

For an answer, she gave him a kick to the groin.

"Oh, fuck!" he yelped.

"Stop fidgeting," the druid ordered.

"But she made me a eunuch!"

"At the very least."

Ailéas had quickly adapted to Sören's group. She got along well with Kyle, chatted all day long with Moira, enjoyed Fergus' compositions—which flattered the ego of the troubadour—and had won Sören's respect in the first week by slaughtering an Englishman who had followed them. But above all, she never hesitated to put Edan in his place with a cackle.

Before anyone else, Fillan spotted a colossal man headed towards them. He was even more impressive than Sören or Wallace, and sported a black beard that he had taken care to braid.

"Sören, can you tell me why you've brought the English to my doorstep?" thundered the mountain of muscle.

Fillan had never had the opportunity to see Sören's face burst into such a smile. Yet that is what happened.

"I'm here to make fun of you! Hail to you, old horn!"

The mercenary laughed, and they patted each other on the shoulder.

"To those who don't know him, Fillan and Ailéas in particular, this is Alexander MacDougall, chief of this rock."

"Watch what you're calling a rock, you northern pest!"

He glanced at them all, one after the other, then stared for a long time at Kyle with a penetrating look.

"Come a little closer, you."

Kyle hesitated, narrowing her eyes, then moved closer to

embrace the man in a firm hug, which despite everything seemed full of warmth.

Fillan opened his eyes wide in shock, and Deorsa couldn't help but notice.

"Well, well," said the spy, approaching. "I was wondering whether she'd told you where she came from."

He couldn't help being smug, which infuriated Fillan.

"Kyle is the daughter of Alexander MacDougall. Only child and true heir."

Fillan felt like the ground was giving way under his feet.

"Don't faint—that would look bad. MacDougall always wanted a son, which is why Kyle was given a boy's name."

"What happened?"

He was angry with himself for playing the spy's game, but his curiosity was too strong.

"The clan chief may have raised his daughter like a man, but the time soon came when he had to follow societal pressures and marry her off. You know Kyle's character—which is not so removed from that of her father, by the way. For a young girl who had been brought up in combat and with the ambition to lead men, to be reduced to a mere wife was unthinkable."

"She ran away," Fillan guessed.

"Always hold on to your intelligence, Fillan. It's an advantage in our environment. You're right. As the wedding approached, our dear warrior turned on her heels and ran. For an entire year, her clan heard no news from her. She joined Sören, and I understand it was Fergus, or maybe Craig, from the same clan, who finally convinced her to write to her father."

"How did he react?"

"When she ran away, very badly. It was an affront to the rival clan he wished to form an alliance with through the marriage. It was an affront to his authority, too. But I believe that today he is no longer disappointed. He knows his daughter well, and that she would have killed her husband within the year, which is also not very good for an alliance between clans."

Fillan finally understood what Moira had implied months earlier. Kyle, daughter of the Highlands, sole heiress of one of the most powerful clans in the north, was truly not just anyone.

"What's going on, Alexander?" asked Sören, with his thumb raised above his shoulder, pointing to where he'd come from.

"The English showed up about an hour ago. They don't do discretion, so I guess it's my stronghold they're interested in. You didn't choose the best time to visit me; war is upon us."

"We actually came to talk with you about revolt and seek your help…"

"You'll be able to do that eventually. I'm surprised to see them this far north. They're up to something, that's for sure. In any case, you are welcome. Don't delay coming in to find shelter."

He left them there before approaching to his men to organize their defenses.

"Sören, this is a disaster," Deorsa said, panicked.

"I bet that for you, a crumb of bread in your bed would be a disaster."

"I am completely serious. The presence of the English around here is no coincidence."

"What do you mean?"

The spy inched closer, speaking lower but still loud enough for Fillan to hear.

"There's only one reason why they'd come so far up into the north when they have no supply point, no support."

"Spill it, Deorsa. May I remind you that an army is about to break in."

"The Templars must have discovered where the Stone of Fal was conveyed."

"Fucking spy!" launched Sören.

Just as they all realized the seriousness of the situation, a war horn sounded nearby.

The English had had time to regroup and were marching on the fort.

32

DUNSTAFFNAGE

The English attacked with such speed that nobody around Dunstaffnage had time to take refuge behind the stone enclosure. While the first battalion rushed forward to the strident sound of the horn, the entrance to the fort descended into chaos as it was located high up and only accessible by a single staircase. A compact crowd pressed together on the stairs in a flurry of shouting and jostling.

Four rows of about ten soldiers each advanced in formation along the coast to the left of the fortress. A horseman directed them from the flank. His red cape flapped behind him in the sea breeze. The first line was equipped with pikes, and all wore metal or leather armor.

"To me!" ordered Alexander MacDougall, to gather the warriors of his clan. "Let's buy enough time for everyone to take shelter!"

With his claymore drawn and resting on his shoulder, he organized a first line of defense at the base of the fortress. The northern men were less numerous, barely twenty or so, but seemed awfully fierce. Only a few wore real armor, and at best there were a handful of leather breastplates dotted around. All wore the clan tartan, the scarlet color of which stood out against the green shades of the plain and the whitish stone ramparts behind them.

Rather than withdrawing, Sören decided to stay beside the Highlander. As usual, he did not impose his choice on the members of his group, who nevertheless decided to stay and fight and grouped together at the center of the line. Not even Deorsa retreated, to the great astonishment of Fillan, who had always imagined that the spy was more adept at stealth than the sword.

Only Moira and Edan did not stay, because of Edan's injury. They were the first to join the protective enclosure of the castle, which did not fail to illicit many curses from the injured mercenary.

"Leave me alone!" he yelled. "I'm going to make them pay!"

"Edan, you do what I tell you, otherwise I'll knock you out with my stick."

Faced with the druid's threats, he stopped arguing.

The sound of the English troops' footsteps approached like the sound of drums.

"Archers!" yelled MacDougall, brandishing his immense sword. "LOOSE!"

From the top of the ramparts, where the clan chief had posted several of his men, the vibration of bowstrings suddenly resounded. A cloud of arrows flew, whistling into the air, to descend among the ranks of their adversaries.

Some arrows hit their targets, who screamed and grabbed at their wounds or simply collapsed. Many arrows merely planted themselves in the ground. Two more volleys followed before the enemy ranks came too close to the clan's front line.

Ailéas and Fillan stood side by side, equipped with their Fal swords that seemed to glow brighter than all other weapons under the rays of the sun.

There was a shouted order, then the first row of the battalion broke apart to charge at full speed. More howls from warriors followed, brutal, calling for blood and death. Most of the clansmen managed to avoid the tips of the spears, and some even broke the wooden handles in half with one powerful strike.

Within the multitude of attacks and blocks, bathed in cries and fear, there was only crushing and death. Ailéas narrowly dodged the tip of a spear, struck against the wooden rod, and cut off her assailant's hand. The man screamed as he grabbed his bloody stump, and she took the opportunity to seize the spear from him and thrust it between the ribs.

The new scream was drowned out by the foaming blood.

Barricade your emotions, feel nothing, only be present in the moment: these were the lessons that Bradley had taught her in order to survive the heat of combat. If she thought for even a second, if she doubted, she was finished. The warriors around her were counting on her resilience.

Another Englishman rushed towards her, his sword raised above his head. She thought she recognized him as one of Bradley's men, who she had known for many months, but immediately blocked that notion from her mind. She stopped him in his tracks by chopping down a leg with the whistle of her blade. The man fainted instantly, collapsing like a rag doll while a reddish wave smeared the bottom of his gambeson.

Fillan also fought fiercely. Two Englishmen had succumbed to his lightning-fast stabbing attacks. A spurt of blood sprayed the side of his head, spreading through his hair and all across his face. He looked like a warrior who had fallen in battle long ago and returned from the Sidh to get his revenge.

Something was different.

He felt it with every blow he landed, every movement of his weapon. More than once he thought he saw his blade gleam slightly, as did his sister's. When he noticed it, all the hair on his body had stood up at once. The swords of Fal gave off a curious energy that drove him more ferociously into battle. Stranger still, the twin blades seemed to answer each other. The more his sister swirled through the confrontation, the stronger he felt, and the reverse also seemed to be true, as if the breath of the gods permeated them with their power.

Deorsa brushed past him as he fended off a burly knight. Fillan barely had time to see the glint of two curved daggers in the spy's hands before his opponent collapsed into the reddened grass.

Sören, Kyle, and Fergus danced with their usual agility, plying dodges, kicks, and hasty attacks. The twins momentarily found themselves back-to-back.

"Who are you?" asked Ailéas, turning to her brother with a mocking look. "Get out of my twin's body!"

"You're not doing too badly yourself!" he said, waving his blade to clear some of the blood that covered it.

"Am I dreaming, or are you showing off?"

He gave her a slight shrug and laughed before returning to battle. Ailéas did the same, leaping and swinging her sword, its sharp edge cutting through armor as if it were made of paper.

The first wave was repelled without too much difficulty and the last surviving English warriors retreated, preceded by the Lann Fala on horseback.

The clansmen let out victorious howls and brandished their weapons.

"We did well," MacDougall said, "but they simply came to see what we were worth. We won't have our advantage for long. These motherfuckers are smart, and they'll bring their archers or their cavalry. Inside, everyone!"

With order and discipline, everyone headed into the fort. No sooner had they ascended the steps leading to the main gate did the war horn sound a new alarm, announcing the imminence of a new attack. After the large wooden doors were closed, the clan chief masterfully organized its defenses. He posted some of his best swordsmen alongside the archers on the ramparts of the fort, to greet the English soldiers who would climb up there.

The entire inner courtyard was transformed into a knot of tensions and expectations. Despite the protection of the walls, the rhythmic sound of the English footsteps resounded. Fillan and Ailéas wanted to fight it out, but both had the awful feeling of being trapped, awaiting the horror to come, just like during the siege of Berwick. Fillan did not dare to imagine what might happen if the English broke through Dunstaffnage's defenses. Due to the narrowness of the fort, it could only be a massacre.

Kyle strode over to him and kissed him firmly, to give him courage, to give herself courage, and so that all her clan could see her. Then she cried out, together with all the other warriors, intending to scare the soldiers who would mount an assault on the ramparts.

"Shields!" yelled a soldier from the wall.

Those who possessed them lifted them above their heads, and the others hunkered down against the stone, trying to make themselves as small as possible. A stream of arrows descended, bouncing against the stone or planting into the wood of the shields.

None hit their mark.

Fillan saw Deorsa getting angry with Sören and headed over to find out what it was all about.

"Who do you think you are?" shouted Sören. "May I remind you that we're stuck here and MacDougall needs our help!"

"If the Templars capture the Stone of Fal, Dunstaffnage and MacDougall will face many other problems—and they won't be the only ones. You know it as well as I do."

"What I know is that I should cut you in half, here and now. Your stories, your eternal struggle—I've had enough. I've already been kind enough to tolerate you on this trip, and look where that got us!"

A clap of thunder, which seemed to shake an entire section of the fort, interrupted him.

"To the doors!" shouted a man from the top of the ramparts. "Barricade the doors! They've brought a ram!"

A group of warriors passed between them, and Fillan bowed his head just in time to avoid a plank they were carrying to reinforce the entrance to the fort.

"Sören, you've turned your back on the Brotherhood, and that's up to you, but you know what the Stone represents and the tragedy it would be if it were to fall into the hands of the Order. This is also your heritage, your destiny…"

"Don't talk to me about destiny." Sören gritted his teeth and grabbed Deorsa with both hands. "You don't have the faintest idea what that means."

"What are you two arguing about?" called Alexander, who approached them, barely out of breath from running everywhere to shout his orders. "We need warriors here, not talkative hens."

"Alexander, is there a way to quietly leave the fortress?" asked Sören after a few seconds of reflection.

"There's an old tunnel that leads to the north beach, but are you really planning to run away while the best is yet to come? I know you love a good battle!"

"I'm only doing it because I have no choice," Sören retorted with a glare in the direction of the spy. "You think you'll get out without our help?"

"You old gull, what do you take me for, a beginner? There's only a handful of them. We'll take a bite out of them and send them back, crying blood into their mothers' petticoats."

"I owe you one."

"You don't owe me anything. You and your warriors have already lent a hand at the foot of my fortress, when I didn't even have time to offer you a cut or a loaf of bread. Nothing forced you to stay. I'm the one who owes you, believe me. We will take care of Edan. Where will you go?"

"We must pass through the Isle of Mull."

"Walk along the beach towards the northern tip; there are boats hidden not far from a grove, if the English haven't burned them yet."

After a brief hug, the clan leader ordered one of his men to tell them where the entrance to the tunnel was, then he rushed to the ramparts, at the top of which the first English soldiers were arriving.

The door continued to shake under the onslaught of the ram. They were about to set off, but Kyle didn't make a move, looking slightly uncomfortable.

"I have to stay to help my clan," she explained. "I've turned my back on it for too long."

"Me, too," Fergus announced.

"I understand," Sören agreed.

"We'll join you at Iona with reinforcements when we're done here."

Sören wished them good luck by gripping their shoulders then turned on his heels, dragging Ailéas, Moira, and the spy behind him.

Kyle and Fillan ended up with only a few seconds of relative intimacy. He handed her Ogme's pendant.

"I have a feeling you're going to need it more than I do," he said.

"You're wrong. I know what awaits me here: a fight, blood, warriors pissing themselves screaming and dying, and a sure victory, considering what my father said. But you, you have no idea what will be on Iona. Keep it."

With her fingertips, she closed her hand.

He thanked her with a brief, hurried kiss that tasted like sweat and smelled of all the blood on his face. At least he had taken the initiative for once.

They parted with a shared look of concern.

Once in the tunnel, the clamor of the fight disappeared entirely. They progressed through a narrow conduit that was completely dark and impossible for everyone to stand up straight. Sören led the way, a torch in hand.

Fillan wondered about this hasty retreat as he thought back on their journey. If the English had discovered where the Stone of Fal had been moved to, it only confirmed once again the presence of a traitor in the ranks of the Brotherhood. Furthermore, it had to be a high-ranking traitor, as few knew where the artifact was taken. He himself had only learned of it at Lanark, when Deorsa had mentioned the Isle of Iona.

He thought again of the spy who had not ceased to be an interventionist since their departure from Lanarkshire, seeking a quarrel for any reason, and being generally unsufferable.

A tiny doubt crept into his mind and began to grow to the point of becoming unbearable.

What if Deorsa was the traitor? That would explain all the information, all the advances that the Templars had gained on the Assassins for a year. First in Berwick, then in Scone, in Lanark where a Lann Fala had popped up in the middle of his mission, and now at Dunstaffnage, where the English seemed to be waiting for them.

What if he was only trying to distract them, stirring up the fear that the Stone of Fal might fall into the hands of the Order, to lead them into a trap as MacDougall's fortress fell?

The thought horrified Fillan and made him stop.

"Well, what's going on with you?" launched Moira, who returned him to the present. "Move forwards, then!"

He absolutely had to tell someone his fears, but not now: Deorsa was right in front of him.

They exited the tunnel through a concealed gap in the middle of a grove. The beach, battered by the rising waves of the tide, opened before them. By following the directions of Alexander, they got their hands on two small sailing boats hidden under dead branches.

"You four, take this boat and head for the Isle of Mull," Sören ordered. "Wallace has a garrison of men who will be useful to us, not far from Loch Uisg."

"And since when do you get to decide everything, all by yourself?" retorted Deorsa.

"If you'd rather I get the fuck out and let you face the Lann Fala alone, don't hesitate to tell me."

The spy cursed under his breath.

"Aren't you coming with us, Sören?" asked Fillan, doing his best to hide the panic in his voice.

"No, I'll go along the coast to reach Iona directly. I will go much faster alone. Maybe I'll even get there before the Templars."

Fillan wanted to yell at his mentor to stop revealing his plans in front of Deorsa, and even more so not to leave without him, but he had no time. Sören approached and grabbed his arm.

"Be on your guard," he said. "I have a bad feeling about this."

"I…"

Sören pushed the first ship into the water and unfurled the sail, which the wind blew.

"Don't delay!" he shouted over the noise of the waves.

Ailéas called her brother to come aboard, and they soon found themselves cleaving the waves of the bay. Back on the peninsula, beyond the grove, the towers of Dunstaffnage appeared. Dark smoke rose from the heart of the fort, growing thicker and thicker.

Fillan wanted to dive into the turbulent waters to join Kyle and help her, but that would have meant leaving his sister with Deorsa.

He clung to the canoe, fighting the apprehension that invaded his mind.

33

DOUBTS

The frenzy of the battle was succeeded by calm, where blood and death were no more than the memory of another world.

The cool, damp wind carried the smell of rain and the storm, and blew without stopping on the Hebrides Sea, where the slender sailboat let herself be pushed at a brisk pace, her sail snapping in the gusts. The surface of the water was strangely serene, contrasted by the storm looming beyond the Isle of Mull in a web of ebony clouds.

Deorsa had taken his place at the front of the boat where he remained alone, muttering between his teeth. Fillan observed this strange attitude, which nourished his mistrust, from where he sat in the middle of the boat, maneuvering the sail.

Ever since he had met the spy at Dalkeith, he'd missed

any opportunity for discussion, gossip or, more simply, a tease.

Moira and Ailéas, meanwhile, sat at the stern and chatted quietly, unaware of Fillan's suspicions. Infrequent snippets of their conversation reached him, but he preferred to ignore them and focus on the waves and on Deorsa, ready to draw his sword at the slightest suspicious sign.

"How did you become a druid?" asked Ailéas, skimming the dark water with her fingers.

The freezing sea washed away some of the blood staining her hands from the fight.

"Like many things, it was written before my birth."

"Do you mean destiny?"

The healer nodded.

"I was born on the Isle of Lewis at the edge of the Highlands, within a druidic circle. All swore by the *Lebor Gabála Érenn**, the story from Ireland that tells how our regions are populated. I was raised among these distant beliefs, ancient practices, and traditions. I did not yet know how to tell that my future was already mapped out: I was going to follow the way of the druids, to become the receptacle of an ancient knowledge, the vehicle of the word of the gods."

---

* An important legend in Celtic Irish mythology, which tells how six mythical beings ruled the world before the human Gaels arrived.

Ailéas felt her curiosity getting carried away, again just a little girl about to discover the mysteries of the world through one of Alastair's stories.

"For a long time, I imagined that my mother was a druid," Ailéas confessed. "I have so few memories of my past, before the massacre of our clan. It's more like they're fleeting fragments that fade as soon as I think too hard about them. Maybe I tell myself these stories because it's reassuring to believe that my mother was different."

"Often our intuitions don't lie," answered Moira, grabbing her hand. "Even if she wasn't one, it is a desire and an energy that you carry within you. Has this been the case for a long time?"

"As far back as I can remember. My roots, those of the Highlands, and these bits of memory have always intrigued me. I felt out of place in Berwick. I had this strange urge to…"

She hesitated, searching for the words with her mouth half-open. She had rarely spoken about this subject.

"To return to the source?"

Ailéas nodded.

"I understand how you feel. Druids are more and more rare. It is a difficult path, and few take it. But it is also a magnificent way to commune with nature and the beings that are a part of it. I don't know of any better way to understand our world."

"I have a feeling this is the right path for me," Ailéas thought aloud, letting her eyes wander across the dark waters. "But…"

"But what?"

"I am a Child of Fal, destined to join the Brotherhood and become an Assassin, it seems."

"It's possible to have two destinies," Moira explained, "two threads woven by providence that come together to form a new one that is more solid, more tenacious."

Ailéas sighed deeply.

"What is it?"

"I have never heard so much about destiny as over the last two weeks. And the more I hear about it, the more it all seems blurry to me."

"If Sören were here, he would tell you that your destiny is in your own hands."

"I quite like that idea."

"Because it's reassuring, but that's only half true. I am convinced that fate is a path traced for us by providence. You can see it as a big, wide track. No one can accurately predict the events that await us. We are free to choose to walk it, but we can also take side roads that turn us astray. But that only lasts for a while; there is always something— an energy buried within us, or the random chance of life —to guide us back to the main path, as a reminder of what really matters."

"A bit like Sören with the Brotherhood?"

Moira looked surprised at first, then smiled.

"You've only been with us two weeks and you've already got the measure of us. Most people have to work hard to read their fellows. That's a druid quality, you know?"

Ailéas felt the color rise in her muddy and blood-stained cheeks.

"Although Sören pretends not to see it and pretends to be free of destiny, each of his decisions leads him back to the Brotherhood. He is a Child of Fal, and the line drawn for him is to protect the heritage of his ancestors. The more he tries to escape, the more the line, stretched like the string of a bow, brings him back to the main path. Don't tell him that—he'll yell at you."

They looked at each other and laughed.

"Destiny is not exclusive to him and the Children of Fal," Moira continued. "Look at Kyle. For a long time, she turned her back on her clan, yet today she finds herself standing with them to defend Dunstaffnage and her family. The circle of fate keeps turning on itself, forming a complex knot."

Ailéas took a moment to mull over Moira's words. She had always believed in providence and now had the feeling that it truly existed. She caught a glimpse of this famous path unfolding in front of her, and it made her dizzy.

"Something is bothering you, isn't it?" said the healer. "Beyond this question of destiny."

"What makes you say that?" she answered, on the defensive.

"The last few days, you've seemed a bit like a hedgehog caught in a trap."

"That's cheating," Ailéas retorted. "You just said that the druids read people."

"What's taking over your thoughts?"

She watched Moira, hesitant. Could she confide in a woman she barely knew? She had already told her a lot, more than anyone.

"I have…"

She broke off, because putting the emotions she felt deep inside her into words was giving them more strength. She found the support she needed in Moira's green eyes.

"I find it difficult to understand my place in all of this. Look at Fillan: he's evolved during this year, he has trained and joined the Brotherhood. As for me, I only suffered and stagnated. I feel out of step, behind."

"I think you're on the wrong track," Moira said, crossing her arms and frowning. "You said yourself that you knew for a long time that your place was not in Berwick, correct?"

Ailéas nodded silently.

"You already felt that your destiny lay elsewhere. You have no reason to envy your brother, for the path he traveled was necessary for him to understand what you already knew.

Your place, which you've been feeling for years, is for you to embrace and make your own choices."

Ailéas meditated on these words for a long time, striving to see the future that could be hers more clearly.

Something else was tormenting her, but she decided to keep it to herself, staring at her brother, as deep in concentration as he was on the tension of the sails.

That something else was him.

For a long time, she had feared that he was dead. For a long time, she had thought she would never find him. Her heart had leapt with joy at their reunion and alleviated the pain caused by Bradley's death. They had experienced horror, death, combat, and had been forced to grow into the opposites of what they used to be. Despite this, she once more felt the wall of ice that Fillan had erected between them in recent years. He had not yet resolved within himself a conflict that she had begun to suspect. She hurt for him. For them.

She squinted in his direction again and saw his face, more closed-off than ever.

The hilly and fractured form of Mull approached and the wind intensified, blowing the sails harder. Fillan was forced to hold on tight to prevent them from capsizing.

"What led you to join Sören's group?" Ailéas asked, watching her brother struggle.

"It's far from a happy story," Moira admitted. "Over

time, I've come to believe that the encounters that form the most solid bonds can only be forged by the saddest events."

Ailéas thought back to the massacre of her clan, which had caused her to meet Alastair, then the one in Berwick, which had crossed her path with Bradley's. Perhaps the druid was telling the truth.

"Sören was still alone when I joined him. It had been some time since he'd turned his back on the Brotherhood. As for me, my clan was massacred by the newly formed Lann Fala."

"I'm sorry…"

"It was a long time ago," Moira said, with a wave of her hand.

"Was it because your circle was linked to the Assassins?"

"You would think so, given our beliefs about the old gods and our desire to protect their heritage, but this was not because of that. All the Order wanted was the knowledge of lost times, which they have thus far obtained only in part."

"This massacre, how did you survive it?"

"Another twist of fate. When the Templars arrived at our dwelling, I had gone to pick a rare plant that does not grow anywhere except the base of the Calanais menhirs. Coming back, the first thing I saw was the smoke. And as I got closer, more and more corpses appeared."

Ailéas shuddered, remembering the streets of Berwick, invaded by panic and death.

"In the end, we've all experienced the same tragedy, for the most part. Shortly after, I swore to become one of the best druid-warriors in Scotland and to perpetuate the knowledge of my kin."

Ailéas would never have suspected that such a tragedy marked the life of the healer, who was always so calm and in a perpetual good mood.

They were quickly approaching to the Isle of Mull. They turned at the mouth of Loch Spelve, which split the coast in two to form a vast expanse of flat, sparkling water. Ten minutes later, they disembarked, soaking their boots in the frozen water and trying to avoid slipping on the pebbles.

"No doubt about it," said Fillan, pointing to the landscape ahead. "The English are already here, somewhere."

Columns of charcoal-black smoke rose from various places on the island.

"All the more reason not to waste a moment!" exclaimed Deorsa, who had stopped mumbling. "Let's get started!"

They dashed off into the grass, and Fillan made sure to always keep his hand on the hilt of the sword at his side. The spy dragged them into a frantic race, as if they were being pursued by the end of time itself. The magnificent landscapes of Mull unfolded before them and seemed to stretch out infinitely under the thundering sky.

After half an hour, Deorsa stopped to look around at the edge of a forest.

"If I remember correctly, Wallace should have posted his men here."

There was no trace of anyone.

"And you have an excellent memory, huh?" Fillan reminded him, no longer able to hide the suspicion in his voice.

The spy looked at him, pretending not to understand what he was implying.

As Fillan was about to draw his sword, several creaks sounded from inside the grove and startled them.

A group of men appeared with their swords drawn.

34

IONA

It didn't take Fillan long to notice that the warriors wore tartans. Judging by their build and their weapons, they were Highlanders, certainly Wallace's men. He stayed in spite of everything his instincts were telling him. The dark vault of the trees overhanging them reflected off his blade.

The first to step out of the shade of the trees appeared in poor shape. They wore makeshift bandages, pieces of cloth torn from their own clothes, soaked in dark blood.

"Who's there?" Fillan called out, without giving Deorsa time to speak.

"Fillan, is that you?"

His fingers stopped tensing on the pommel of his sword. He knew that voice.

"James!" he said, relieved.

Father Thomas's apprentice left the shelter of the forest.

He was limping and a large gash on the side of his skull had let enough blood run down his neck to smear the top of his gambeson.

"James?" repeated the spy, visibly annoyed. "But what the hell are you doing here?"

Fillan wanted to jump at his throat. Couldn't he just be happy to see a familiar face? It only served to deepen Fillan's mistrust.

"As soon as Master Wallace learned that the Order discovered where the Stone of Fal was to be taken, he commanded me to come this way."

"William knows? Since when?"

"A little over a week. We were stopping in Glasgow when he cornered a Templar informant. It didn't take long to make him talk. I came as fast as possible; I only arrived this morning."

"Why didn't Wallace tell us?" Fillan hastened to ask.

"He tried. He sent many messages to clans where he thought you might go."

"Since we've been traveling the whole time," Moira mused, "it's no wonder we missed them."

"How did you know that the Order marched on Iona, then?" prompted James.

"We were at Dunstaffnage when the fortress was attacked by the English. Deorsa was the first to suspect the danger, because they were far too north."

"And Sören?"

"He set sail to reach Iona as quickly as possible. He asked us to find the garrison to bring reinforcements to the island."

"You're out of luck on that front," James replied, gesturing pitifully at the wounded warriors.

"What happened?" asked the spy in a loud voice, not wanting to be left out of the conversation.

"When I arrived on Mull in the morning, the Lann Fala and several Englishmen had already landed. I dashed to the garrison, but William's men had already engaged a detachment led by a Templar. We got rid of them, but…"

"You mean you're the only survivors?!"

"Many perished," James confirmed. "However, when they saw the English land, a few headed straight for Iona to reinforce the defense of the convoy."

"Where's Wallace?!"

"When I left him, he was leading a rebellion against an English garrison, not far from Gilshochill. He wanted to join us but was slowed down."

"And the English?" Deorsa continued.

Fillan stared at him darkly. He got goosebumps of dread seeing the spy glean every fragment of information, so as not to lose track of everyone's movements. He could easily imagine how much this manipulator studied every eventuality to feed his own purposes, whatever they might be.

James half-slumped in exhaustion. Moira, who had rushed to help several warriors, came to tend to him.

"They're on their way to Iona. Maybe they've already reached the island. We're only alive because they were in a hurry. This forest is just a mass grave."

He spat a glut of blood onto the ground.

"We don't have a second to lose," said the spy, ignoring the apprentice's moan of pain. "Do you have horses?"

"They ran away during the fight," said one of the wounded warriors. "We only managed to recover three."

"That'll do the trick anyway! James and one of you," he said to the wounded, "you're coming with us. We'll set off in pairs."

The apprentice rose to fetch the horses.

"We'll help you!" called Fillan, grabbing his sister's arm to lead her away, seeing an opportunity to escape the eyes and ears of the spy.

They plunged into the woods with long strides.

"What's going on?" asked Ailéas once they were sufficiently separated from the others, recognizing that her twin seemed worried.

"It's Deorsa. I suspect him of working for the Order."

"It's true that he's an asshole," said Ailéas, "but moving from that to betrayal is a big jump…"

James took in the corpses strewn over the humus of the forest, thoughtfully, before asking:

"Did you tell anyone else about it? Sören, maybe?"

"I would have liked to," replied Fillan, "but we ran all the way here from Dunstaffnage and I had no chance to do it. I couldn't even say anything to Ailéas."

"Is that why you were so tense in the canoe?" she realized.

"Yes, I was waiting for him to let the mask slip from one moment to the next. James, you don't seem surprised."

"Thomas has been harboring suspicions for a few months. There is a traitor within the Brotherhood. My master suspects that it is a high-ranking individual. His doubts first fell on Amy Comyn at the end of the autumn, but he investigated, and she'd done nothing wrong. They then looked into the case of Deorsa."

"And what did they discover?" asked Ailéas while repositioning the stirrups of one of the horses.

"Up to now, nothing at all. Spying on a spy is no easy task. Most of the informants they could think to talk to are already embedded in his meticulous spider web. But the fact that the Templars discovered the whereabouts of Lia Fàil only reinforces the suspicions against him."

"We have to be on our guard," Fillan agreed, grabbing the pommel of his weapon.

"That's for sure!"

They climbed onto their mounts and returned to the others at a trot. They immediately set off.

Deorsa rode with one of the Highlanders, Ailéas with Moira, and Fillan with James, who he was forced to hold tightly onto as they crossed the island because he was so exhausted from the fight. He almost fell off their horse several times.

The Isle of Mull could have been beautiful.

Mossy rock sprang up amongst the rolling green hills, which created irregular chains culminating in fractal compositions beneath the stormy sky that loomed in ruptures of hues. Yes, the Isle of Mull could have been beautiful, were it not for the charred dwellings, the corpses that the Templars had left in their wake, and the abominable sense of imminent danger.

They were speeding through a glen[*] when Fillan had a sudden feeling of déjà vu. He thought he recognized the peak of a mountain here, the curve that opened out to the river in the hollow of the valley there.

He'd walked this earth before. He felt it deep inside his being.

Perhaps it was in this life, when his clan had not yet suffered the wrath of the Templars. Or perhaps it was in another life, the memory of an important event that had taken place there inscribed in his genes, passed down through the mist and the drizzle of ancient times.

[*] Long and deep valleys common to Scotland.

He turned his head, sought Ailéas's gaze, and saw in her eyes that she felt the same thing.

Both now understood just how important their link with the Highlands really was.

During their breathless race, they didn't encounter any Lann Fala, or any English soldiers, which only increased their apprehension.

The time ticked by under the hammering of hooves while the sky became so dark it looked like night.

The east coast of Mull appeared, and with it the Isle of Iona, whose curves seemed to spring from the ocean.

"The Templars have already crossed the arm of the sea!" shouted Moira, pointing to new columns of smoke.

"Do you hear that?" Fillan called out.

All fell silent to listen to the wind howling in their ears, carrying the sound of the waves. The clink of weapons and the screams of terror added to the soundscape.

"Weapons! They're still fighting," guessed Deorsa. "The Templars and the English must not long have reached the island."

He spurred on his steed, shouting, and the rest all imitated him.

When their cavalcade exited the beach, they found themselves face to face with a detachment of soldiers who had remained behind to defend a wooden wharf. There were eight of them, including one who looked like a colossus.

"Oh, crap!" Ailéas cried.

"What do we do?" asked James.

Deorsa drew one of his daggers.

"They've seen us," he said. "We have no choice but to rush into the fold."

They all drew their weapons and charged.

Fillan was the first to reach the group of warriors. As he drew level with them, he twirled his sword of Fal and beheaded one of them. Ignoring his wounds, James swung a vertical blow that disfigured another of their opponents who screamed abominably as he collapsed on the ground, holding the shreds of his face.

The rest of the troop did almost as much damage. By the time they dismounted, their horses having exhausted the last of their strength, four Englishmen were still fit to fight.

The twins went into battle without thinking or consulting one another. They moved with incredible speed, using erratic movements to confuse their opponents.

One moment they were sprinting in a straight line, the next, they'd take a sidestep before jumping in the opposite direction.

Both made contact with a huge warrior, whom they massacred in a few seconds. Fillan chose an upward attack, taking care to aim for his opponent's groin from where a stream of blood gushed out almost immediately upon contact with his sword. Ailéas had jumped up to slice her weapon across the collarbone of the colossus, whom she wouldn't have been able to fight in the traditional way.

The sky seemed to explode as a flash lit it up.

The heavy air was broken by rain, first as fine as silk threads, but which soon became hailstones. Thunder rumbled and the ground shook.

"Come and get me, demons!" shouted one of the last two surviving Englishmen to Fillan and his sister.

The water streamed down his helmet and echoed off the metal of his armor. The hand that held his sword was shaking.

Fillan was about to pounce, but there was no time. Ailéas rushed into contact with both warriors. She dodged their attacks, crouched down and slid across the sodden ground to finish her run behind their backs. She pirouetted and, swishing Fal's blade through the air, she struck the two warriors in the head at the same time. They collapsed with a gasp. Only the sounds of the tapping of the downpour and the thunder remained.

Everyone was flabbergasted by the show of force that she had just demonstrated. Fillan, too. Despite all the training he had undergone, she remained a better fighter than him by far. Moira approached the teenage girl.

"And you think you're lagging behind?" she breathed. "You are exactly where you should be, perfect and strong."

Ailéas brushed away a sodden lock of hair from her face and smiled.

Meanwhile, Fillan approached James, who seemed on the verge of fainting. He placed the apprentice's arm around his neck for support.

"Leave me here," James said. "I'll slow you down. There's no more danger. Or at least I think so."

"Shut up, you're coming with us."

"Do you think we have time to chat?" yelled Deorsa. "Let's take these boats and get to Iona."

They pulled two small boats into the water and jumped inside.

It only took a few minutes to reach the other side. They moved quickly because the storm was growing, angrier than ever, and provoking powerful waves. Soon further crossings would be impossible.

They barely had time to disembark before they saw a massacre much worse than that of Mull. The bodies of island residents—monks, nuns, and simple peasants—lay everywhere, lifeless.

"By the Sidh…" Moira whispered, tears in her eyes.

"Where are we headed?" Fillan asked.

"The monastery," Deorsa said simply. "The Stone was to be transported there. Maybe Wallace's men had time to get it to safety."

"I doubt it," James said, pointing his sword at the bodies of Highlanders bathed in mud pools mixed with blood.

There were also the corpses of many English soldiers,

and even those of the Lann Fala. The horror had taken place only a few minutes before their arrival. Some bodies were still twitching and moaning in agony, while others were simply and silently bleeding to death.

Fillan could not help but look for the body of Sören, a lump in his throat.

They resumed their quest at full speed, ignoring their fatigue. They were nearing their goal and Fillan sensed that James had regained some energy, as he no longer needed to support him. The monastery was not difficult to find, because Iona was sparsely populated. They glimpsed the Stone of Fal, which had been hastily abandoned near the gaping entrance of the building.

But it was not alone.

Cornavii, whose deer-antler helmet was slashed by the wind and rain, stood beside it, slaying the last of its guardians with his broadsword. Two other red-cloaked warriors accompanied him, killing poor souls.

A new flash lit up the heavens, making their armor gleam, and the thunder clapped nearby with a bestial roar.

35

THUNDER

The rain was so heavy that the entire landscape of Iona disappeared beneath sheaths of gray. In the distance, the clouds looked like they were falling from the heavens, like the claws of giants eager to grab the earth.

Cornavii leaned his huge blood-covered sword on his shoulder and stared at each of the new arrivals. Facing Fillan, the deer-antler helm stilled for a long time. The warrior's eyes were barely visible but stared at him intently.

"I have hunted you for eight years, Lowlands to Highlands, but in the end it's you who's come to me!" he sneered. "You are not a Child of Fal for no reason."

"Shut up and get away from the Stone!" spat Fillan, putting up his guard.

He felt an inconceivable rage boiling inside him that ignited his entire being. The fear that once paralyzed him had definitively dissipated in favor of anger and a desire for revenge that made his head spin.

"You've learned to bark since we met in Scone. We'll soon find out if you also learned to bite."

Fillan gripped his sword tighter.

"Is that the Claidheamh Fal you're holding in your hands there? So, you've become a filthy Brotherhood pig? That would explain why we had such a hard time flushing you out. No matter, it won't protect you."

"He told you to shut up!" roared Ailéas, stepping forward to stand at her brother's side.

The Lann Fala barely turned his head to look at her.

"You… To think you were right under my nose all this time!" He burst into laughter that sounded demented and terrifying. "Oh, how the gods do like to play their little games," he said, raising an arm towards the clouds like a madman. "I suspected that old codger Bradley Dacre would be a problem, but I never imagined he'd be so quick to betray England. He got the death he deserved, skewered like a pig. Did you kill him, kid? After he helped you hide all this time?"

Fillan pursed his lips, a gesture that the Templar did not fail to notice, which evoked a new tirade of ghostly sounding giggles.

"Oh, I see! Surely you acted on behalf of the Assassins, eager to rouse this pathetic rebellion, imagining that we would see nothing but the fire. You're no more than a puppet swept along by the winds of fate and the will of the Brotherhood. Pathetic. Perfectly shabby. Tell me one thing, kid: was it really your decision, or was it just that the Brotherhood knew how to use you at the right time?"

The words cut deep, sharp as a blade. Fillan had asked himself this question dozens of times since Lanark, resonating with Sören's advice.

"That's enough!" Deorsa called out. "Let's get this over with!"

Out of the corner of her eye, Ailéas glimpsed a movement among the rainfall pounding the heights of Iona Monastery. She forced herself to act as though nothing had happened, because she was the only one who could see it from where she stood. Her heart began pounding; she had to buy some time.

"Why hunt us down?" she asked.

"There's no point arguing with him!" said the spy.

"Ah, why not, after all?" retorted the Lann Fala. "These ignorant kids are going to die, anyway. I am a merciful man. In any case, I am much more so than the gods who pull their strings to lead them more quickly to their deaths."

Assured of his victory, Cornavii became talkative. *It couldn't have worked out better*, thought Ailéas, risking another look upwards.

"Understand one thing," said the warrior to the twins. "In the beginning, it was nothing personal. The Children of Fal are an error, a degeneracy engendered by a god who allowed himself to be misled by the Gaels. Your existence is an insult, an aberration. Your destiny is to join the Assassins; mine, as well as that of the Lann Fala, is to eradicate you."

Ailéas caught a glimmer on the building tiles in the pouring rain.

"I failed to kill you eight years ago. Can you imagine the affront? I, the leader of the Lann Fala, unable to flush out and kill two filthy brats?"

"You failed eight years ago. You will fail again," she said confidently.

"Oh, I don't think so. Not now that I have this in my possession."

He put one knee on the ground and moved his hand towards the Stone of Destiny.

"Lia Fàil," he whispered.

Seeing him do this, Moira was about to scream, but at the same time a shadow leapt from the roofs of the monastery, illuminated by the lightning that spread across the sky in a long tear.

With the exception of the Templar, everyone saw what Ailéas had barely been able to make out. Sören swooped down on Cornavii, the blade drawn from his leather armband.

"My Lord, behind you!" shouted a voice at the top of their lungs, trying to be heard over the rumbling thunder.

There was another flash, and chaos erupted.

Stepping aside, Cornavii dodged Sören's attack, and he landed heavily in a puddle of water. He tried to get up but received a powerful kick to the face that sent him rolling to the ground.

Meanwhile, Fillan, Ailéas, and Moira watched Deorsa in horror.

Two bulging and amazed eyes sat above a half-open mouth from which a stream of blood poured out, diluted by drops of rain. James had just sliced him with a short blade across the throat, as if to silence him.

Yet he was the one who had alerted Cornavii to Sören's attack a few seconds earlier, not the spy. The thunder rumbled loud enough to burst their eardrums.

"You?" Fillan exclaimed in a barely audible whisper.

"Kill them all!" Cornavii shouted, swinging down his immense sword onto Sören, who narrowly blocked the blow by brandishing his own blade.

James took advantage of the element of surprise and leapt up to cut the throat of the Highlander soldier who had been looking joyfully at the lifeless body of Deorsa slumped in the mud.

A second passed. There was a trickle of blood. And a hiccup.

Once his second victim hit the ground, he went up against Ailéas with a lightning-fast stabbing attack. His dagger bounced off her sword of Fal as she dodged with agility, not taken by surprise. He showered her with blows and forced her into defensive postures, which made her use all her flexibility and speed. She kept blocking and wouldn't leave him any openings as she retreated without managing to strike a single blow.

Fillan could not believe his eyes; every word that James had spoken flooded his mind in a wave of lies and deceptions.

He shook himself to go rescue his sister but found himself up against another of Cornavii's acolytes, armed with an extended spear. The other red-cloaked soldier rushed at Moira.

Every single one of them was battling as nature itself unleashed its savagery. After another roaring thunderbolt, hail pelted down for a few moments, forming a thin layer of slippery diamonds.

By turning about, Fillan dodged a blow from his opponent at the last second. He saw that his twin was losing ground. After a flurry of blows, James had used the unsuspected momentum to circumvent Ailéas and position himself behind her back. His blade was pressed against her pale throat. Ailéas, terrified, tremblingly spread her arms in surrender.

"Nooo!" yelled Fillan, awkwardly pushing away his own attacker.

"Kill her!" Cornavii bellowed. "Kill her if you want to keep your place at my side in the Order!"

Forced to turn in the wrong direction to avoid the sickle blade that brushed his arm, Fillan had to think fast.

"James!" he yelled. "Glory in death is no glory!"

He wasn't sure where that phrase came from, but the apprentice who had seemed so sure of himself a second earlier hesitated and stopped moving.

"Ailéas, close your eyes!" cried Moira.

She threw a vial on the ground that produced a blinding flash as it broke. Disoriented, James released his grip on Ailéas as he flung up a hand to shield his eyes. He did not see her blow coming. Her Fal sword pierced his abdomen. The tip of the blade, beaded with red, poked out on the other side between his shoulder blades.

"Damn, what was that?!" she cried.

Too busy with her own fight, the druid did not answer.

Ailéas joined her brother in a few strides to lend him a hand against his assailant.

"I'm here!" she exclaimed.

"I'm doing just fine on my own!"

She stared at him blankly, hurt.

"Sorry... I..."

The Lann Fala made no allowances for such heart-to-hearts, and he slashed at Fillan's shoulder, eliciting a scream. Ailéas charged, and the twins fought side by side, both trying not to get in the way of each other's attacks.

Moira was struggling, too. She could be formidable,

for she wielded her staff and her long, tapered dagger with incredible dexterity, but the Lann Fala she fought was a colossus. She used her blinding vials twice. The first one let her get in a slash to the side and the second, to the thigh. Her opponent did not flinch, however, and resumed the assault by bellowing, turning into a real maniac.

"You are tough little thing, my boy!" she said. "Why don't you just give up before you get hurt?"

The man growled and spat.

"As you wish!"

She planted her stick in the ground and used it as a support to push the warrior back with a mighty kick. Utilizing the newfound distance between them, she aimed and threw her last vial, which shattered on the Lann Fala's face. A blinding flash was followed by a howl of pain and a trail of blood that mingled with the water pooling on the ground. At the exact moment of the burst of light, the druid had thrown her dagger between the two eyes of the Lann Fala.

"Always listen to a druid," she muttered, retrieving her blade with a spongy noise.

Fillan and Ailéas also reached the end of their fight. After the first few minutes of their dual clash, they had synchronized their movements. Their swords moved with such fluidity that they seemed to fly on their own through the air, giving the impression that they were wielding the twins and not the other way around.

The Order soldier collapsed with his skull split open.

Fillan felt like giving a shout of victory, but the most dangerous of them all was still alive.

Near the Stone of Fal, Cornavii and Sören were fighting fiercely. The mercenary used all his talent and exhausted all his techniques to try and defeat the Templar. He moved swiftly through the mud and rain, leapt and arched back with a flurry of various attacks. His usual dance of death was more terrifying than ever; there were moments when he almost felled the helmeted warrior, brushing him with the edge of his blade or narrowly failing to unbalance him.

The leader of the Lann Fala was as steadfast as a mountain and returned blow for blow with disproportionate brutality. It was as if he read and anticipated each of the Norwegian's movements. By evading a close-range attack, he was able to land a violent punch to the mercenary's face before propelling him back with the edge of his blade against the wall of the monastery, squirting blood into the air.

"Sören!" Moira and the twins cried.

He fell to his knees and, just before collapsing completely, they distinctly saw the blood flooding down the front of his leather armor.

Cornavii looked around at the inert bodies of his warriors and made a show of stretching and cracking his neck.

"This little game has gone on long enough," he said.

He knelt before the Stone of Fal, removed one of his gloves, and put his hand on the soaked rock.

"Lia Fàil!" Moira groaned, clutching her staff in panic.

They saw the Lann Fala's lips move but could hear nothing through the storm. A new flash, which seemed as supernatural as it was bright, fell on the monastery and set fire to its frame. Sunken into the ground softened by downpours, the Stone of Fal gave off a faint glow. Droplets of water that rained down hovered inches away from the rock, beating against an invisible barrier.

Mysterious arabesques began to glow on the block of sandstone and a stream of golden energy emanated from it to surround Cornavii's hand.

"Oh no!" Moira continued to moan.

"What is that?" Ailéas wondered.

"The power of the gods."

"What can we do?"

The druid reached for the pouches attached to her waist, but she had no more vials. She went on the attack alone, uttering a cry of rage under the bewildered eyes of the twins.

"What are you thinking, poor puppet?" laughed the Lann Fala in his horrible voice.

He stood up, drawing the energy of the Stone towards him and extending his hand. Moira staggered in the middle of her run, as if hit by an invisible force. She fell to her knees, dropped her staff and dagger, and put her head in her hands.

"Look upon my power, vile creature!" sneered Cornavii, whose eyes shone a fiery yellow.

She began to scream, louder and louder, drowning out the cacophony of the storm.

"You see! I told you I wouldn't fail! Not with the Stone of Fal under my control. I will kill you, avenge the affront of your escape, and regain my honor with the Order."

Driven by the increasingly abominable cries of the druid, the twins charged into battle, but Cornavii sent a new wave of energy that knocked them down.

They collapsed to the ground like puppets.

Fillan felt like his head was exploding. Visions of horror invaded his mind, and terror paralyzed his body. He saw himself destroying familiar members of the Brotherhood in order to establish his dominance within the organization. In this nightmarish dream, he massacred, conquered, and plundered to get what he had always dreamed of: fame and wealth.

Overtaken by the influence of the Stone of Fal, he was only rage and envy, before being swept away in another flood of emotions.

A new scene unfolded in his mind, in which he stabbed Ailéas in the middle of the night without an ounce of hesitation, and rejoiced after killing Sören. Thus, he became the only Child of Fal, the only descendant of the Gaels and heir to the gods.

Fillan opened his eyes, trying to fight against those thoughts that weren't really his.

Less than a yard from him, he met the emerald green eyes of his sister, filled with tears.

She had the pleading look of a little girl whose only hope was to wake up from the nightmare she was living.

He stared intently at her face, clinging to it like an anchor to remain grounded and extricate himself from the harmful influence of the artifact.

Ailéas grimaced, moaned, and Fillan felt a barricade give way in his mind, as if he had already experienced this before.

A memory surged.

9

The dark furrows of the fire blew to the unsteady rhythm of the wind.

"Hide under there and do not come out under any circumstance. I will find Ailéas."

Fillan obeyed without taking the time to look one last time at his mother's face or to kiss her. He slid his little body under the cart cluttered with straw, canvas bags, and hid. She released his hand after a final squeeze that panic only allowed him to do with his fingertips.

By the light of the flames that lit up the night, he saw her boots walk away from the carriage in long strides. The ground trembled in a pounding of hooves, then a sharp, heartbreaking cry rung out and he saw her slump to the ground around the corner, broken.

He waited for her to get up, watched for a movement, but another galloping horse trampled her. She rolled two yards before falling still, covered with earth.

New tears mingled with those that had already flooded the child's cheeks when he heard the first screams.

Under cover of the soft light of twilight, he had been playing in the street, not far from the well and his house when the tumult had erupted. The warriors had arrived in a whirlwind from the north of the village and had massacred the first members of the clan without asking any questions.

From his hiding place, he could not help but watch the horror that was spreading everywhere. Everything was just a mixture of menacing lights and fleeting darkness.

A smell of urine filled his nostrils. It was his own. He felt ashamed, as he hadn't done that in years. What would the warriors of the clan say if they saw him like this, his hose soaked? His father would be furious when he found out.

People ran in all directions. They weren't just black, fleeting, and impersonal shapes that howled in the night. They were people who, every day, he rubbed shoulders with, played and laughed with, and yet in their terror and suffering they became foreign to him. Death had this curious power.

"Fillan!" whispered a small voice.

He turned his head and his heart jumped when he saw Ailéas across the street, under the awning of their house. She was squatting under a pile of crates attached to a barrel.

9

In silence, he gestured for her to join him, but she shook her head.

She was too afraid, because from where she was, she could see a towering form that moved in the misty darkness and which was growing clearer and closer.

By the glow of flames and to the rhythm of heavy and terrifying steps, glinting deer antlers emerged.

The two children made themselves smaller than they already were, trying to disappear.

Astride a stallion robed in darkness, a warrior more colossal than all the others slowly emerged from the smoke and ashes. He looked like a gigantic deer with the helmet he wore, adorned with metallic antlers. He swung his sword with a stroke of rage and made a runner collapse on the ground, right beside the cart. Despite the blood, Fillan recognized Argyll, the blacksmith's apprentice.

He clapped his hand over his mouth to keep from moaning in fear.

"Find me the kids!" ordered the deer-warrior. "All the kids

of this rat hole! And take them to the central square! You better not have lied to me," he shouted to something he dragged behind him at the end of a rope.

It was Rhona, the village druid.

They disappeared in the plumes of smoke.

Fillan chewed his lower lip with all his might to keep from screaming. He knew what awaited him if he were to make a noise. The livid eyes of the lifeless body that lay before him kept reminding him. He heard a creak and saw the flames spread at full speed, engulfing his house in a fierce crackling.

Ale! I have to go save Ale! *he kept thinking.*

Paralyzed with fear, he couldn't move.

The screams of other village children broke out, and he tried to cover his ears without success. The vociferations faded away, one after the next.

Ailéas got up, having finally found the strength to join him once another red-cloaked warrior had crossed the street. About to take off, she barely had time to awkwardly protect her face. A beam had given way in a series of creaks and the house collapsed on her.

For a moment the sky lit up, creating new stars from the embers that faded silently.

The little girl disappeared under the rubble and the burning wood, letting out a short cry.

Fillan felt his heart rip but couldn't do anything, paralyzed.

He lay on the ground, feeling the flames slowly gnawing at the cart and roasting his back.

He had just enough time to see the rain falling in torrents, then he fainted.

9

A few hours later, a fist that pulled him out from under the cart woke him up. He tried to scream, but his throat was so dry that he only managed to choke.

"Don't worry," a hooded man reassured him, checking his wrist. "I'm here to keep you safe."

He gave off an unpleasant smell of blood. But at least he wasn't wearing a red cape.

Fillan let himself be picked up, not even having the strength to cry.

The stranger took a large step, but the child gripped so tightly to his shoulder that he was forced to stop. The child had seen a ragdoll stained with blood on the ground.

"What is it?"

Unable to speak, the little one just pointed at the rubble.

The man hesitated, but faced with the persistence of the boy who was using his last strength to pull on his fur coat, he moved closer.

A small hand, inert, protruded from under the smoking ridge. He freed her after putting the boy down and discovered the body of a little girl, covered in ash and soot.

Her belly slowly swelled with the rhythm of her breathing.

"Well spotted, child! She's alive!"

"Ale…" whispered Fillan.

Now in the arms of the stranger, tossed about by each of his steps, he stared at his sister's slack face.

Blood dripped from a long gash across her left eyebrow. He grabbed his sister's hand and shook it, using the little strength he had left.

"Ale, I'm sorry, so sorry…" he repeated to himself until fainting again.

The memory came flooding back to him.

At the time, he had concealed it in the deepest reaches of his being, locked behind an unreachable door. This amnesia was the only way his mind had found to bury the guilt that gnawed at him for not having rescued his sister, who'd come so close to death.

The scar on her face was proof of his monstrous selfishness and his weakness.

He had buried it and the emotion had metamorphosed: rather than hating himself, he had come to hate her. He couldn't bear that she regularly did what he himself had been unable to do, and save the other. The smallest disagreement was the opportunity to push her away, to raise a wall of ice between them to further lock the door behind which his past and his suffering kept knocking to get out.

"Your guilt is twofold: one recent, the other older," Tilda had told him. It was only now the door had been flung wide open that he understood how much the old druid had read him like an open book.

9

In his ears resounded the words of little Ailéas who he had seen that same night, and he understood that it was time. To forgive himself first, but also to get up and act, to not have similar regrets in the future.

36

LIA FÀIL

The rain smattering against his face brought him quickly back to the present.

The flames that had taken hold of the abbey had been extinguished in the deluge. Not a single wisp of smoke remained.

Fillan felt a penetrating, visceral fatigue. Every muscle, every joint, every bit of his body screamed for rest, to give in. In a flash, an unspeakable weariness overwhelmed him and he contemplated abandoning everything to disappear into the nothingness of the Sidh.

Less than a yard away, Ailéas watched him with pleading eyes. Her scar was dripping with rain and stood out from the white of her skin. She held out a hand that he seized for an embrace with the tips of his fingers, with as much strength as he could muster.

He felt dizzy, like he had just woken up from an endless nightmare. It cost him terribly to escape the harmful influence diffused by the Stone of Fal. He gripped his sword and stood, staring at Cornavii who was still in front of the artifact, haloed with light.

"How can you get up?!" the Lann Fala asked, annoyed.

He extended his hand to project a new wave of energy.

Around the rock, the light trembled, hesitant, before obeying and spreading, unleashed.

Fillan saw succeeding fragments of scenes that were neither memories nor dreams, just horrific projections. He anchored himself in reality, the present, but above all, in his emotions. Every step he took drove away his childlike guilt, for he was accomplishing what he had been unable to accomplish years before.

"You are not worthy of the Stone," he said in a low, broken voice.

The words had mysteriously sprung from his mouth, and he had no idea how they came to him. Cornavii watched the energy flowing from the rock with an unhappy air.

Fillan charged forward, brandishing the sword of Fal with all his strength. The Lann Fala was forced to wield his broadsword with one hand to block, the other hand too concentrated on the artifact.

"You don't stand a chance, kid."

The gigantic sword swung in a brutal arc, hissing in

the air as it whipped through the rain. The tip of the blade brushed Fillan's throat, who almost fell backwards. He retaliated with a series of short sequences and realized that, as he harassed his opponent, Cornavii had been forced to release his control over the Stone and the glow surrounding it was shrinking.

Lying on the floor, Moira stopped screaming.

Ailéas woke and stared at the cloudy sky. The visions of horror that had invaded her mind at first matched the nightmares that had plagued her dreams for years, until exploding to become even more terrible, making her relive perpetual massacres.

She took a deep breath to calm her racing heart and heard the clang of metal. Her brother was no longer beside her. Ignoring the dizziness that assailed her, she stood to join him. He was dodging a side attack from Cornavii.

Upon seeing her, Fillan's heart lightened. He was glad that she stood at his side to face the one who had made them orphans, twice.

Cornavii blocked a dexterous attack from the teenager by leaning his blade into his back and used the opportunity to deliver a powerful kick to Fillan, which made him double over. After this reprise, he approached the Stone of Fal, which he placed his hand on again.

The golden flow hesitated once more, longer this time, before increasing its power.

The surge of energy left the twins staggering and dazed, and the Lann Fala tried to take advantage of this by thrusting the sword in a devastating downward attack.

Ailéas felt the blade brush against her shirt and whoosh past her neck. Her brother blocked the resulting sweep to protect her and heaved a muffled curse. Under the power of the blow, the pain in his shoulder returned and restricted some of his movements. She in turn moved forward, aiming for Cornavii's side without success.

She took advantage of the movement of his weapon's backswing to modify the angle of her arm. The blade thrust up, slashed the Lann Fala's breastplate, and hit the helm on its way, snapping one of its antlers clean off.

"You filthy bitch!" he growled, his ghostly voice becoming more snake-like than ever.

He returned the attack, furious.

The confrontation persisted as the rain continued to pour, and the thunder and lightning still shook the ground. The twins had coordinated well to stand up to Cornavii, using tricks and ingenuity, but he was talented and clever. He used the power of the Stone of Fal to create openings in their defense or to dodge fatal blows, making the energy that surrounded it explode to form a blinding shield.

This advantage made him unbeatable.

Ailéas was the first to understand that she and Fillan would soon succumb, seeing how much their strength was weakening. On the verge of losing hope. As she pulled out of a dodge, she saw Moira who had knelt, trembling and trying to be heard over the din of the storm.

"Lia Fàil… Your swords…" said the druid with difficulty. "Strike… Stone…"

Ailéas stared at the blade she held in her hand.

She saw it glow faintly, as she had seen it do before when she fought alongside her brother at Dunstaffnage.

It didn't take her long to understand.

"Fillan, keep him busy!" she yelled at her twin, who was trying to repel an attack by holding his weapon with both hands.

"I'm already doing that!" he yelled.

Sensing that she was up to something, Cornavii turned towards her, but she dove in the mud to duck his blow. Now in front of the Stone, she raised the sword of Fal above her head and struck with all her might.

The blade became covered with curious writings, and then Iona exploded in a myriad of lightning that set the sky ablaze. The artifact unleashed a wave of energy that knocked them all down and disintegrated the monastery, the stones of which flew away.

The island remained frozen for a few moments as the storm died down.

"What have you done?!" yelled Cornavii as he rose, leaning on his weapon, his eyes fixed on the Stone.

The blast had ripped off his helm, revealing an emaciated face covered with scars.

The twins, regaining their strength, were already charging at him.

Each performed a series of moves and attacks that managed to send the Templar's broadsword flying into the air.

"It shouldn't be like this!" cried Cornavii. "My destiny…"

Weapon in hand, Ailéas approached cautiously. She met the eyes of the Lann Fala, filled with excessive hatred, and read him like a book. Beyond the rage, she saw something else as she probed the warrior's mind. First she discovered a mixed ambition of shame and ego, flouted by failure, experienced as an affront.

Delving deeper, she discovered a slump of inextricable emotions; he was oozing with envy and suffocating like a dog trained by suffering for the simple purpose of killing obsessively.

The demon from her nightmares stood before her, just as vulnerable as she had felt on the worst nights of her life.

She raised her sword.

"The Order," he stammered. "The Order will find you…"

The blade struck across his neck.

He slid slowly to the floor.

Even after his body was no longer twitching, Fillan dealt another blow.

"I think he was already dead," Ailéas said, raising an eyebrow.

"Just to be sure."

They fell into each other's arms but cut short their embrace to rush to Moira, who was struggling to get up.

"Sören…" she said. "Take me to Sören."

The Norwegian slumped at the foot of the shattered monastery, breathing shallowly. The druid lay him in the mud as best she could with the help of the twins to remove his armor and assess his wounds.

"So?" Fillan asked impatiently.

"He will live."

He sighed in relief.

"He has a long gash in his abdomen that will require some time to heal. He's going to have to stay still for a while."

"I'm sure he'll love that," he joked.

She smiled, then tended to the wound with what little she had to hand. Instinctively, Ailéas assisted her. She disappeared after a few moments into the abbey, only to return with the holy water font full of clear water that allowed them to clean the wound.

Fillan watched them while massaging his shoulder, exhausted. He had learned to fight, to kill, to see blood flow, but the sight of skin being sewn up, pulled by a thread, made him shiver.

"There," Moira sighed after applying a dressing. "That's all we can do for now."

A few patches of blue sky started to appear between the dark clouds.

Feverish, the druid approached the Stone.

"Lia Fàil," she whispered.

"How did you know to hit it?" asked Fillan.

She smiled weakly.

"Thanks to knowledge inherited from your circle?" ventured Ailéas.

"Partly, yes, but I wasn't sure of anything. With such a precious but distant legacy, being sure of anything is difficult. Much has been lost and the fragments we have do not make it possible to fully understand everything. The breath of gods flows through Lia Fàil, there can be no doubt of it after what we just experienced. An identical breath travels in your weapons. It made me think of an old bas-relief that I visited during a trip to the north of Ireland."

"How can the breath of the gods have such a … horrible effect? I feel like I've been through hell."

"Me, too. I believe Fillan was correct when he said to Cornavii that he was not worthy of the power of the Stone. The Lann Fala was blinded; he thought he controlled the Stone, but this was just an illusion."

"I got the feeling it was resisting him."

"And it was, my boy. It would have ended up annihilating him, and us with it."

"Did we destroy it?" stammered Fillan as he approached the Stone of Fal.

"If you had, it would be broken. I get the feeling you've just disabled it. But truth be told, I don't really know. Despite everything I read, I didn't know how to use it."

"It would seem that the Order outstripped the druids and Assassins on this subject."

"What are we going to do with it?"

"The Stone was not brought to Iona by accident. Help me to get it up into the monastery."

They complied and moved towards the entrance of the building. They passed the body of James on the way.

"I still can't believe it," Fillan murmured. "I was so convinced that Deorsa was a traitor, and I didn't see James coming."

"Deorsa?" asked the druid in surprise. "No. If he had wanted to betray the Brotherhood, he would have taken the path a long time ago."

"Why would James do it?"

"Would knowing why ease your pain?"

He shrugged.

"Insatiable ambition is more than enough to tip the balance one way or the other. He didn't show it, but James was full of it."

They entered the remnants of the monastery and, clinging to their arms, the druid led them to a hidden staircase.

"If I remember correctly, it must be that way. Ailéas, grab that torch."

At the end of the steps, they discovered a maze of narrow corridors. Without Moira, they would have both lost their way, and there were many dead ends. At the bend of a corridor more endless than the others, the walls became dark.

He squinted.

"You recognize that smooth, black stone, don't you, Fillan?"

He nodded his head. The same material was in the depths of Scone.

"What is that?" whispered Ailéas.

"A creation of the gods."

Moira grumbled in agreement.

In the light of the flame, a dead end appeared. The twins observed the druid without understanding.

"Lia Fàil would have been safe here, no matter what," she explained, placing her hand on the smooth wall. "But the Brotherhood is far from stupid… They must have known."

"What do you suspect?"

"That something is beyond this wall. They were probably hoping to figure out how to open it, as is the case beneath Scone Abbey."

Ailéas noticed symbols similar to those she had seen

gleaming on her sword and touched the smooth coldness. With a rumble, the wall split into two parts that slid away.

"What did you break?" Fillan asked.

"Nothing, I just put my hand there!"

They looked at Moira again with wide, interrogative eyes.

"Stop staring at me like that! I don't know everything about everything!"

"You still know a lot about it," retorted the teenager. "More than anyone."

The druid observed the gaping opening before looking at them alternately.

"It must have something to do with the fact that you are Children of Fal."

"How can a rock realize that?" wondered Fillan.

"I haven't the faintest idea, but that's the only explanation that I can see."

"We truly are their heirs…" whispered Ailéas, as if she were only now aware of this reality.

"As well as those of the Gaels," added Moira. "Cornavii did not lie about that."

Beyond the passage, a room like that in Scone was plunged in darkness, invaded by mist.

"We should take advantage of it to lay the Stone here," said Moira. "And when I say 'we', I of course mean you. If I try too hard, I'll pass out, and you will have to carry me."

They accepted with enthusiasm, happy to be able to bring the artifact to safety, but became disillusioned when they had to carry the rock that weighed the same as them up the stairs.

They placed it in the center of the room while Moira illuminated the way at arm's length. When they emerged, the walls slowly slid back down into place.

"And so the true Lia Fàil disappears from the eyes of the world," said the druid in a solemn voice.

"Will it be safe here?" asked Ailéas.

"I hope so, but it is impossible to be sure. We all have our own destinies, but so does the Brotherhood and the Order. Only the gods know if their conflict will drive them to pull Lia Fàil out of these depths, for better or for worse."

They turned on their heels and the noise of the dark rock that came together to reform the wall behind them echoed loudly.

EPILOGUE

The waves lapped the shore of Iona, breaking softly.

Sitting in the sand, Ailéas and Fillan watched them in silence, their swords lying beside them. They looked terrifying, covered in mud and blood, hair stuck together on their faces.

In the distance, two large sails sporting a raven, the symbol of the Clan MacDougall, had just appeared along the shores of the Isle of Mull and begun their approach.

"And now?" asked Ailéas. "What do we do?"

"I would have answered you with certainty a year ago, but today…"

"Aren't you going to stay in the Brotherhood?"

He watched the sea foam without saying anything.

"Is it because of what Cornavii told you?"

"I don't know. Moira can say what she wants; I like the idea of having my destiny in my own hands."

They turned their heads to look at the druid, who was watching over Sören.

"That's reassuring," replied Ailéas, remembering their discussion on the Hebrides Sea. "Do you really feel like that's what's happening with the Assassins?"

"Not completely, no. It's more about fear. Maybe because of what Sören told me, or what happened with Bradley Dacre. But I know there's a lot to accomplish. Especially now."

He thought of Deorsa, of James' betrayal, of what the Assassins had lost despite their victory over the Templars.

"After seeing Cornavii abuse the Stone's powers," he continued, "I think I have a better understanding of what's at stake."

"That Lann Fala ass tried to throw you off balance. The way of the Assassins has changed you a lot, for the better. If you feel that that's where you belong, you don't have to hesitate. And if the time comes when your doubts are confirmed, there will always be time to close the door on them."

"You're right," he agreed. "Since when have you been so wise?"

"I always have been! You were the one who didn't want to listen!"

"I know how hard I've been on you lately."

For the past few years, he thought.

"I'm truly sorry, you didn't deserve it."

"You've finally made peace with yourself," observed his twin. "It's about time."

"I think so, and then… Wait a second, how do you…?"

"Long before the Berwick massacre, I suspected something was eating at you. Something that didn't concern only you. What was it?"

He stared at her, embarrassed.

"Do you remember the day our parents were killed?" he asked.

Ailéas smiled sadly.

It was the phrase she repeated to him every day after her nightmares, hoping to share the burden of her pain.

"Too well, unfortunately."

"I couldn't bear the thought of not saving you that day."

She felt tears well up in her eyes as she imagined the guilt he must have felt and pressed her forehead against her brother's.

"There was nothing you could do," she whispered. "I am glad you finally figured that out."

"You have a gift for reading people. You always had it."

"I know, Moira already told me."

"And what about you? Which path will you choose? That of the Assassins or that of the druids?"

She pulled her head back, surprised.

"What?" he laughed. "I may not have the gift of reading people, but I know you."

"Both interest me. A druid Assassin. I believe that would be useful, especially given what we just lived through."

"I think so, too."

The ship approached, gliding on waters that reflected the ever-clearing sky. Kyle was stood at the bow, her loose hair flying in the wind.

Fillan watched her, unable to help but smile.

"I wonder if Kyle would make a good Assassin?" he teased his sister.

He gently pushed her with his shoulder, and they laughed without noticing the elegant raven which, after performing many circles in the air above them, headed towards the north with a cry.

CHARACTERS

ABBOT THOMAS DE BALMERINO*: Leader of the Abbey of Scone. He plays an essential role in the Scottish Brotherhood, like a keystone.

AILÉAS: Scottish girl, sixteen-year-old twin sister of Fillan. Lives in Berwick and dreams of one day finding her roots in the northern wilds.

ALASTAIR AITKEN: Wealthy tailor from Berwick, who took Ailéas and Fillan in after their clan was massacred.

AMY COMYN: Member of the Scottish Brotherhood.

* Editor's note: a * means the characters are historical figures who really existed. The author was loosely inspired by their life trajectories to bring you the story of Fillan and Ailéas.

CORNAVII: Warrior and head of the Lann Fala, servant of the Order of the Templars. He is a specialist tracker and fanatic, responsible for numerous massacres in Scotland.

CRAIG: Mercenary in Sören's group, armed with an axe. He is a member of the MacDougall clan and cousin of Fergus.

DEORSA: Master spy of the Brotherhood. He is the main informant about everything that happens in Scotland. He and Sören hate each other.

EDAN: An inexhaustible and lewd mercenary in Sören's group.

EDWARD I*: Duke of Aquitaine, King of England and Lord of Ireland. After the treason of John Balliol, he declared war with Scotland. He is counselled by the Order of the Templars.

FERGUS: Bard in Sören's group, cousin of Craig.

FILLAN: Scottish boy, sixteen-year-old twin brother of Ailéas. He dreams of becoming a famous tailor.

JAMES DE CRANNACH: Apprentice of the Brotherhood under Abbot Thomas.

JOHN BALLIOL*: King of Scotland. He had sworn allegiance to Edward I of England but betrayed his vow when he forged an alliance with the kingdom of France.

KYLE: Talented warrior, eighteen years old, and member of Sören's group.

MOIRA: Druid and member of Sören's group.

SÖREN: Direct descendant of Norwegian Vikings, he is the leader of a group of mercenaries in service of the Brotherhood.

WILLIAM WALLACE*: Full member of the Scottish Brotherhood, he wishes to make the Scottish people rise up against the English and to use the revolt to work against the Templars.

For more fantastic fiction, author events,
exclusive excerpts, competitions, limited editions and more

VISIT OUR WEBSITE
titanbooks.com

LIKE US ON FACEBOOK
facebook.com/titanbooks

FOLLOW US ON TWITTER AND INSTAGRAM
@TitanBooks

EMAIL US
readerfeedback@titanemail.com